The Wicked Kind

John Turner

Every day in America 2,300 people go missing
Many of them are adults
Most are never heard from again

The rules do not apply
To people in love
—Jerry Harrison

The Wicked Kind

Regrets

Everyone has them.

For some, they are as plain and as obvious as the nose on their face. And depending on your level of self-awareness, the acknowledgment of those regrets can be a good, or a bad thing.

My regrets are sneakier. Just when I think I've got a handle on them they pull a fast one and morph into something else entirely, forcing me to rethink all that I know. But my core regret, the one from which all others flow, can be easily identified and narrowed to a specific time and place. Yet no matter how hard I try to come to terms with the past, it eludes me, taunting me with endless questions that have no answers. The simple act of reflecting on that time fills me with immeasurable sorrow, and nothing even resembling closure.

Closure. That's a hell of a concept. It looks real good written down in some book collecting dust on a therapist's shelf.

A friend once told me it isn't what happens to you in life that matters, it's how you deal with it. He was a good friend and I miss him deeply. He's dead now, and when I think back on my forty-odd years of living, all of the highs and the lows and the in-betweens, it always comes down to that one simple fact. He's dead now. Maybe I had something to do with it. Maybe I could have prevented it. In the end, I nearly died avenging it.

Sure, regret can be a real bitch. This is mine.

Part One

Missing

1

Bear Valley, California
November 1989

The first big storm of the season is always the best. Later ones might pack a bigger punch, dial your thrill meter a few clicks higher, but the first is always the sweetest. For it signals the end of the drought, the many months spent wandering in the weeds, languishing through another long, hot summer. Granted, the rocks can trash your boards, and the base hasn't built up enough for killer moguls, but so what? In the end, you just can't top the feeling you get from the first run of a new ski season.

Every year it's the same, and come the Indian summer you search the weather forecasts for signs of where it will hit, the anticipation building with each new day. You shake out the gear, tune-up your skis, and you wait. Out here in California we're pretty fortunate, and by Thanksgiving weekend there is usually at least one resort open for business and ready to go.

It was Sam who suggested Bear Valley. I had never heard of the place, though I had spent time around that part of the Sierras, up near Yosemite. Angels Camp was the nearest town, more than an hour south on Highway 4, in the heart of the Gold Country. The resort itself was fairly small and unassuming, more of a locals-only type of place.

I would have preferred Mammoth or Tahoe, but unfortunately the big boys were sitting high and dry, while this obscure little nobody had snow to spare.

The only problem was, it seemed every skier in California had the same idea as us, and all the lodging from Angels Camp to Bear Valley was booked solid. Sam was all for throwing caution to the wind and taking our chances something would come up, but I wasn't too keen on that, the prospect of driving nearly six hours only to find ourselves homeless in the mountains not very appealing. Eventually Sam wore me down, and visions of dropping in on a nice fat run of fresh powder sealed the deal. And so we found ourselves sitting in the lodge that afternoon, with nowhere to go and no place to stay. Oh, but what an awesome day it was.

We'd driven late through the night after Thanksgiving dinner spent with our families, arriving at the resort early on Friday morning before the lifts opened. It felt good to be on the road, to get out of town for a while. I'd been dealing with things lately that weighed heavily on me. Some of it work related, some of it family, some of it just the general bullshit that crops up in life and tries to drag you down.

Sam had his own share of issues confronting him, and some big decisions to make as well, and I knew that he'd looked forward to this trip as much as I had. He held things together pretty well for a twenty-one-year-old, but there was a lot on his plate and it was definitely time to blow off steam. We had loose plans for a very full ski season, the centerpiece being a long-planned trip to Jackson Hole, but I wasn't sure how much of it we'd be able to accomplish. Despite being just a few years removed from high school, it seemed like life had come at us fast, and it became harder than ever to do the things we wanted to do, rather than the things we had to do.

But this weekend none of that mattered. This weekend we were free of troubles and responsibilities and of demands put upon us, of pleasing someone else and living up to their expectations. Driving through the San Joaquin Valley, the highway deserted save for long haul truckers and Johnny Law, I was determined more than ever to hold onto that feeling of freedom for as long as I could, to never grow old before my time.

Once at Bear Valley, we found a turnoff near the resort and parked the car, settling in for some much needed rest. We got up with the sun and hit the local greasy spoon for omelets and java, and boogied straight for the slopes. I was rusty and a little unsteady at first, but a summer of mountain biking kept me in good shape, and before long I fell into the rhythm of the mountain, the glide of my powder boards smooth and controlled, the familiar feeling coming back like it was yesterday. Just like riding a bike.

The rush of the high country and the drop of some big runs pushed away my fatigue, and with it my burdens fell. Sam and I worked that mountain hard, like so many others over the years. We'd been at this for a long time and the bond we'd forged transcended friendship, defied description. Sam Stoneman, *The Stone Man*, the brother I never had and the best damn compadre a guy could ask for. Indeed, Sam was an able-bodied wingman ready for action at the drop of a hat. You get the picture. We were tight.

All that was missing was Kelli, Sam's fiancée. She used to be my girl, but that was back in high school. She was my first love and she broke my heart, crushed it actually, into a million little pieces. She left me for Sam, and even though he wasn't the instigator, it led to a period of time where Sam and I weren't so tight. I didn't *want* to blame him, but I did. Pain can make you do funny things. After a while emotions cooled and things settled down, and since they're both good people and I'm the forgiving sort, the three of us remained best friends. He's Sam after all, and the truth is, I never stopped loving Kelli.

Sam and Kelli and Mason, the Three Musketeers.

Yeah, I know it sounds corny as hell, but it's true.

So this time out it was just the two of us. Kelli couldn't take time away from her sick mother. Terminal cancer is what I heard, but Kelli didn't talk about it and I don't push. Sam dealt with it the best he could. He liked to keep things light, and at times I wondered if anything was truly important to him. But you can stuff your feelings for only so long before it all comes out sideways, and for Sam, with Kelli and her mom's illness, the strain was starting to show. Don't get me wrong, Sam was not a shallow guy, he just kept a tight lid on his emotions.

By contrast, I'm what you might call emotionally complicated. I wear my heart on my sleeve and I don't suffer fools, and mixed with that is a bad temper driven by impatience, which all too often leads me into trouble. Maybe that's why Kelli chose Sam over me. He was always lots of fun and easy to be with, whereas I'm a little more work, take some getting used to. But that's what makes us human, right? We can't all be the same, and besides, while the differences may make us unique, it's the similarities that bring us together.

Our perfect day on the mountain led to an afternoon of brews and bullshit. It doesn't get much deeper than a lodge full of skiers telling tales and scamming snow bunnies. Something about that thin mountain air combined with testosterone seems to push the boys into overdrive.

We hooked up with some dudes from the Bay Area and stayed way later than I wanted to, but Sam was digging the scene and he seemed to forget all about our predicament. That was always the dynamic, fun-loving Sam versus practical Mason. It's not that I don't like a good time, but someone has to keep their eye on things, and left up to Sam we'd never get a damn thing accomplished. Yin and yang, the way of life.

For a brief period it looked like we might be able to snag a place with the crew from Frisco, but the next thing I knew, they were gone and Sam and I remained, homeless and a little drunk. The lodge had emptied out and by the time we got to our car it was the only one in the lot. It was a lonely scene that made me feel sad, but not in any specific way. Winter in the mountains always brings out the melancholy in me, and in keeping with the season of hibernation, I tend to turn within, becoming more introspective than usual.

I sucked in some clean mountain air, thankful to be alive, thankful for time spent with my friends. When I turned to say something to Sam, I saw him fumble with his keys. He dropped them and giggled, leaning against the car door as he bent over and dug through the snow, clearly amused with himself. He stood and I gave him one of my looks.

"What?" he said.

"What do you mean, what?"

"You got that look, Mason."

"Which one is that?"

"The parental one. Damn, brother, you look like my mom."

"Well, have *you* got a plan? We're a little stranded here."

"No worries, dude, we'll figure it out."

He flashed his toothy grin, with that shock of curly hair hanging down over his eyes, and I turned away to keep from laughing. What I wanted was to be pissed. The thing is, with Sam it was hard to be pissed.

"Mason?"

"Yeah?"

"Turn around. I've got something for you."

I turned and caught a snowball square on the forehead. I wiped the snow from my face and Sam laughed, and I did too. The wind kicked up and blew through the tops of the trees. The air felt brittle as a thin sheet of glass, the black sky illuminated by the thousand tiny pinpricks of stars dancing in and out of the fast-moving clouds.

"Storm's coming," Sam said. "Should dump big tomorrow."

"Yep."

We stood on opposite sides of Sam's car, wordlessly staring up at the sky. I've thought often of that time, found myself wishing there'd been someone around to snap a picture. Sure, I remember it clearly. But to have photographic evidence would be priceless, to hold in my hands a perfect moment between friends, never to be diminished by the passage of time or failing memories. That was a good day. It was the last good day we ever had. Sam turned to me.

"Hey, Mason, let's go find a place to stay, and tomorrow we'll slay this goddamn mountain."

He slid in behind the wheel and I got in beside him, and we took off down the road, our whole lifetime laid out in front of us, there for the taking.

2

Fifteen minutes later the sky opened up, dropping big fat flakes of wet Sierra snow. The temperature had dropped to below twenty and visibility on the road was cut in half. It was shaping up to be a tough night. With at least forty-five minutes to go before we hit Angels Camp, and that was in good weather, there was no guarantee we'd even be able to find a room when we got there.

Sam didn't seem too concerned about it. But then again, he was always more comfortable flying by the seat of his pants. I prefer a little more planning, like to have at least a general idea of where I'm headed and what I'm going to do when I get there. We drove on for a while longer, barely covering a few miles, and the conditions worsened. After another mile we came upon a roadhouse, the neon outline of a mountain range atop a steel pole visible through the snow. As we neared, I made out the name on the sign, *Val's Mountain Inn*. Sam looked at me and shrugged. I nodded back and he turned off the road and into the parking lot. Sometimes it went that way with us, like sign language.

The lot was nearly full and we found a spot near the back. Sam parked the car and we got out, stood there a moment to take in the scene. The gently falling snow deadened your senses, like layers of gauze covering your ears. Smoke billowed from the top of a wide stone chimney set into the middle of the low-slung, wood-framed building. From inside came the muted sounds of music and conversation, the side windows revealing a lively crowd bathed in yellow glow, distorted eerily by condensation frosting the glass.

"Looks warm in there."

"What're you saying, Sam?"

"We could hang out here a while, wait for the weather to clear." He got that wily look in his eye, and I knew better than to resist.

"It'll mess up our plans."

"What plans?"

"Exactly," I replied.

BY MIDNIGHT the action at Val's was winding down and the crowd thinned out fast as the band finished their last set. I was ready to do the same, the prospect of finding a place to stay putting a serious damper on my attitude. We'd had our fun and now it was time to take care of business. Sam was oblivious.

He was sitting at the bar engrossed in conversation with some guy we'd met earlier. It was one of those casual *how ya doin'* things that happen when guys belly up to the bar for drinks and make bullshit small talk with whoever happens to be standing there. As soon as we had our beers in hand a couple of seats opened up next to the stranger, and Sam continued to engage the guy. Thirty minutes later I grew uneasy and tried to steer the conversation to a close, but Sam wasn't picking up on my cues, so I got up and drifted away.

The guy's name was Gary and he was full of shit. It wasn't any one thing he said or did, it was his whole vibe. You ever meet someone who claims to have been there and done that? Well he was *that* guy. No matter what we talked about, Gary had done it before, twice. Sam either didn't notice or didn't care. But that was always Sam's deal, he was easygoing that way, willing to sit for hours talking to all kinds of lowlifes and lunatics and lost souls and never bat an eye. I've got limits, and when my radar blips, I'm done.

But beyond his bullshit nature, Gary just plain gave me the creeps. It wasn't necessarily his appearance that did it. He was dressed normal enough in blue jeans and flannel shirt and work boots, and he was clean shaven, with no offensive body odor or anything like that. His teeth were bad, but he didn't show them much, and he smoked like a chimney, but so did half the people in the bar that night.

More than anything it was Gary's eyes that bugged me. They were weird eyes, crazy eyes, with a lifeless quality that belied his attempts at casual repartee. His manner seemed off to me, charged with some kind of strange energy, and I felt uncomfortable sitting next to him. Why Sam didn't pick up on it I'll never know. Maybe he was simply bored, content to mindlessly kill time talking to a creep. No matter, the whole thing turned really strange a short while later.

I'd circled back around to the bar after spending too much time chatting up a couple of cute girls over near the bandstand. Under different circumstances I might have made a play, but that night it wasn't happening. Sam was alone at the bar, and he had some kind of sheepish look on his face when I asked him where Gary was. Back in the head, he told me. That was my opening, but when I tried to get Sam out the door he stalled, and out of the blue he hit me up with the crazy idea of us staying at Gary's house for the weekend. Apparently it was something they'd been discussing, and Sam got it in his head that he'd found the perfect solution to our dilemma. He mumbled something about Gary living nearby and a few other details, but I wasn't having it. I was restless and ready to hit the road, and there was no way in hell I was spending the weekend with some mountain weirdo.

"So, what do you think?"

I looked at Sam blankly. "I don't want to do that."

"Why?"

"I need a reason?"

"Well, yeah, I think you do. You can't say no without a reason. We're kind of stuck here, Mason, and Gary's offering to help. What's the problem?"

"The guy creeps me out, okay? I can't explain it any better than that. I don't trust him."

"How do you get that?"

"Remember earlier, when I was talking about my trip to the Cottonwood Lakes, up by Lone Pine?"

"Sure. You said you fished lake number seven, camped overnight near Stevens Pass. What about it?"

"Your buddy claimed he was up there a month before me, talked all about the monster trout he caught in that same spot. The problem, Sam, is there's no lake number seven up there. Hell, there's no Stevens Pass, I made that up, and Gary took the bait and threw out a line of shit."

Sam shook his head, skeptical. "Maybe he just got confused."

"No, he didn't. He's trying too hard to be cool with us, to make a connection. He's playing us. For what, I don't know."

Sam waved me off dismissively.

"You want more?" I said. "When I mentioned working construction, he said he did that too, knew all about my trade."

"So what? Maybe that's what he does for a living."

"Okay, fair enough. But then how is it he can set you up with vendors in the Bay Area?"

Sam worked for his dad in an antique clock business. They made reproductions and sold wholesale all over Southern California. Gary claimed to be in the business of supplying chains of home furnishing stores, said he wanted to discuss a distribution deal with Sam.

"Maybe he does both," Sam replied weakly. "Or maybe he did construction for a while and gave it up. What the hell are you so suspicious for? The guy's trying to help us."

I was losing patience with Sam. For all our brotherly love, at times he could be a stubborn mule, and once he got onto an idea it wasn't easy talking him out of it. I tried a different approach.

"Listen, I'll make you a deal. When this dude gets back, you tell him you changed your mind about staying with him. If he accepts and says nothing more, then I'll reconsider. But if he keeps pushing and tries to convince you otherwise, then you agree to bail on this whole idea. Deal?"

Sam considered my proposition. He drained his beer and slid the empty bottle across the bar, and he turned to me smiling, a confident look in his eyes.

"All right, Mason, I'll play along."

GARY RETURNED from the restroom sweating, his face flushed, and when he sat down I noticed his jaw muscles working. He kept sniffing and messing with his nose, like he had some kind of sinus problem. I figured the guy did some blow in the can, and for me that was strike two. Now it was up to Sam.

"This place is closing up," Gary said, his voice pinched. "It's time to roll on outta here. We can do after-hours at my place." He forced a thin smile, revealing his crooked and stained teeth, and he lit a cigarette, inhaling deeply. I gave Sam the fisheye, and tilted my head slightly towards Gary.

"Speaking of that, we decided to head down the road and find a hotel for the night." Sam did it right, he said it with conviction. Gary responded as I expected.

"That's a bad move, Sam. I'm telling you, this whole valley is sold out. The only thing you'll find down that road is a long drive to disappointment."

Gary gave out a weird little smirk.

"Shit, you'll end up in Modesto before you're through. But stay at my place and you'll be on the mountain first thing in the morning, no hassles, no bullshit."

I glanced sideways at Sam as he watched Gary smoke. Gary took slow drags on his cigarette, his lifeless eyes drawn to slits, fixed on an arbitrary point behind the bar, as if contemplating some deep thought. The vibe got weird and the creep factor notched by degrees, the reality of it dawning on Sam.

"I appreciate the offer, Gary," he said. "And believe me, it's tempting. But we may not even ski tomorrow. I twisted my knee earlier today and now it feels stiff. I may have to pack it in." He extended his leg and grimaced. That was a nice touch; Sam was all in.

And Gary was out, and not looking too happy about it.

"So rest up at my place, and if you want to split in the morning, go for it. If not, we can hit this joint tomorrow night. They got a killer band playing. Slingshot." He pointed to a gig poster hanging on the wall. "Those dudes rock it, bro, and they bring in the honeys. This place'll be crawling with wall to wall gash."

There was an edge to Gary's voice and his body language was all wrong, and I had the distinct impression that he didn't give two shits about a roomful of gash.

It was at that point I noticed something that had slipped by me earlier, but now I saw clear as day. Gary was completely ignoring me, his attention focused solely on Sam, as if they were the only two people in the room. The realization twisted a knot in my stomach, and I knew beyond a doubt that this guy was trouble.

"I'm not too sure about that, Gary," Sam said. "I've got my own sweet little honey waiting for me back home. I don't think she'd appreciate me trolling while I'm out here on the road."

Sam gave me a sly wink and a surge went through me. Jealousy perhaps? Even though it had been a couple of years, I'd never completely accepted Kelli and Sam together. I'd learned to live with it, but the hurt never went away. I allowed a small grin and spoke directly to Gary, shifting my body to block Sam from view.

"So that's it then. We're heading out now."

I kept my eyes locked on Gary's, sensed a heat rise inside him as he grew visibly agitated and the jaw grinding worsened. He tried to hide it but failed miserably in the process. He slid sideways a step to look at Sam, and I nearly laughed out loud it was so pathetic.

"I'm telling you, Sam, that's a huge mistake. My place is only two miles from here. We could walk there if it wasn't snowing. Come on over and I'll set you up in my guest house, we can party all night."

Gary stood rigidly, a sheen of sweat visible on his forehead. A predatory look fired his eyes, any pretense of friendliness abandoned now, and I saw the understanding come over Sam in full bloom. Now he got it. Now he knew this guy was bent and we had no choice but to bail on him immediately. He took his jacket off the back of the chair and put it on, turned to Gary and reached out his hand.

"Thanks anyway, but Mason and I are going to split. You've got my business card, so call me if you still want to get together on the clock deal." Gary hesitated before giving Sam a limp handshake. Sam turned to me. "Let's roll, Mason."

I stepped away from the bar, making no effort to offer my hand. On my way to the door I glanced once at Gary. He was lighting a cigarette, and through the smoke I saw him stare, eyes on mine. In that moment, and for no reason I could ever explain, I had the overwhelming feeling I'd looked into the heart of darkness.

3

Back on the road we laughed nervously about it, throwing out bad jokes about creepers and slashers and things that go bump in the night; gallows humor to ease the tension. I hadn't realized the depth of the funk inside Val's until we'd stepped out into the cold night air. The snow had let up and the sense of relief was palpable. We were no closer to finding a room, but I felt good nonetheless, and I was glad to put some distance between us and Gary.

I replayed the scene in my mind, just to check myself, make sure my intuition was correct. At times, Sam could be so easygoing that by comparison it made me look like an old maid, like the guy who was always pouring water on the fun. But after thinking it through, I was sure we'd done right by leaving that guy in the dust. Sam seemed to pick up on my thoughts.

"I'm sorry about that back there," he said.

"Hey, no worries. I know your freak radar isn't as finely tuned as mine." I tilted my seat back and closed my eyes. Sam was quiet for a moment, and when he spoke again he went in a completely different direction.

"I'm not talking about that, Mason. What I meant was the thing I said to Gary about my girl back home. That wasn't cool, and I'm sorry."

14

I knew that Sam still harbored guilt over what went down with Kelli. The thing is, he shouldn't have, for he was simply an innocent bystander. Kelli had aggressively pursued him before completely breaking it off with me. If anyone deserved blame it was her. But of course I loved Kelli too much to see *that* truth, so I focused instead on Sam, and in the process nearly ruined our friendship. Sadly, I was young and stupid and knew nothing of the ways of love, with a schoolboy's understanding that barely went skin-deep.

"Man, you don't have to tell me that. But I appreciate it anyway. I know you and Kelli are good together. Do I wish it had been me? Sure, I can't lie to you, buddy. But if not me, well then who better than the Stone Man?"

I rocked my seat upright and playfully jabbed at Sam. He looked like a scarecrow stretched out behind the wheel, his lanky frame all angular and wiry, curly hair that was unruly yet somehow always stylish. Sam was a true free spirit, unencumbered by worry and self-doubt, and he was the perfect foil for my more complex worldview. He was the straight line running through the peaks and valleys of my psyche, and I could always count on him to balance out the rough spots.

We drove along in silence, the low hum of the car's heater soothing in the background. Visibility had improved but it was still slow going. Thick stands of pines framed the road, shrouded in heavy mist, creating a tunnel-like effect as we worked our way down the mountain. There were no other cars to be seen, the sense of isolation magnified by endless miles of snow-covered forest. Occasionally we'd come upon an intersection, the blacktop to the right or the left of us boring into the mist, fading into nothingness. The world seemed to close around us and my thoughts turned inward, and I felt compelled to speak, to broach a difficult subject.

"She needs to talk about it," I said. I was thinking about Kelli and the walls she put up as she dealt with her mother's illness. "She doesn't want to burden you. But she's trying too hard to be strong, and it's taking a toll."

It hung there between us as the car sloshed down the highway, laying down a steady groove against the rhythmic sweep of the wipers, every eight seconds, back and forth. Sam drew in a breath, his eyes fixed straight ahead. He let it out slowly, turning slightly to fog the side window.

"I know it, Mason, believe me I do. It's hard though. It brings it all back for me, and that's a box I don't want to open."

Sam's mother died of cervical cancer when he was fifteen. She was thirty-five and she went quickly. It seemed like one minute everything was fine, and the next, we were standing at the cemetery listening to Pastor Murphy recite the Lord's Prayer. They lowered Katherine Stoneman into the ground and along with her went a piece of Sam's heart. He was an only child, and his dad managed the best he could under the circumstances. He was a good man who always put Sam first in his life, but in time he leaned too hard on the bottle, and by Sam's senior year, Bill Stoneman was deep into an alcoholic haze. Sam had to grow up fast and learn some hard truths in the process. He bypassed college so he could help run the family business, and he basically managed his dad's affairs. Yet through it all he never complained, exhibiting a temperament beyond his years.

I thought back to the day I first met Sam. It was the Bicentennial year, summer of 1976, and my family had recently moved from Long Beach to Costa Mesa. During the move an antique Regulator clock was broken, and once discovered, my dad set out to get it repaired. I went along with him that day, to a little clock shop called *Styles in Time*, tucked in a strip mall on Fairview Street, not far from our new house. Bill Stoneman greeted us in his shop, and while my dad showed him the damaged clock, I wandered around bored to tears. There was a small showroom at the front of the shop, filled with various wall-hung clocks and tall floor models, and the constant ticking and chiming of the mechanisms was nearly unbearable. In the back there was a workshop, and after a while I noticed a kid moving past an open door. I got curious about that kid, mostly because I was so bored, and as my dad and Bill gabbed away about our new house and their jobs and life in Costa Mesa, everything *but* broken clocks, I slipped through the door.

"Hey," I said to the kid. He looked at me quizzically, no doubt wondering who this intruder was. "Hey," he said back.

We stared at each other, a couple of eight-year-olds taking each other's measure. He held a skinny piece of wood in his hand and stood in front of the strangest looking contraption I'd ever seen, scraping sawdust out of its nooks and crannies. He told me later that it was a lathe, and that it "makes square wood round". He was a little taller than me, with very curly hair the color of beach sand, and there was a light in his eyes I remember clearly.

"What's your name?"

"Mason," I said. "I'm Mason Tanner."

"Hi, I'm Sam. My dad owns this clock shop." He offered his hand and I shook it, and he said, "Doesn't all that ticking out there make you crazy?"

We both laughed uncontrollably then, and I knew right away that Sam Stoneman was my kind of kid. It turned out he lived in the same neighborhood as us, and soon after that encounter in the clock shop we became inseparable. The timing was perfect too. I'd been feeling anxious about the prospects of starting third grade at a new school, and meeting Sam was a godsend; now I wouldn't have to go it alone.

The memory filled me up, and I wanted to reach out to my friend in a meaningful way, to be there for him like he had always been for me. I put some words together, tried to convey them the best I could.

"Maybe you can take it a little at a time, open it up some and let her in. As much as it hurts you, Sam, your experience can help her." My words felt awkwardly spoken, but I could tell they hit home.

"You know, Mason, I'm going to consider that. I always knew you were good for something, besides saving my ass from pervs." Sam laughed big then, infectious in a way you couldn't help but join. "Throw on some music, man, liven this ride up."

I reached into the back seat for the tape box, opened it and scanned the selections. The obvious choice jumped out. I grabbed the cassette and held it up.

"Fogelberg?"

"Do it."

I popped the tape in and twisted up the volume. The first notes of *Aspen* filled the air, the violin and piano intro gentle in its beauty and simplicity. The accompaniment kicked in, building to a tasteful peak before fading into the little piano figure at the end. Then the acoustic guitar of *These Days* played, rhythmic and strong, and Sam and I started singing along.

I used to think of myself as a soldier, holding his own against impossible odds…

The music felt awesome and pure, honest, the promise of the future and the pleasures of the past all rolled into one. Dan and Sam and Mason, singing together in the car.

Oh but these days, are just like you and me…

4

I had just flipped the tape to side two when Sam slowed the car to a crawl. The conditions had suddenly worsened and visibility was less than a hundred feet. It felt like we'd never get down that mountain.

"Mason, take a look up ahead."

I turned the stereo off and stared through the windshield, saw a pair of taillights haloed by fog. It was the first vehicle we'd seen since leaving Val's.

"That's weird," I said. "Looks like it's just parked there."

We approached the vehicle, an older model Ford pickup truck with a camper shell on the back. The truck was dark in color, a film of dirt streaking the lower half from end to end, the shell one of those cap types with tinted windows. An arm poked out the driver's side and motioned us forward. Sam stopped short. The arm waved us on.

"What the hell?" Sam looked at me. My pulse quickened and I shrugged.

"Maybe he broke down," I said.

"Then why's exhaust coming out of the tailpipe?"

Sam pulled even with the truck. My window was fogged and all I could make out was the bare outline of a person illuminated by dash lights. I turned to Sam and he slid his hand to the power window button. I heard the glass squeak on the rubber seal, saw Sam's eyes widen and I jerked my head around, my jaw dropping as my heart leapt into my throat.

It was Gary sitting in the cab of the truck, his ugly teeth clenched on the filter of a smoldering cigarette. He tried to look casual about it, like sitting on the side of the road in the middle of a snowy night was the most natural thing in the world, but his dead eyes betrayed him.

"Thanks for stopping," he said, his voice deep, almost guttural, different than it sounded back at the bar. "I wasn't sure I'd be able to find you."

I was too dumbfounded to speak. How did this guy get down the road without us seeing him? We hadn't encountered a single vehicle since leaving Val's, and every side road we'd passed was deserted. We may as well have been on the Moon for all the people we'd seen. Yet this freak shows up out of the blue?

"What's going on, Gary?" There was an edge to Sam's voice. He didn't often show it, but Sam Stoneman had a temper, and when he got there, you knew it.

"I was kickin' it at my place, it's just down the road here a ways, and I got to thinking about your situation. I decided to come up here and wait for you to pass by, convince you to change your mind before you made a big mistake."

He took a deep drag off his smoke, studied the burning end like it held a secret, hit it once more and flicked the butt out his window, sent it bouncing off the hood of Sam's car in a mini plume of sparks and smoke.

"Listen, man," I said, my voice tight. "We told you back at the bar that we appreciated your offer, but no thanks. Are you confused by that? Do I have to spell it out for you?"

Gary said nothing, his eyes fixed on the hood of his truck, his jaw working and knuckles white as he gripped the steering wheel. I had an immediate sense of danger. Maybe he had a gun. Maybe he was getting ready to lurch forward and block our path with his truck, force a confrontation right there in the middle of the road. I tensed in my seat, ready to react.

"Thanks anyway, Gary," Sam said. "But we've got things figured out from here, okay? So we're going to split now. Be cool, dude."

Sam powered up my window and drove away. I looked behind us, saw the truck's headlights fade into little white dots in the mist. And then they were gone.

"Jesus, that guy is strange," Sam said.

"No shit. Did he really think we'd follow him at this point? Anywhere?"

"You know what's really weird?"

"All of it?"

"No, think about it, Mason. Back at Val's, Gary said he lived what, two miles from the bar? He said we could walk there if it wasn't snowing."

"Yeah, so?"

"Well just now he told us he lived down the road. We've been driving for at least forty-five minutes since we left Val's. How many miles do you think that is? More than a few, that's for sure. *That's* what's weird."

I saw Sam's point. It hadn't occurred to me earlier. It was nice to see he was thinking like me for a change. "Well to hell with him," I said. "He's history now. Makes you think though, about guys like that, what their deal is. You hear about serial killers and all that crazy shit, but still, you wonder how that kind of thing even happens. How it is a guy can gain someone's trust enough to get one over on them."

Sam had an odd look in his eyes. Maybe he was thinking about how close he'd come to going along with Gary, and how hard he tried to talk me into it. He might even have felt foolish about it now.

"Holy shit, that was close. I must've lost my mind back there at the bar. Thank God you were able to knock some sense into me, Mason. That could have been a total horror movie. Jeez almighty."

One thing about Sam, when he got it, he *really* got it.

"No worries, buddy," I said. "That's what I'm here for."

The road conditions improved quickly, as if that one rough patch was brought along by Gary as a means to hide his bad intentions, and Sam hit the high beams and accelerated. It felt damn good to finally have some wind in our sails. Even though it was after one in the morning and we still had no place to stay, I saw light at the end of the tunnel. I hit the stereo and turned up the volume, side two of *Captured Angel* starting, and I closed my eyes and thought of tomorrow, and the awesome day of skiing that surely lay ahead.

5

We passed a sign indicating fifteen miles to Angels Camp. The weather had cleared up completely and the sky was brilliant with stars, like a painting or something too perfect to be true. Puffs of clouds hung suspended, illuminated like neon in the moonlight. The forest thinned out and a smattering of houses appeared alongside the road. Up ahead on the left I saw the lighted sign of a country store blinking through the trees. Sam saw it too.

"Let's stop and pick up some supplies"

"Good idea," I said.

Sam pulled into the empty lot and parked in front, and we got out. The air temperature was ice, easily single digits, and we walked quickly up the concrete steps that led onto a wooden porch set under a deep eave. The porch wrapped around both sides of the building and it was bordered by a hitching post railing. A couple of split-log benches and a newspaper rack framed the front door, along with a large bulletin board covered with flyers and business cards and local announcements. I peered through the window, saw a typical mountain store filled with fishing gear and groceries and souvenirs. At the corner of the building was a sign with an arrow pointing to a pay phone around back.

"How about I go make some calls, see if I can find us a room?" I said.

"I'll stock up. You want some beer?"

"Sure, get Coors. Bottles."

Sam moved towards the door, stopped short and turned to face me. His sleepy eyes brightened, and I prepared myself for a blast of Sam Stoneman's wry humor.

"What?" I said.

"Oh nothing, Mason, just thinking."

"Yeah? About what?"

"What a good dude you are."

He brushed his hair back, and walked inside the High Country Market.

I WAS IN THE phone booth for fifteen minutes. I know this because I checked my watch. Fifteen minutes was all the time it took for my life to change forever. I've often wondered if a few less minutes would have mattered.

It's shocking how quickly things can change, how randomly and inexplicably fate can swoop down and deal you a losing hand, forever altering the course of your life. I never used to think of such things. Since that day in Bear Valley I can think of nothing else.

I made reservations at the Sycamore Inn. It was the second place I called. The first was sold out. More questions. What if they hadn't been sold out? I would have finished in the phone booth precious minutes earlier, maybe with enough time to make a difference.

I hung up the receiver and dropped the directory, listened to it bang against the glass, swinging on the metal chain. They don't make phone booths like that anymore. Hell, you can hardly find a public phone these days, everyone carries a cell. Stepping out of the booth I slid the door shut, heard it squeak loudly on its hinges. I think about that phone booth now and again, hear the sounds, smell that old phone booth smell; it's strange what your mind holds onto.

When I turned to meet up with Sam, I nearly had a heart attack.

Standing in front of me was a man with dead eyes. He was a man who wouldn't take no for an answer, a man who embodied the darkest of fears. I staggered back against the phone booth, unsure of what I was seeing. My breath came fast and I felt a surge of adrenaline, the fight-or-flight instinct kicking in big time.

"Hey there, Mason," the man with the dead eyes said. "It was Mason, right? I'm kind of bad with names. Sam I remember, but you, man it's easy to forget guys like you."

Gary bit down on a burning cigarette with his dirty teeth, his eyes squinted. My heart beat wildly as my mind raced. How did he do it? How did he get here without us knowing it? Is this guy even real? And then I saw red and I felt an all too familiar feeling, one of violence bursting at the seams, blind aggression fighting for release.

"What the fuck's your problem, man? I mean seriously, what in the hell is your deal? We told you we want nothing to do with you, and yet here you are, following us like some kind of faggot."

Gary showed no recognition of my words. He just stood there unmoving, smoking his cigarette while I seethed. Three feet separated us, and I calculated how many times I could hit him before he reacted. He matched me in height, about five-eleven, and he might have had thirty pounds on me, but they were soft pounds and I was lean and hard, and I was sure I could take him. He sucked down his smoke and flicked the butt over my shoulder, a stray spark nicking my cheek. "Sorry," he said.

I paced my breathing, tried to shake the light-headed feeling coming over me. "I'm going to give you exactly ten seconds to get out of my face and leave me and Sam alone. If you don't, I'm going to fuck you up, Gary. Do you hear me? Are we clear on that?"

He took eight seconds by my count to speak.

"Okay."

That was it, a single word spoken as casually as a wave to a passerby. Gary brushed past me, a musty smell like mothballs lingering, and I heard his footsteps on the wood planks. I turned and watched him walk down the steps leading to the rear parking lot. But there were no vehicles back there, no old pickup truck with a camper shell. I shouted at him, a parting shot fueled as much by fear as by anger.

"Hey! What the hell kind of person does that anyway, follow guys around, pushing yourself on people who want nothing to do with you. Tell me, man, what kind of person does that?"

Gary stopped twenty feet from me and turned his head, his face a mask of dread, those dead eyes joined by an ugly grin. He held that look without speaking, and I should have walked away, but something kept me there, waiting for whatever would come. When Gary spoke, his voice was like sandpaper on bark.

"The wicked kind."

He gave out a sick laugh and walked away. I looked down at the ground, breathing deeply. When I looked back up, Gary was gone. My hands shook and I reached for the wood railing next to me, squeezing it hard while leaning forward, slowly regaining my composure. I stared at the parking lot, and it struck me that I'd heard no engine start up when Gary left.

How in the hell did he get here? And how did he leave? Did he fly away? It was weird and creepy and so absurd that I began to doubt it had even happened. I straightened and headed for the front of the store. When I turned the corner and saw our car in the lot, it brought a huge sense of relief.

I went inside the store but did not see Sam. The clerk was asleep behind the counter, a kid, younger than me. The store was eerily quiet, save for the kid's light snoring, and my intuition vibed trouble. Where the hell was Sam? I walked the aisles, all four of them, and went to the back and opened each of the coolers, calling Sam's name to the stockroom beyond. Nothing. Panic rising, I ran to the front and leaned against the counter, raised my voice to the kid to wake his ass up. He yawned and stretched and I shouted, asking him about Sam. The kid stared blankly and he shook his head no, then the awareness took hold and he looked at me like I was nuts.

An image flashed in my brain.

The wicked kind.

That's what Gary said. That's what he called himself. A sick feeling tore through my guts, a fear so immense I nearly blacked out. Staggering through the front door, I shouted Sam's name, praying to God he was out there somewhere, taking a leak or playing some shitty-ass joke on me. I saw the car and the empty parking lot and my breath steaming in the frozen air, but not Sam. The walls closed in and I went dizzy. I stumbled two times around the building calling for Sam, my voice echoing forlornly in the darkness. When I reached the front of the store the clerk was standing outside and I ran into him hard, knocking us both down. The kid scuttled back on his haunches, fearful and confused, and as I got to my feet, reality hit me like a sledgehammer between the eyes.

Sam was missing.

Part Two

Redemption

6

Newport Beach, California
November 2009

The dream arrived as expected.

I knew it would come and it did not disappoint. It had been far too long for it not to.

I lay in bed listening to the pounding surf, a swell borne of a monster storm in Tahiti, generating incredible energy as it surged across four thousand miles of ocean before finally landing on the beaches of Southern California, the pure beauty and immutable power of Mother Nature on display for all to see.

A salty breeze blew in through the open window, the billowing curtain throwing dancing shadows on the wall, filtering the emerging light of dawn. The air smelled of rain, heavily laden with moisture as the barometric pressure dropped fast. I contemplated patterns on the ceiling while putting the details of the dream in the correct order. Feeling alternately tired and awake, I readied myself for the task at hand.

A few minutes later I was out of bed and coffee was brewing, the kitchen filled with the rich aroma of freshly ground Kona beans. I retrieved my worn, leather-bound journal from a place only I knew, the embossed pattern on the cover familiar to my touch, the weight reassuring in my hands. I opened it to the first page and studied the childlike scrawl, the barely formed thoughts made more cryptic by words that seemed to run together. A bottle of Jack Daniel's at five o'clock in the morning will do that to you.

I traced my finger across several of the lines, stopping on four perfectly formed spots, stains on the paper made by falling tears and ink smeared mid-sentence, rendering the words indecipherable. An image came to me, and I saw those four tears as they fell onto the page, I felt the rage and the fear and the guilt rise up from the depths of my soul and forever mark my pain in that one moment in time.

Closing my eyes, I inhaled deeply, tried to find my center. But my mind remained jumbled, the faint stirrings of anxiety tingling inside me. I knew I should start writing or the details might be lost, but I wasn't ready. I opened my eyes and exhaled, closed the journal and trusted my instincts. The writing would wait. The dream would be remembered. It was time to hit the water.

THE DAY AFTER Thanksgiving and the beach was deserted. The mist shrouding the coastline kept even the hardcore cyclists and joggers indoors. I looked north up the bike path and saw only gray, and to the south, the dim lights of the Newport Pier. I turned and faced the ocean, steadied my longboard and took off running across the sand, my stride even and sure. My legs burned as the blood pumped, my body generating warmth inside my wetsuit. I hit the waterline without hesitation and skimmed out on my board, paddling with even strokes through the whitewash, up and over a small roller. I torpedoed under a bigger wave directly behind it and paddled hard until I was a hundred yards out. When I finally stopped I was alone, save for a few gulls swooping down and calling to one another. I lay back on my board and rolled with the swell, and I recalled my dream. It came to me whole, and I knew that later I'd be able to put it down exactly as it was, documenting it next to the others. Satisfied that all was in order, I rolled over and hit the surf. I worked those waves hard, just like I used to work the ski slopes a lifetime ago.

BACK HOME AFTER a two-hour session in the water, I brewed up another pot of Kona and sat down to write. I opened my journal to a clean page and contemplated where to start. At the beginning I suppose, but have you ever tried to recall the beginning of a dream? I don't write down all of my dreams, only this one. Today marked my twentieth time doing so.

Let me back up a bit and explain.

The initial dream, the one that started this tradition, if you will, came to me the day after Thanksgiving in 1990. It was one year to the day after my friend Sam Stoneman disappeared.

Sam was never found. The police investigated, but the complete lack of leads or any physical evidence of wrongdoing eventually pushed his case into the black hole of unsolved mysteries. I was sure that creepy guy from the bar was responsible, but the Mariposa County Sheriff found no evidence of any such person. Interviews with regulars at Val's Mountain Inn turned up nothing, and despite claims that he owned a house nearby, tax records showed only three property owners in the area with the name Gary, and none of them fit the description. Whoever Gary *really* was, he simply vanished, as if he'd never existed in the first place. Just like Sam.

After many months spent waiting for news or a break in the case, I finally admitted defeat and buried my friend in my mind. Sam's father refused to hold a real burial, steadfastly holding onto the belief that to have a funeral for his only child would kill the small shred of hope he clung to as if his life depended on it. In time even that failed, and Bill Stoneman died six years after Sam went missing, as surely from a broken heart as from the fifth of Maker's Mark he drank nearly every day in the last year of his life.

For me the pain of losing my friend—and indeed it seemed as if I'd *lost* him that day, just like you'd misplace your car keys or your cell phone, because when a human being disappears into thin air like that, what the hell else do you call it?—the pain of that singular event marked me for life, and it set me on a path I almost didn't return from. Call it survivor's guilt or remorse, whatever you choose, but the self-loathing brought on by pure helplessness, and a year spent stuffing those feelings and making believe I was okay, nearly killed me.

It culminated in the first dream, the one where Sam came to me and pleaded for help. Gary was there too, with his dead eyes and his fake camaraderie and his leering countenance, and those words he spoke upon leaving, *the wicked kind*, ran through my brain like the crawl on a twenty-four hour news channel.

The dream was horrific, the details so disturbing that when I finally put pen to paper I wasn't sure I could do it. I don't even know what compelled me to write it down. Certainly there was no sense that it was anything other than a random and appropriate nightmare associated with an event that was still fresh in my mind. But I did put the words down, and when the same dream came the following year I was glad that I had, because now there was a point of reference, and by the fourth year I knew I was in for the long haul; this would be my penance for living, the price I would pay for my failures that night in November so long ago.

The dreams continued once a year, always on the day after Thanksgiving, each one the same yet different. And as the dreams evolved so too did the record of them, my writing becoming more elaborate, more critically nuanced as I tried to work out on paper things I didn't even know I felt. I played amateur psychologist with myself for a long time, until the day came when I finally surrendered and sought professional help for the demons that plagued me.

My performance for that first dream was surely epic, for I was hopelessly miserable and blind drunk and about as close to suicidal as a man can get. It all poured out of me then, a year's worth of denial and running from the one thing I could never escape, and a year's worth of tears, memorialized forever by those four little stains smearing words that even today scare the living shit out of me.

So here's how it went down.

One year to the day after Sam and I went skiing at Bear Valley, I awoke long before sunrise, wasted from the whiskey bottle I'd cracked open after getting home late from my parents' house and a Thanksgiving dinner I sat through in body but not spirit. The bad juju was just starting, I could feel it creeping in like a tide, anxiety pushed along by memories of what had happened a year earlier. My family knew something was wrong, they sensed my discomfort, but there was no salve for what ailed me, and when I abruptly told them I was leaving they did not stop me.

I drove to Sam's house, parked in front and sat in my car, lost in that place where all the hurt goes. The house was dark, and if Sam's father was home I couldn't tell. God only knew what that man was going through. I drove away at midnight, got to my apartment and hit the bottle, and man did I get drunk. When I eventually passed out the ghosts came for me, and they brought the dream, and upon waking in the false dawn it felt like I was losing my mind. I reached for the whiskey bottle and finished what I'd started, if only to stop the pain.

I drank and I wrote, and when the words ran out I cried, and after crying I raged and put my fist through a wall, breaking my hand. But even that wasn't good enough, so I got in my truck and drove down to Newport Beach, hit two cars along the way and parked it in the middle of the street near the Blue Beet, the old jazz club down on the peninsula, and left the motor running. I jogged down past the pier, fell three times and tore up my arms and stopped once to puke, and I kept going, as if by sheer force of will I could push out all the bad.

When I finally stopped running I stood there and looked out at the ocean, mesmerized by the waves. I'd lived near the beach my whole life yet never once surfed. A thought came to me then, and looking back, maybe it was because I wanted to die. How else do you explain stripping down to my boxers, stealing a surfboard from some guy's patio, and paddling out into sixty degree water and a seven foot swell?

I don't know how long I was out there, but when I was finally pulled from the water by two strangers, the stolen surfboard lost at sea, I was on the verge of hypothermia. The cops came and arrested me and my truck was impounded, and I was carted off to the hospital and after they stabilized me I went to jail.

But the dream was saved, tucked away in my journal for eternity. It isn't really a journal in the true sense of the word, for when I sat down to write that morning the only paper I could find was in an old day planner my mother had given me as a gift a few years earlier. There were times I thought about getting a proper journal and rewriting the previous entries, but I never did, for the simple fact I'd lose the page with those tears, and that was something I could not bear.

So I improvised, and since that day in 1990 I've documented twenty dreams. Twenty dreams for twenty years, including today's. And every year after the writing is finished I go out in the water, because you see, I'm a surfer now, ever since the drunken debacle that nearly cost me my life so long ago. I'm pretty good at it too. Maybe not as good as I was at skiing, but still I'm good.

And speaking of skiing, I don't do that anymore. Not since the day Sam went missing. It wasn't a conscious decision on my part, it just worked out that way. I don't know what to say about that, other than in life, some things cannot be helped.

7

The storm passed and the weather cleared. I did a few chores, ate a late breakfast, and afterwards took a nap. A short while later the telephone woke me up.

"Mason?" the voice on the line said after my hello.

"You were expecting someone else?" I heard a familiar giggle and it made me smile.

"No, silly, you know what I mean."

"How are you, Kelli?" I said after a pause.

"I'm good. And you?"

I sensed a tentative drag to her words that bothered me, and I hesitated while my thoughts formed.

"Mason, are you there?"

"Yeah, sorry about that, you caught me napping is all."

The line went quiet, as now *she* hesitated. It seemed to me this phone call needed a do-over.

"Did you go out this morning?" Kelli said, her voice small, like it got whenever she had things on her mind.

"Yeah, I did."

"How was it?"

"Rough, but good."

"That's nice."

"How's your dad?"

"He's okay, all things considered. But his memory is slipping and he's having trouble getting around. I'm afraid I'll have to take his car soon. He gets confused and the

38

driving worries me. A neighbor told me that last week he took off for Auburn and ended up in Truckee. The Highway Patrol turned him around. Dad's told me the story a few times and it's always different. Once he said he drove to Downieville, in another version it was Stockton. I don't know what to do about it, except to stay up here a little longer and try to figure it out."

I thought about Kelli's father.

Tom Flynn never cared for me, for reasons that were unclear. Who knows, maybe it had something to do with what happened to Sam. I hadn't even seen the guy in more than five years, ever since he retired to Grass Valley, up in Northern California. Every time Kelli went up there to visit I begged off with some kind of excuse, and she never pushed the issue, which only troubled me more; shouldn't she care?

"Did you hear me?" Kelli said.

"Yes, I did. How much longer will you stay?"

"I'm not sure, maybe another week. Are you okay with that?"

"Sure, whatever you have to do. I'll be fine. I've got to get a couple of bids out anyway, and you know how that goes. This way I won't have any distractions."

I chuckled suggestively, but Kelli was silent and the smile left my face. I blurted out something about getting my year-end tax stuff together and some errands I had to run, my mind preoccupied by thoughts I had no business with, and the more I talked the more it felt like Kelli wasn't even listening, so I steered the phone call to an end.

"So yeah, go ahead and take your time. I'll be busy until you get back."

"Thank you, Mason, I appreciate your understanding."

"No problem. I'll let you go now. Take care, Kelli. I hope things work out with your dad."

"Thanks again, Mason. I'll call you in a day or two."

"Okay." Hanging up the receiver, I pulled it quickly back to my ear. "I love you, Kelli," I said, before realizing she'd already hung up.

THE CALL PUT me in a funk for the rest of the day. That's just how it went with Kelli. Even though our relationship was going strong, doubts remained. Granted, they were all mine, but Kelli's elusive nature and the way she loved did little to calm my deep insecurities. It would be easy to say it was because of Sam, but that doesn't tell the whole story.

Kelli and I came first, and even though our initial relationship could rightfully be written off as high school puppy love, *my* feelings were never in doubt. When she got together with Sam it shook me to the core, and while I tried to take it in stride, it ate at me. Seeing them together triggered a profound need unlike anything I'd ever felt, and as the years went by I'd built my love for Kelli into something akin to myth, a truth that could not be denied.

We reconnected at our ten-year high school reunion. The night was a total disaster, but a seed was planted, and in time it grew in ways I could never have imagined. I hadn't seen or heard from her for a long time, yet our common loss forever bound us together. The intervening years and our individual life experience helped to reset the board, and it laid the groundwork for us to start over, though it didn't happen right away.

Kelli's path since the day Sam went missing was altogether different than mine. She suffered a dual loss back then, her mother passing away within days of Sam's disappearance. I spoke to her only a few times by phone in the aftermath, during the long week I spent in Angels Camp, desperately trying to find out what happened to Sam. The calls were hard, filled with long gaps of silence, and an emotional weight just starting to descend upon me; a fear that all who loved Sam would find fault with *me* for living, and more importantly, for not knowing a damn thing about what happened, outside of an enigma named Gary and the feeling I had in my gut that he was responsible.

I beat myself up over that for a long time, the not knowing. I couldn't describe Gary's truck accurately, and I never saw the license plate. His last name was a mystery, and I couldn't recall if he even gave it to us. When it came time to work up a police sketch the details eluded me, and the finished product never quite jibed with the image of a man I felt, but couldn't put into words. There was talk of using hypnosis to break free the details from my subconscious, but for some reason it was never arranged.

But there was something else at play besides my inability to provide any details. It was the sense that somehow I'd set the whole thing into motion by my open hostility towards Gary. Perhaps there was a more subtle way I could have handled the situation, and maybe my heavy-handed approach is what pushed Gary over the edge and caused whatever fixation he had with Sam to turn dangerous. Yeah, it took me a long damn time to reconcile *that* guilt.

After a week spent in Angels Camp spinning my wheels with nothing to show for it, I finally gave in to hopelessness and poverty—my wallet empty and my sole credit card maxed out—and I drove Sam's car home. At first I wasn't sure how I'd get home, the car keys having disappeared along with Sam. But then I remembered the hide-a-key he kept under the right front fender of his car. I think about those car keys from time to time.

When tragedy strikes it seems the inconsequential remains, magnified into importance beyond the simple absurdity of small things that cut so deep: missing car keys, a suitcase filled with clothes, a pair of snow skis strapped to the top of a car, a postcard bought for someone dear but never sent.

Yet life goes on, despite the horrors that living brings. Friends go missing and mothers die, shit happens. I drove

Sam's car home in a reverential silence that nearly killed me. Looking back, I should have had the damn thing towed and taken a bus.

When I got to Orange County I took the car to Sam's house. But Bill Stoneman wasn't home when I got there, even though I'd called ahead and told him when I expected to arrive, and while I didn't want to read too much into it, somehow it felt intentioned. Maybe Sam's father couldn't bear to see me. Maybe he blamed me for what happened. Hell, maybe the guy simply had things to do that day. Regardless, I never found out the reason, and I was left with a nagging feeling that eventually grew into the kind of overblown self-pity that puts people in the ground.

After dropping off the car I walked to my apartment. It was a long walk, five or six miles at least, and the whole way there felt strange to me, as if I'd been transported to some alternate universe and dropped into a place where I didn't belong. It was the end of the innocence, and my world had irrevocably changed. When I arrived at my apartment I didn't go inside. Instead, I drove my car back to Sam's house for my ski gear and duffel bag. Bill had not returned, and after waiting a short while I scribbled him a note and stuck it to the front door, dropped the key to Sam's car in the mailbox, and I drove away feeling like the biggest piece of shit on the planet.

I went straight to Kelli's house, and when she opened the door I lost it, the events of the week having drained me. We hugged and we cried, and we drove down to the beach and sat there until dark, and when I left it was a long damn time before I saw her again. Seven years to be exact.

KELLI RAN OFF to Europe, where she traveled for a year before settling into school in France. She studied for three years at a liberal arts college near Paris, fell in love with some French dude who came across in the letters she wrote as being too much like Sam, suffered a broken heart at the hands of said French dude, and eventually fled Europe for the comfort of home. She finished up her degree and got an MBA, and started selling real estate in South Orange County.

She was a natural, her easy manner and flawless beauty a compelling combination. People *liked* Kelli, and they were drawn to her in ways that sometimes made her feel uncomfortable. After a few years spent working for a local realtor, she went independent, and eventually she partnered with a high-profile broker out of Newport Beach. When I asked her once why her name wasn't on the letterhead, she had no answer. But that was Kelli, she shied away from the limelight, felt uneasy being the center of attention. And that was a huge part of her appeal, because she had the goods but didn't flaunt it.

The night of our reunion found me in fine form, pig-eyed drunk and glad-handing, hoping desperately with every cocktail I put away that no one would ask me about Sam. I felt their eyes on me, watching me, feeling sorry for me, some of them surely judging me. I was a mess that night, the trajectory of my life peaking on its self-destructive path, and as much as I tried to hide it, I knew it was futile; I wore my pain poorly, in the undignified manner of a coward.

I'd alternately hoped for and feared seeing Kelli, and when the time came I posed and postured and acted like an asshole. She reached out to me on a level I didn't understand, and I responded by pushing her away and lewdly hitting on her friends, before finally drifting off and spending the rest of the night hanging out with a group of guys I couldn't stand back in school, but that night I treated like my long-lost buddies. We had ourselves a good old time acting like fools, up until the point in the reunion where they paid homage to our dead classmates, and then the walls closed in.

I wasn't expecting it. You'd think ten years on there wouldn't be any deaths to report. But in our class there were three: one girl the victim of a drunk driving hit and run, one guy dead in a car wreck down in Mexico, and Sam. I didn't stick around to see if they said that Sam had died or simply gone missing. Without a word I split out of there and never looked back.

Once at home I numbed myself with more booze. I had a hell of a drinking problem in those days. That night I drank until I blacked out, and thankfully my dreams didn't include Sam. But I knew they wouldn't, because *that* dream only came once a year.

When I woke in the morning I felt horrible. It wasn't the hangover that made me feel that way. It was the note I found in my pants pocket when I was looking for my smokes. I unfolded the paper and saw it was a message from Kelli. I had no idea when she put it there; it might have been when we hugged upon first meeting, or maybe she had a friend slip it to me later. Her message was a simple one. Kelli told me she understood my pain. She said she hurt too, and that we could help each other, if only I would try. She left me her phone number. It took me more than a year to call her.

8

That last year was a real bitch.

You hear stories about people hitting rock bottom, watch movies and TV shows about it, read novels based on protagonists whose lives are so miserable you wonder how anyone ever got to such a point. I lived it.

Drinking and smoking, brawling and reckless living, behavior designed to either destroy me or prove me worthy of life. I bounced from job to job as a carpenter in the construction industry, building up trust only to knock it down with my indifference and impulsiveness, using up every marker I had while leveraging those who saw the core good in me, until they too were forced to lose my number.

I was a one-man wrecking crew driving balls to the wall, hell-bent on oblivion. To this day it amazes me how much you can run and still not get anywhere. The incident with the stolen surfboard was only the beginning, unleashing in me a self-destructive streak I never knew existed, its origins buried so deep it took years to uncover. My sisters and parents tried in vain to help. Intervention didn't work. Tough love was a joke. Poverty was merely a temporary inconvenience. Nothing was going to change until I was good and ready for it. My salvation finally arrived one day out of the blue.

I was searching through my closet for a purpose long since forgotten, when a box literally fell on my head, spilling its contents on the floor. My temper flared and I kicked the box, and a single photograph was cast off as if by fate. I bent down to look at it, the image stopping me cold. I wanted a drink, but the mere thought of it disgusted me. It was a picture of Sam Stoneman at the top of Mount Whitney, in the summer of 1988. I was standing next to him, both of us smiling wide, the satisfaction of accomplishment written on our faces.

I scooped up the photograph and looked at Sam, felt myself transported back to that day, the two of us standing at the top of the mountain. I closed my eyes and felt shame, and I prayed for my friend and for myself, and for every life touched by the senselessness of what had happened. When I opened my eyes I knew clearly and with absolute certainty that the course of my life was wrong, and that Sam would have kicked my ass hard had he been there. He would have admonished me to accept life's trials and tragedies with grace and dignity, to step up and move beyond that which we cannot control.

Try harder, Mason. Be a man. Do not let what happened to me define you. I expect more of you, my friend, and I will accept nothing less.

From that moment on, I turned the wheel of my life in a new direction. I set out on a path to mend fences, repair damaged relationships. I checked into rehab, joined a twelve-step group, and defiantly said *no* to all of my destructive urges. Out went the drinking and the smoking and the rage directed randomly and without reason. I reconnected with my family, nurtured the few friends who'd stood by me, re-established my professional reputation within an industry that had grown to distrust me, and more importantly, I reached out to Kelli. I took the note she'd written the year before, on a night when I'd made a complete mess out of our own personal reunion, a scrap of paper I'd kept prominently displayed on the door of my refrigerator under a Corona beer magnet, and with shaking hands I called the number, only to find it was no longer in service. I could have stopped right there, could have rationalized that I'd done my part; it wasn't my fault she'd moved on.

But that would've been a cop-out, the same shitty behavior that got me to rock bottom in the first place. Forcing myself to do it differently, I sought out Tom Flynn and asked for his help. He reluctantly gave me Kelli's new phone number, after a stern admonishment to let the past be, that whole sleeping dogs bullshit. He'd heard the rumors like everyone else, about what a mess I was, how I'd never gotten over what happened to Sam, and that my obituary was already written, just waiting to be published.

I bit down on my anger at Tom's words and I wanted to tell him to fuck off for judging me, but instead, I assured him that my intentions were genuine. I stopped short of telling him that I was clean and sober and had my act together. That seemed phony to me, and I'm sure he wouldn't have believed it anyway. Better to let things run their natural course, and if it was meant for me to prove myself to Tom Flynn, well then so be it.

Later that day I called Kelli. But I had to work up the courage first. I did it by distraction. Two hours at the gym, a long session in the water, and a marathon cleaning of my tiny apartment. When I finally ran out of things to do I made the call. It was after dark and I dimmed the lights, burned a couple of candles and put some vinyl on the turntable, Daniel Lanois, *Acadie*.

It was all so dramatic. But like I said earlier, I'd built my feelings for Kelli into something mythic, and I'd convinced myself that so much remained unresolved. Like a scene from a movie I picked up the phone and dialed the number, heard the ringing on the other end. I felt scared and energized, on the verge of being reborn, and I knew that no matter what the outcome, no matter if she heard my voice and slammed down the receiver, or cursed me for my selfish destructiveness, I would be all right.

On the eighth ring I was about to give up. Take the needle off the record, blow out the candles, go to bed and try again another day. On the ninth ring she answered. And though what I'm about to tell you may seem completely made up, I swear to you it's true. On the ninth ring Kelli's voice came on the line.

"Hello, Mason," she said. "What took you so long?"

9

L ife is what took so long. Life, and all that gets in the way of living it. All the mislaid plans and endless good intentions, the putting off to tomorrow the things that should be done today, that *must* be done today, for tomorrow is not guaranteed. About the only thing you can be sure of is the course of your life will never go as planned.

Kelli and I talked for a long time that night. We had a lot of ground to cover. And in the days and weeks and months following we talked some more. I didn't see her right away, though she'd wanted to meet. It felt more honest to talk from a distance, away from the lure of her beauty, the enticement that would no doubt come from physical proximity. Quite simply, I didn't trust myself around her, and I needed to know where I stood first, not with her and any feelings she may have had towards me, but within myself and what my expectations were. Could I be there for Kelli with no strings attached? It's true I still loved her, but I had to cleanse myself of all that, establish a true friendship that was not tainted by feelings of lust or need or some crazy notion in my head that we were meant to be.

We talked so much back then, but so little of it was about Sam. When we did go there it was good, and in a lot of ways the words we spoke were the same ones we would have shared had there been a funeral for Sam. But there never was, because Bill Stoneman refused to do that, and he went to his grave believing that one day his son would return.

Through those long talks I learned of Kelli's time in France, all of the things I didn't know after the correspondence from her stopped abruptly in the spring of '91. It was because of the French dude, her going incommunicado, and though it was uncomfortable hearing the details of their love affair, I forced myself to listen.

Later, when it came my turn to share, I felt the heat of embarrassment as I admitted to Kelli my failings in the area of romance. The series of bad relationships with vacuous women who were fun as hell while pounding drinks in the bar and knocking out sex through the night, but come the cold light of day represented no better stab at love than the transactions of some tired old whore long past her prime. It was all just so much bullshit. About the only thing those women and I had in common was a miserable void in our souls that we tried vainly to self-medicate.

Sure, a lot of that can be attributed to the foibles of youth and the time-honored quest of all young men to sow their oats, but the truth is, I'd been running for a long time, and all those lousy relationships were just par for the course.

For her part, Kelli didn't judge, and she made it easy for me to bare my soul simply because of that. All through those weeks and months of calls we wrote our story, made it possible for Mason Tanner and Kelli Flynn to begin anew, to bridge the years of heartbreak and disappointment and shared loss, and to help each other grow in ways I never thought possible. We remained friends for years before we became lovers, and for me those years were a lesson in patience and letting go. While things between us didn't move as quickly as I'd wanted, in truth it could not have happened any other way.

When we finally arranged to meet we did it on neutral ground, Diedrich Coffee, down on Seventeenth Street in Newport. It felt like a first date, and I was nervous as a teenager the whole way there. When I saw Kelli and she hugged me, my nervousness fell away, and I knew I'd finally come home. We spent the morning at the coffeehouse, and when we parted, I floated away on a cloud of bliss, with no more expectation than was warranted, yet hugely thankful for the opportunity to just be there. It wasn't that long ago the odds were even money Mason Tanner wouldn't make it to thirty. Well screw fate's oddsmakers, because I was twenty-nine years old and the sky was the limit. I'd beat back my demons and made my amends, took a hard look at myself and said yes to life and no to anybody or anything that did not contribute to it in a positive way.

In short, I took Sam's challenge. It may only have been a challenge in my own mind, the result of having seen that photograph of us standing at the top of Mount Whitney, but it was as real as if Sam himself had issued it. And I met that challenge, and in time I came to know that no matter what happened, no matter what fate threw at me, I was going to be okay.

My mantra became truth and truth became my life, and in living it differently I gained far more than I ever could have imagined. Looking back, I can see the tumblers falling into place, the Big Clock ticking its way towards my destiny. For in my future there would be a different kind of reconciliation, and while I could never have known it then, God had a plan for me. It would take years to come to fruition, and when it did, it brought me face to face with Sam Stoneman's killer.

10

Saturday morning I woke early and rode my bike to my office, located a couple of miles south down the peninsula, near the Balboa Pier. The weather had cleared and the sun was out, and it was a beautiful day for it.

I went around to the alley and opened the garage, chose my beach cruiser over the road bike. Today wasn't about speed or endurance, it was about enjoying a fine November day and taking it easy. I straightened some things and came back around to the front of the house and locked up, and I took a moment to *see* things. I did that often, making a conscious effort to stop and look and listen, to take the time necessary to truly appreciate the gift of life.

I had a lot to be thankful for. Business was good, my health was good, and more importantly, Kelli and I were good. We'd recently moved in together after dating exclusively for five years. While the subject of marriage never came up, I think we were both looking for something more. I certainly was.

So I finally said goodbye to my crummy apartment in Costa Mesa and moved into Kelli's house in Newport Beach. Friends of mine scratched their heads at why I continued to live in the same place I'd moved into a year after graduating high school, back when money was scarce and all I could afford was a one-bedroom over in the seedy side of town. It was never my intention to stay in that apartment for as long as I did, yet somehow it worked out that way. About all I can say to that is, the years go by a lot faster than they have a right to.

Kelli's house was built in the 1930s, one of those quaint little beach cottages that evoke a simpler time. It was a modest place with shingled sides and sash windows and a covered porch set back from a small yard shaded by a lemon tree. The bay window in front offered an unobstructed view of the ocean and the Newport Pier to the south, and Kelli had modernized the house in a way that made it both functional and comfortable, yet still retained the flavor of old-Newport.

So far our little experiment was working out well, though in my worst moments even our living together could not quell those lingering doubts, the ones that said it was all some kind of put-on. The fact is, I was much needier than Kelli, and the reassurances I craved were not easily given. Kelli loved without condition, but something in her wiring made it all seem so elusive, temporary in an unsettling way. The bottom line is, living with Kelli Flynn was strictly a one day at a time affair, and to ask for more was to invite emotional disaster.

Standing there looking at her house, *our* house now, touched something in me, and my thoughts came back both troubling and strange. I thought of Kelli's phone call from yesterday, the sense I'd had of her holding something back. And now she was extending her stay with her father. It seemed so easy for her to be gone like that, a few days, a week, sometimes a month back when we first got together. I felt an ache in my heart, a feeling of sadness taking root. What the hell was I looking for? Words professing love and devotion?

While I might have felt something was missing between us, for the life of me I couldn't pin it down. And that's always the worst kind of feeling, that thing just under the surface, the itch that can't be scratched, yet still you try.

Too much head-tripping, that was the problem. At times like this I had to remind myself to take a step back and let it be. Just for today life was good, and that's about all any of us can ask for.

I got on my bike and started riding.

I'D ONLY MADE IT a short distance when I came to the Newport Dory Fish Market. They were wrapping things up, the day's catch long since sold out, and I waved at a few people I knew. The dory fleet had been operating continuously from that location since the late 1800s, at the foot of the old McFadden wharf, known today as the Newport Pier.

The McFadden brothers bet big on Orange County back when it was still wide-open rolling hills inhabited by ranchers and Indians and desperadoes, and Newport was nothing but a swampy marsh, belying no hint of its future as the center of power and wealth in the county. They built their wharf and the railroads came, and soon they lorded over a thriving commercial enterprise. When the Federal Government started financing the development of a new commercial harbor thirty miles to the north in San Pedro, the brothers saw the writing on the wall and got out while the getting was good.

I made a mental note to come by early the next day and pick up some fresh fish for the barbecue, and I'd started on my way when I noticed a familiar sight huddled on one of the concrete benches near the ramp leading up to the pier. I got off and pushed my bike that way. As I neared, the man looked up at me. Bewilderment crossed his dirty face, and he appeared to shrink back as I got closer.

"Pete?" I said to the man.

He seemed to gather his thoughts. "Who dat?" he said gruffly.

"Mason Tanner."

The man on the bench was known to locals as Pete the Fisherman, an odd name, seeing how I never once saw him fish. He was a Cajun, come to Newport Beach by way of New Orleans, the circumstances changing with each telling. He was one of a handful of homeless people who inhabited the peninsula and managed to evade the Newport PD in their efforts to rid the city of lowlifes and undesirables.

I leaned my bike against a light pole and took off my sunglasses, looked Pete straight in the eye. "You okay, friend? I haven't seen you around in a while."

"Been doin' some t'ings over across de river," Pete said.

When guys like Pete mentioned the *river*, it usually meant the Santa Ana River. I wondered what he was into lately. Maybe he'd actually done some fishing.

"Me and some fellas, we got sumptin' goin' down to de river. Makin' plans for dem boys got no bidness bein' anywheres near where I'm at. You seen dem boys, Mason? One a dem's a big nigger, ugly bastard he is. I'm gonna get dat boy, he keep messin' wit' ol' Pete."

"I'll keep my eyes peeled. If I see that dude, I'll holler at you." Pete stared back absently, and I thought of something. "You eat yet today, friend?"

"Huh?"

"I said you eat anything today?"

"Eat? Naw, I ain't done anyt'ing like dat. Why you ask?"

"Sit tight, buddy, I'll be right back."

Ten minutes later I walked back to the bench from Seaside Donuts. I wasn't too worried about leaving my bike with Pete. He was a homeless person, not a thief, and despite some people's bias, one didn't necessarily mean the other. I had some coffees and a sack of donuts and ham and cheese croissants, and I gave two of the coffees and the food to Pete. I've always had a soft spot for the down and out, the forgotten ones pulled under by addiction and mental illness, the misery of life gone wrong. It wasn't that long ago I was on a road that could have very easily led to the spot Pete now occupied.

There but for the grace of God go I.

That's a lesson we all should learn.

Pete sipped from one of the coffees, and he carefully chose a donut from the bag and spread a napkin on his filthy lap. He broke the donut into four equal pieces and slowly ate each one. He seemed to forget I was standing there, and as I watched him eat I thought of what would come of him tomorrow or the next day, next month, next year. I felt the weight of sadness then, for all those cast off from love and happiness and peace of mind. It's a big, bad world out there, and damn if we aren't the lucky ones for making it through in one piece.

I wished Pete a good day and got on my bike, and as I rode away, I had the strange feeling that old Cajun and I would cross paths again soon, and when we did, nothing would be the same.

11

Thirty minutes later I rode past the plaque marking the location of the old Rendezvous Ballroom, the massive block-long dance hall that hosted countless Big Bands back in the 1930s and 40s, and was ground zero for the surf guitar craze in the early sixties; move over Benny Goodman and Stan Kenton, here comes Dick Dale and his Del-Tones. The Rendezvous burned down in 1966 and was replaced by an apartment complex, and even though I was born way too late to experience what *Look* magazine called the *Queen of Swing*, just standing next to that stone marker conjured up vivid images.

I've always been a bit of a history buff, and Orange County possesses a rich past deeply woven into the fabric of California as a state, and a *state* of mind. Secrets abound for those willing to seek them out, and links to the past are never far away. I'm tempted to say I have an old soul, but I find that saying a bit too New Age for my tastes. What I have is an overdeveloped sense of nostalgia, tinged with a healthy dose of melancholy, and at times I've felt a greater connection to the past than to the present, whether it's something I've experienced directly or just read about in a book or saw on the television. Granted, the reality of those bygone times would surely never measure up to my romantic notions, but it's still fun to imagine.

Kelli would sometimes tease me about that, playfully accusing me of being stuck in the past, and even though I took it well and in the spirit intended, I couldn't help but feel there was more to it. Kelli lived in the moment, and it's one of the things I found so appealing about her. She could make you feel so important right *now*. When she looked at you with those almond-shaped eyes, a blue so clear and deep they drew you right in, you knew beyond any doubt that she heard you, felt what you felt, cared deeply about whatever was important to you. There was nothing flirtatious in her manner, yet she exuded a subtle sexuality that was felt, a heat you wanted to be close to, a manner of being that brought out intense feelings of longing and lust, possession and protection. A lot of men have loved Kelli Flynn, and many more have wanted to, but she knew nothing about that because she didn't see it, and at her core that's what made her so damn attractive.

Turning onto Main Street, I pedaled towards the Balboa Pavilion and cut over to East Bay Avenue, coming up behind my office. I unlocked the back door and pushed my bike inside. The office was cold and I noticed the cleaning people had not been in because of the holiday.

I ran a small general contracting business, Tanner Builders, specializing in custom homes and room additions. Most of my work was along the coast, as far north as Long Beach and south down to San Clemente. Business was good, and every year since I'd hung my shingle in 2004 was better than the last. I had a freelance estimator and a general foreman named Mark Johnson who'd worked with me from the start, and a pool of tradesmen to draw from. With each new project Mark and I would put together a team to handle the work we did in-house, and I'd subcontract the rest.

I'd started working in construction while still in high school. At first it was just a way to earn some walking around money, but in time I discovered that I really liked the physical aspect of the job and being outdoors. After graduation I stumbled through an uninspired year of community college before dropping out and taking on a full-time job as a house framer. Once I had enough money put away I moved out of my parents' house and into the Edgewood Apartments with a kid I knew from the high school track team. Unfortunately, that fool kid split on me, and it led to a lean period where things got really tough. Somehow I managed to hang on, and six months later I was thrown a lifeline from a guy named Mike Cook.

Mike and I used to be close, and when the opportunity came to join his dad's commercial framing company I jumped at it. We partnered together doing piece-work, and we were fast and we were good. But Mike was also one of the biggest drunks in town, with a vicious temper on top of it, and hanging out and drinking with him in the years after Sam disappeared brought out the worst in me. We'd disrespect bartenders and harass women wantonly, and start fights for no reason, wearing out our welcome in far too many shithole bars for me to remember.

The end for us came one night at Blackie's by the Sea. We got into it over some thing or another; maybe it was a woman, maybe we were just too drunk to give a shit. Anyhow, the end result was the same, and after throwing his punk ass through the front window of Blackie's, I was ejected through that very same window by the massive cooler who worked the front door. Mike and I rolled around on the bike path beating the shit out of each other before finally calling it a draw, and from that day forward I never worked with him or for his father again. After that I never kept a job for longer than six months, and even that was rare. Yeah, those were the good old days all right.

12

I turned on the computer and answered some emails, made a feeble effort at reviewing the drawings for a custom home project in Palm Springs, then I got hungry. I still had to get some paperwork together for my accountant, but my growling stomach distracted me too much for that right now. I eyed the Balboa Saloon across the street, thinking one of their custom-built sandwiches was just the ticket, and off I went.

The Balboa Saloon was one of the few beachfront joints I still frequented; most of the others brought back way too many bad memories. That, and the fact I didn't drink anymore, made those places strictly taboo. The Saloon was your typical funky seaside watering hole, both a local hangout and a popular tourist spot, being as it was close to the Fun Zone and the Balboa Ferry.

I walked through the front door, saw my good friend Larry Peters tending bar. Larry and I went back a long way, to my first years at the Edgewood Apartments. He lived next door to me and had an insane roommate at the time, a guy whose name I can never remember, and the two of them together kept the scene rocking seven days a week.

I still remember the first time I met Larry. He was hanging out in front of his apartment, smoking a cigarette, and this guy pulls up in a Jeep out on the street. Walking past Larry on the way to my car, I heard him say out loud,

"Fucking Jeepster." I thought he was talking to me, so I turned and stared at him. Larry pointed to the guy in the Jeep, decked out in tight Wrangler jeans and a pearl snap western shirt, sporting a stiff white cowboy hat. I shrugged my shoulders and Larry pointed to the apartment unit directly above us, to where an insanely hot chick named Jill lived, seemingly by herself. Every guy at the Edgewood had it bad for Jill. I looked at Larry in confusion, and he said, "Can you believe that's her dude? I mean seriously, what's a honey like that doing with a goddamn cowboy, one who drives a Jeep no less?"

I laughed out loud, and when Jeepster walked past he shot me an unfriendly look. The guy threw off some serious attitude as he huffed up the stairs to Jill's place, his snakeskin boots clomping on every step. On the balcony, the front door opened and shut loudly, and Larry looked at me and busted out laughing.

Ever since then we'd been friendly, the orbit of our lives regularly crossing. And being as he was slightly less crazy than most of those I hung with back in the dark days, and the fact he walked the same sober path as me, we remained good friends.

"Mason!" Larry shouted upon seeing me.

"How's it hanging, Big Larry?"

The moniker amused me. Larry was about five-eight and maybe one-twenty soaking wet. Clearly he was far from big. But that was always our thing, crazy nicknames we gave each other that didn't make a lick of sense.

"Hey, brother, I've got some mail here for you. Actually, it's for Kelli."

"Huh?" I said.

"Shit, you know how it is with that squid Willie. He can never get his program right."

Larry reached under the bar and pulled out a large manila envelope. The Willie he referred to was William Stinson, a friend of ours from the neighborhood who also happened to be the mailman for the area. Willie was renowned for his ability to completely fail at just about everything he endeavored to do, including the simple job of delivering mail to the correct address. Since my office was close to the Saloon we got our stuff mixed up fairly regularly. About the only thing that kept poor Willie from being fired for pure incompetence was the fact letter carriers damn near never got fired, and besides, everyone around here liked him—or simply felt sorry for him—and they picked up the slack.

"You know," Larry said, "maybe if the dude would lay off the weed with his morning coffee he might make a better go of it."

"Really? And what about your part, serving the guy on his lunch break, how's that working out? That's what you call a contributing factor, not to mention a violation of Postal Service rules."

Larry smiled sheepishly and raised his arms in a placating gesture. I sat on a bar stool and picked up the envelope, noting the return address from a realtor in Bridgeport, a small town located about an hour north of Mammoth Lakes. Getting Kelli's mail at my office was not unusual, seeing how it used to be her real estate office, and it seemed a lot of her clients hung on to that old address. But I don't believe I ever saw anything from out of town, not from another realtor at least.

Holding onto the envelope, I thought of Kelli, and felt a strong urge to call her. It went like that sometimes, usually when I had nothing much to say yet simply wanted to hear her voice. We both had fairly busy lives professionally, though in truth mine was a cakewalk compared to the hectic schedule Kelli kept. Lately it seemed difficult to carve out time for each other, quality time as they say. Now that we lived together it got better only from the standpoint of us sharing the same space, so by virtue of that we saw each other a lot more. But still, days would go by where it seemed we never connected, and much of our interaction took on a superficiality I found unsettling.

"So what's cookin', Mason?"

Larry's voice pulled me from my thoughts. I decided I would call Kelli as soon as I returned to my office, if only to tell her about the envelope and to see if her plans had changed. Larry slid an iced tea in front of me and after a long drink I brought him up to speed.

"Things have slowed down the last month or so. But you know me, Larry, I like to ramp it down at the end of the year."

"I hear that. Work to live, that's what I always say. Too many cats got their priorities wrong on that one, and living becomes nothing *but* work. Screw that noise."

"Amen to that."

"So what's on the horizon? Anything I'd be interested in?"

Larry was a tile setter and he was damn good. But he was also hard to pin down, and even though he didn't drink anymore he was still a nut. I always enjoyed hanging out with Larry Peters. He was one of the good guys.

"I've got something lined up in Palm Springs," I said. "A nice custom home, very high-end. The tile scope will be big."

"Whoa, the desert? That's getting a little too far inland, isn't it?"

"Maybe. But then again, you consider everything east of the 405 freeway to be a different country."

Larry laughed out loud and he topped off my iced tea. He definitely had a big man's laugh.

"The money made me do it," I went on. "It was too damn sweet a deal to pass up. I'm getting double my fee and the material markup alone will be huge. The owner is a friend of my dad's and he's building his dream home, and he's got a boatload of bread and a burning desire to spend it. And he's a nice guy too."

Larry whistled. "You don't see that combo often, that's for sure. Speaking of Mr. Tanner, how is your dad?"

I thought about that question. How's Dad? Damn, where do I start?

Well, he and my mom finally split-up a few years ago, after spending far too long trying to pump life back into a dead marriage. Dad remarried quickly, and as an added bonus he found God along the way. Today he lives in Fallbrook, down in San Diego County, and he's a big wheel in the little church he centers his life around. Which is strange, because my father was hardly a religious man when I was growing up. About all I can say to that is, people change.

Dad's retired now and he's pushing seventy, and it shows; he's definitely lost a step or two in the last few years. He spent nearly forty years working for Hughes Aircraft as an engineer, most of it at their massive facility in Fullerton. Dad claims I met Hughes once in 1973, during the time Howard was living in Las Vegas at the Desert Inn, surrounded by all those Mormons, his mind thoroughly baked by that point. We were on a family vacation at Lake Mead, and my dad took me along with him when he went to Vegas to drop off some important documents. I'd like to tell you I remember all of it clearly, maybe even share with you a cool anecdote about weird Howard, but unfortunately, five was a little young for it to make much of an impression on me.

When I finally answered Larry, I told him my dad was doing okay and left it at that. Then I shifted gears. "So, you want in on the Palm Springs deal?"

"When're you getting to finishes?"

"Sometime in the summer, just in time for all that nice desert heat. You going to be around?"

"Barely," Larry said. "Check this out, bro." He reached under the bar and pulled out a brochure for surfing expeditions in Vietnam. I flipped through the pages quickly, instant flashbacks popping in my head.

I'd done a fair amount of traveling in my time, and back in the lean years I'd perfected the art of the cheap vacation, my destination anywhere sunny and close to the water, where I'd spend money recklessly and drink myself to oblivion, causing all manner of mayhem along the way. While my sense of nostalgia likes to view those times as my halcyon days, the reality is something completely different; there was a lot of bad stuff associated with those trips, and some of my traveling companions were not of the highest caliber.

"Vietnam?" I said, handing the brochure back to Larry. "For surfing?" I hadn't thought about my traveling days for a long time, but damn if that itch didn't come right back.

"Hell yes, didn't you ever see *Apocalypse Now*, that scene down there on the beach with Robert Duvall?" Larry struck a pose behind the bar. "I love the smell of napalm in the morning," he said in dramatic fashion.

"I'm envious," I replied half-heartedly, thinking that it just might be true.

"You should be." Larry winked at me. "I'm going with a couple of guys from Huntington. You remember Charlie Burke and Brett Anderson? I think they might've done some work for you before."

The names didn't ring a bell, but that wasn't unusual. In the beach communities the construction trade was transient, with workers coming and going like the tide. As soon as you found a good, seemingly reliable tradesman, he was off on a new trip. Guys like Larry were rare, guys you could go back to and count on to produce at a high level.

It seemed like nothing endured down on the coast, and for a long time that's exactly why it felt so right for me to be there. But lately I'd found myself chafing at that, the lack of permanence feeling wrong, the sense that no one wanted to commit to anything pissing me off. Was I growing old? It sure seemed that way. Pretty soon I'd be yelling at kids to get the hell off my lawn.

My food came and I ate. Larry served a few customers and came back around with more details about his upcoming surfing expedition. The more he talked about it the more I realized that I *was* envious, and jealous as hell over Larry's seemingly absolute freedom in the way he lived. While I would have never traded away my life with Kelli, and I was certainly wise enough to know that the grass always looks greener on the other side, I still felt the pangs of what if?

What if my wandering years had not been wasted in an alcoholic haze? What if things had turned out just a little bit differently? What if I had the chance to do it over, would I take it?

I smirked inside at the folly of my thinking. I had a great life, yet here I was analyzing the shit out of it because my friend told me he was planning a vacation. I was truly my own worst enemy.

The conversation drifted off and I finished my lunch. Larry and I made plans to get together on Sunday if the waves were good. Getting up to leave, I thought of my encounter with Pete the Fisherman, and I asked Larry if he knew of any problems Pete might be having with anyone, maybe a black guy. Larry said he hadn't seen Pete in more than a month, and he knew of no trouble like that. I asked him to keep his eyes open, thanked him for the excellent lunch, and left the Balboa Saloon for my office.

LATER THAT DAY I was back at home searching for the box containing financial documents I needed for my accountant. It wasn't at my office or the storage unit I used for construction supplies, but I wasn't too concerned, figuring eventually it would turn up. I called Kelli a few times that afternoon but all I got was her voicemail. It bothered me I couldn't reach her, but I tried to keep it in perspective. I'd been feeling low all throughout the long holiday weekend, depression hovering along the fringes, fighting its way in. It was to be expected, and I dealt with it the only way I knew how, by filling my time with activity. I kept myself busy and it kept the wolves at bay.

Back to the task at hand, I searched a few likely places with no luck. Then I remembered the attic above the garage, a crawl space that Kelli used for storage. I couldn't recall ever putting anything up there, but it was worth checking out. I took a ladder from its hook on the wall and positioned it under the access panel. There was no light in the attic, so I grabbed a flashlight from the workbench. At the top of the ladder I slid the panel back and poked my head up.

I saw holiday decorations and realtor signs from Kelli's old business, boxes of books and photo albums and other artifacts, everything labeled neatly in Kelli's distinctive writing, and I knew there was nothing of mine up there. I'd started down the ladder when something caught my eye. It was a newer looking box set off to the side, one with no writing on it. The accumulated dust on the floor of the attic was undisturbed, except for the area directly in front of the unlabeled box. Clearly, Kelli had recently taken it down.

For reasons I'll never understand, that box piqued my curiosity, so I stepped back up the ladder and studied it more closely. I actually felt my heart shudder when I reached for it. The box was full but not heavy, and when I put my hands through the holes in the side I felt papers. I stepped down the ladder and set the box on the workbench, but hesitated before taking the lid off. I don't know why I did that, or why at that particular moment I felt like having a drink. Was it premonition? Perhaps. Or maybe it was simply fate calling me out. For inside that box was something that nearly destroyed me.

13

I finally spoke to Kelli at nine o'clock on Sunday evening, after playing phone tag with her since the call on Friday morning. While I was relieved to connect with her, at the same time I was at odds with myself, and the conversation was difficult.

I'd been out surfing earlier in the day with Larry Peters. It was a good day for it and we had a long session in the water. But I was distracted all day, and later, when we went for fish tacos, I told Larry what was bothering me. It was that box I'd found in the attic. Larry was a good sounding board, and he gave me some useful advice on how to handle the situation, most importantly to not make any assumptions about it. The truth would be revealed in its own time.

I tried to keep that in mind when Kelli and I spoke, and despite the emotions raging inside me, I managed to keep myself in check as Kelli told me about her dad and the decisions she'd made regarding his condition. But soon I felt myself drifting, disconnecting from the call, and when the conversation turned to small talk I steered it to an end. For once, Kelli's voice brought me no solace. She said she'd be home by Friday and I was good with that, as it would give me time to get my head together and prepare for what would come.

I avoided the box all week, tried to keep my mind clear of it. This was only after I'd spent some time going through its contents. I was both intrigued and repulsed by what I'd found, and a crushing sense of sadness came over me when I was through with it. I also opened the manila envelope addressed to Kelli. I knew it was a major line to cross and there would be no way for me to cover it up, but I did it anyway. It was that damn Bridgeport return address, and the feeling I'd had that it was connected to the box from the attic. Ultimately, I deemed the consequences of violating Kelli's privacy worth the information gained.

As Friday neared I began to feel anxious, and wished there was some work to keep me busy. But things were slow, as they always were at the end of the year, and after I got a couple of bids out I had nothing to do but surf and read and wait. I looked for Pete the Fisherman but couldn't find him, and no one I spoke to had seen him around. For reasons I can't explain, my intuition said to find that old Cajun and make sure he was okay.

I did a lot of reflecting that week, about my life and my motivations, about family and what it meant to me. On Wednesday evening I took my mom to dinner and spent some time at her house. Thursday I drove down to see my dad in Fallbrook. I felt a pull to do so, and while a phone call would have been easier, I wanted to see Dad face to face, give him a hug and tell him that I loved him. We spent a good afternoon together, and even though I didn't tell him what was on my mind, he seemed to sense my unease, and the things he said to me that day helped me greatly. Dad had a lot of wisdom, and despite it being couched in too much religious mumbo-jumbo, the gist of it remained.

By the time I left Fallbrook I felt better, or at least more settled, and I knew that in less than twenty-four hours Kelli would be home and we'd get the chance to talk and clear the air. I trusted her implicitly and I loved her deeply, and

I knew that whatever the hell she was up to, it was for a good purpose.

14

Kelli looked at me and I grew uneasy, the intensity of those blue eyes drawing me in with a pull so strong, so all-encompassing, that I felt consumed by doubt. From the minute she walked in the door it had all gone wrong. I'd had a number of scenarios mapped out, but none of them were *this*.

I had hoped we could spend some time together before broaching the subject of the box from the attic, dinner and a walk on the beach, maybe some lovemaking afterwards. I mean, isn't that what people in love are supposed to do after they've been apart for a while? A familiar hunger came over me, and as was so often the case, the more I hungered the more she withdrew. Her hug felt rigid, her kisses forced, the whole of her so completely out of sync with my desires that you would have thought we were mere acquaintances.

The part of Kelli I wanted most had shut down, and while I'd like to tell you the reasons meant something to me, that would be a lie. Her manner forced me inward and from there I grew insecure, old voices in my ear, and I was off to the races. It became all about *me* then, all about my needs and my hurt and my anger, and even though I knew this was a tough time for Kelli, I chose to ignore it. After all, she lost her fiancé all those years ago, the man she wanted to spend the rest of her life with.

And me? I only lost a friend.

It didn't escape me that had Sam Stoneman lived, he'd be here right now, likely in this very house, probably with a few of his kids running around. I've often wondered if they would have made it this far. Would they have made it to the wedding? Who knows? When you're young lots of things can happen. Things *did* happen.

And where would I be today? Certainly not standing here arguing with Kelli Flynn, feeling like I do. Sometimes it seemed so impossibly complicated, so hopelessly entangled, that I wondered if it wasn't all one big dream, or worse, a twenty-year nightmare.

The situation derailed quickly and soon I was treading water. To be fair, it was all my fault, as I'd left the manila envelope sitting out in the open, and once Kelli saw it I was sunk. I had not planned on owning up to that little transgression until after we'd discussed the other thing, but Kelli's immediate and almost visceral reaction to what I'd done put me on the ropes.

I've never been a very subtle guy, certainly not when my back is up, and I'm probably a lot more prideful than I have a right to be, so like a fool I dug my heels in, which was exactly the wrong thing to do. Kelli dropped the boom on me hard, and the words she spoke cut me, not because they were filled with anger—that I could have handled, could have countered it with my own sharp tongue—but because they were so plaintively real, and they spoke of a hurtful realization in her heart; I'd crossed a major boundary, and no amount of bullshit double-talk on my part would change that.

"Damn it, Mason, it's a trust issue. You may be living with me now, but that gives you no right to open my mail. Why would you do this to me?"

Kelli's eyes turned cold and in them I saw an awakening, and I knew that we faced a defining moment. And yet I was determined to fuck it all up, because deep down inside, a part of me never really believed I deserved Kelli, and because I didn't deserve her our life together was a lie, and what better time to expose that lie than right now.

"Trust? You're going to go with that are you?"

My tone verged on a sneer. I was looking for a reaction now, being an asshole for no other reason than to be an asshole. I'd had good practice at that too, and even though I'd buried that part of myself when I stopped the drinking and reckless living, it frightened me how quickly it all came back.

I felt betrayed by what Kelli had done, or at the very least, left out of something I deserved to be part of, because damn it, I was *there* when it happened. My nerves fired and I wanted a cigarette, and that old craving for booze jumped on my back and wouldn't let go. I channeled all of it into my outrage, and I went for broke.

"If you're all about trust, then explain what the hell this is."

I picked up the box from the floor, where I'd concealed it alongside a bookshelf, the plan being to ease my way into it. There was no easing into anything now, and when I flipped the lid, Kelli looked stricken.

"How did you find that?" she said.

A stab of emotion went through me, the feeling that maybe I'd gotten this all wrong. I'd made too many assumptions, all of them bad, one built on top of the other until I was convinced of some plot against me. But when I saw Kelli look down into that box, her eyes tentative, almost wondering, every bit of justification I'd held onto went out the window. Yet still I plowed ahead, a hard-ass to the end.

"I found it in the attic. When I was looking for my business records. I wasn't snooping around, Kelli. You know I'm not like that."

She gave me an odd look, like maybe she thought I *was* like that, and I had the inexplicable feeling that we really didn't know each other.

Kelli didn't speak. She stood rigidly in front of me, and even though she was a tall woman, what they used to call statuesque back in my dad's time, she seemed to shrink into herself as she stared into the box with a faraway look, like she was seeing through the bottom of it into the depths of some unknown thing. When she raised her eyes to mine, a world of hurt obscured their beauty.

"Sit down, Mason," she whispered. "We need to talk."

15

The box contained evidence of two decades of suspicious disappearances from small towns throughout the Sierra Nevada Mountains, all of them seemingly linked, and they began with Sam Stoneman's disappearance in 1989. The information was gathered by Kelli and put together like a puzzle, until slowly a picture emerged. It was a picture of heartbreak and loss, of lives ruined by the vagaries of life and the whims of a sick mind, and the haunting uncertainty that comes from never knowing the truth.

Kelli had marked up a map indicating each town and date where a disappearance occurred, a trail of red dots running north from Bear Valley on Highway 49, straight through the Gold Country. The trail turned east at Auburn and worked its way along Interstate 80 to Reno, where it turned again and followed U.S. Route 395 south, to the final red dot dated three weeks ago in Bridgeport.

One person missing every year since 1989, all of them young men, none of them ever heard from again. Each incident occurred during a defined period of time, between October and November, and the evidence pointed to one man as the perpetrator. A man I'd met once before.

There were police reports and witness statements, newspaper clippings, Internet documents, contact names and numbers, maps and minutiae, all of it organized into file folders broken down by year. Sam's folder contained the police report I'd filed back in '89, along with a copy of the police sketch of Gary, and even though the picture never quite captured what he really looked like, seeing the image now made me shudder so thoroughly that I reached out to steady myself.

"When did all of this start?" I said. "And how?"

The heat was gone between us now, the fight having drained out of me, a sense of foolishness taking its place. Impatience has always been my downfall, and far too often I've sabotaged myself by jumping to conclusions before knowing facts. I pulled back on that part of myself, and even though the minutes stretched out unbearably, this was not the time for me to force anything. I'd pushed Kelli so much already it would be a miracle if she didn't kick my ass out when this was finished.

"It was summer before last, when I went up to my dad's place to help out after his operation. Do you remember?"

She stared at me unfocused, eyes rimmed by fatigue, and I knew that I had completely steamrolled Kelli after what was certainly a difficult week for her. Her face looked tired and drawn, but her natural beauty could never be concealed. At forty, Kelli was just starting to show the slow creep of middle age, and I found her far more attractive now than when we were eighteen and had the world at our fingertips. She'd filled out in all the right ways, and she carried herself with a grace that age would surely never diminish.

"Yes, I remember."

"I was reading an article in the local newspaper. It was about a young man who went missing in Truckee a few years earlier, under mysterious circumstances. A witness reported seeing a suspicious man hanging around at the time, and his name was Gary. When I read that my heart about stopped."

"Gary?" I said.

The name came back to me weirdly, and I felt my throat go dry. Random thoughts and images hit me in quick succession, and in that moment the past crashed violently into the present. I repeated the name distastefully, Kelli's eyes seeming to apologize for it.

"Yes, and the description of him fit. And the circumstances fit too."

"Circumstances?"

"To what happened with you and Sam. Two friends were skiing up at Donner and they hooked up with some guy in a tavern. The next day one of the friends went to the local sheriff's office and reported the other missing." Kelli looked into my eyes, as if gauging my reaction. "Strange, isn't it?"

"Yeah, strange. But all this," I said, pointing to the files. "How did you get to this?"

"The article linked the disappearance in Truckee to another incident a year earlier in Colfax, and a third kid who vanished in Auburn a year before that."

"Linked in what way?"

"All three times it was two friends out drinking. They encountered a stranger in a bar and one of them disappeared later that night. The name Gary didn't come up in those other two cases, but the description of the suspect was the same. The victims were all close in age and their descriptions were similar, and similar to Sam's too."

"And you think they're related, those three and what happened to Sam?"

"Yes, I do."

"But we're talking a big time gap, Kelli, between Sam and those other guys."

"That's true, and at first I didn't give it much thought beyond my initial reaction. But then it occurred to me that if a link did exist, the police might know about it. It seemed to be a logical starting point, to find out if there was any official record of such a thing. So I contacted the sheriff up in Mariposa County, asked him—"

"You talked to Terry?" I blurted, cutting Kelli off. Terry Stuart was the sheriff I'd dealt with back in '89.

"No, Terry passed away a few years ago. I spoke with a detective named Michael Jeffcoat. He said he knew of no ongoing investigation into serial disappearances. Later, after he checked some things out, he called me back and told me that as far as he could tell, it was never an area explored after Sam went missing."

I noticed Kelli used the word *disappearances*, and not *killings*, to describe the crimes, a telling distinction. But of course Sam was dead, and if the cases in those file folders were the work of the same man, then all of those people were dead too, and what we were looking at was a serial killer operating on a major scale. How could the cops not know about this?

"What did you do next?" I said.

"For a while I did nothing. But I couldn't get the story out of my head, so one day I started searching the Internet, just throwing keywords out to see what came up. Fairly quickly I found two other cases that seemed to fit, Placerville in '95 and El Dorado in '93. That's when I put together the map, and the visual was startling. I literally had a trail moving north from Bear Valley, and I was convinced more than ever that I was onto something significant.

"I got serious about it then and I signed up for one of those public records research sites, and pretty soon I had more articles about missing persons than I knew what to do with. At first I concentrated on the area between Bear Valley and Lake Tahoe, but pretty soon I expanded it to include the Eastern Sierra. I filtered out everything prior to 1989, and later I went back several years earlier to test my theory that all of this started with Sam."

"And?"

"I found no common denominators, so I knew I was on the right track. Whenever something promising came up I contacted local authorities for more information, and I also spoke with some of the people directly involved. I found a lot of similarities in their stories. A black pickup for instance, with and without a camper shell. The suspect named Gary, and his claim that he lived nearby. There were even some accounts that the suspect followed the victims, like what happened to you guys. It's been hit and miss though, and at times I've considered hiring someone to help me with it, like an investigator or a researcher."

I stared at Kelli for a long minute, uneasy with what she'd said.

"Why the look, Mason?"

"I'm wondering why you never shared this with me, or asked for my help."

Kelli scrunched her face, her eyes wandering. "I'm sorry about that. But you have to understand, there was never any conscious plan behind this. I guess I just got so caught up in it I lost perspective."

"But shouldn't I have been a part of it? Am I not entitled to know?"

With that my tone veered into accusation, and I checked myself on the attitude. Kelli reached across the table, took my hands in hers. She melted me with her touch, and if there was anything in this world I felt compelled to resist, I was powerless to do so.

"But now you do. And it was never my intention to mislead you. Maybe I did by omission, but eventually this was meant for us."

She swallowed me with her eyes, and I knew what Kelli would say next, I felt it in the center of my soul, and it scared the hell out of me.

"For us?"

"Yes, Mason, for us. So we'd finally know the truth. It's right here in front of us, and I know you want it as much as I do. Our whole lives we've been missing a piece of ourselves. It's the part that feels wrong. And if we can find it and put it back where it belongs, then we can truly move on."

Kelli's eyes held mine and the tears came, and she turned slightly to wipe them. The years fell away and we were young again, sitting on the beach after it happened, mourning a loss the enormity of which we could never fully grasp.

But in truth I feared it, the finding out, and a part of me wanted to turn selfishly away, shield Kelli and protect *us* from it, because something deep inside said if we went down that road, we wouldn't make it back. Not together at least.

Kelli Flynn was a very intuitive woman, and she could plug so completely into you it was unnerving, the sense that she knew your thoughts. Like right now.

"Listen to me, Mason." She looked at me in that way of hers, the one that said nothing else existed but for this one moment. "I love you. I have for a long time. But I also loved Sam. And that's not to say it was a better love or a deeper love or anything like that. It was different, that's all. And in truth, our love never had a chance to grow, because he was taken from me, and it still hurts, it…"

Kelli's voice faltered and I looked away, emotions piling up inside me. She reached out and touched my face, turned my head gently, and she brought her other hand up and held me like that.

"I know this is hard for you and that you've struggled with it, and I know you have doubts. God knows I've tried to ease them. You can be such a complicated man, Mason, but that's one thing I love about you. So please hear me when I tell you that finding out what happened to Sam doesn't change anything about us. I need to know, that's all. *We* need to know. And finally Sam can rest in peace."

Kelli slipped her hands from my face. I closed my eyes and saw it all then, and I knew as much as I knew anything in my life that it was time. It was time to confront the monster in the closet, the one I may have beaten into submission, but never truly vanquished.

"What do you want, Kelli?"

"I want the truth."

I opened my eyes and looked at her, and I knew with absolute certainty that I would follow this woman to hell and back, if that's what it took.

16

Later we made love. When Kelli took me inside her, the entire world ceased to exist, the flood of emotion so strong it felt unreal. We took our time with it and I made myself slow down, rein in the part of me that was always on the move, always ready for the *next* thing.

Kelli gave herself so fully to me I felt ashamed for having doubted her in the first place. We made love twice that night, and afterwards, when Kelli lay sleeping and my mind would not slow down, I slipped out of bed and dressed in the other room.

I left the house and started south on the bike path. I often went out late at night, walking aimlessly along the shore, the rhythm of the waves rolling in one after the other calming to my shifting moods, the vastness of the ocean spread out before me affording a perspective that said I was insignificant in all things, and therefore all that I worried over was insignificant as well. It was during those walks that I felt an appreciation for the simplest of life's pleasures, a feeling that often evaded me in the frantic hustle of day to day.

It was late, after eleven at least, and the cold temperature kept the bar action along the strand subdued. Come summer the scene would be crazy, with all manner of knuckleheads and fools and scammers coming down by the carload to live it up Newport-style. In short order it all grew so tedious, and I saw a day when Kelli and I would leave this place for good, move somewhere where the pace was slower, less hip. With the money we were making we could bankroll enough to buy some land, a big spread near Deadwood, or maybe Colorado, somewhere down around Pagosa Springs. Sure, that'd be nice. It's always good to have dreams.

I made it to the pier and kept going, coming up a few minutes later on a pile of old clothes next to a bench. As I neared, I saw it was a man bundled against the cold. I recognized the faded Army jacket and dreadlocks poking out from the dirty trucker cap, the bill pulled down low to conceal the man's face. It was Pete the Fisherman, and he looked like a homeless Buddha, sitting upright and cross-legged alongside the bench, layers of clothing bulking up his thin frame.

Pete looked up at me as I stood in front of him. I'd learned from past experience that you had to approach street people cautiously, not out of any fearful reasons, but because the mental afflictions so many of them suffered from made them unpredictable and prone to jumpiness, and the constant hassling by the cops caused guys like Pete to view every encounter as potentially dangerous.

"Hey, buddy," I said. "How are you?"

"Who dat? Do I know ye?"

"It's Mason. You remember, we talked a few days ago?"

"Aye, Mason, how you be, friend?" Pete pushed his cap to show his face. "Why you be out on a cold night? You got bidness wit' de Fisherman?"

"Not tonight, Pete. I'm out for a walk, doing some thinking."

"T'inking eh? What you t'inking 'bout? You gots troubles?"

"Life's good. How about you? You work out that business at the river?"

Pete guffawed loudly and slapped his knee. "Ha! Dem boys, dey learnt some t'ings 'bout messin' wit' de Fisherman. I showed dat big ol' nigger how we do it down in Nawlins. Yessir, I done took cared all dat."

Pete snorted and mumbled to himself, seeming to slip away, and I thought about the depths of confusion he surely confronted each and every day. Sometimes I felt that guys like Pete the Fisherman existed solely to give the rest of us an appreciation for the gift of sanity and peace of mind, and to expose the ridiculousness of our self-absorbed ways. Unfortunately, most people viewed guys like Pete with disdain, and they wouldn't piss on him if he were on fire.

It occurred to me that I'd never seen Pete drinking, and he'd never once asked me for booze or implied in any way that he was a drunk. I felt a kinship with that, and a hope that maybe someday Pete would find his way to better days. I asked if he'd eaten lately. Pete thanked me and said that he wasn't hungry, maybe tomorrow he'd be.

"I won't be around next week," I told him. "I'm heading up to Bridgeport in a few days. I'll check on you when I get back."

It was then that I knew I'd made the decision, and it felt completely natural telling Pete about it. When Kelli told me earlier that she wanted to go up there and look around, see what we could find out about the twenty-one-year-old named Ted Parker who vanished three weeks ago, I found myself shrinking back from everything we'd talked about, the honesty we'd bared. It all sounded good on paper, but the idea of actually investigating such a thing triggered all kinds of alarms in me. What was I afraid of? I wish I could tell you.

But fear it I did, and I'm sure that's what made me restless, and it was the reason I was out that night walking along the beach, subconsciously sorting it out. And now I'd told Pete about it, and in telling it I felt more confident that it was the right thing to do.

"Where dat?" Pete said.

"Bridgeport?"

"Yeah, where dat place, Mason?"

"It's up north, near the mountains."

"It snow in dat place?"

"Some. Not too much though."

"Cold, eh?"

"Yes, very cold," I said.

"Ha! Ol' Pete don' like none a dat, snow and such. Cold ain't bad, it's cold in Nawlins, see, but no snow. No sir, Pete don' like dat snow."

Pete retreated into himself, mumbling about the cold and the snow and something about the Mississippi River. I left him then, knowing that in his own way, Pete was living the best life he could. I felt sadness for him but no pity. To pity Pete the Fisherman would be to disrespect him, and I suspected he had plenty of that in his life already.

I turned and walked back home, thinking of what the future would bring, wondering if Kelli and I would really be able to bridge two decades and uncover the truth of what happened to Sam.

17

Bridgeport, California
December 2009

We pulled into town at three o'clock on Monday afternoon. The drive up U.S. Route 395 was pleasant and we took our time with it, eating lunch at Jack's in Bishop and stopping at Mono Lake to take some pictures. The weather was mostly clear and the road conditions good, and though we hit some light snow going over Deadman Summit, it barely slowed us down. I was told once by an old-timer up in Lee Vining that the pass was named for an actual dead man, a murder victim who was found decapitated nearby in the 1860s. While the tale may be apocryphal, the telling of it does make for a nice bit of creepy trivia.

Bridgeport is located about a hundred miles south of Reno, not far from the California-Nevada border. Situated along the East Walker River in the middle of a fertile grazing basin hemmed in by the Sierra Nevada Mountains to the west and the Bodie Hills to the east, the town's main source of income is outdoor tourism, hunting and fishing and the like. I hadn't been there in nearly fifteen years, when I made a gas stop as I headed to Reno for a friend's wedding and a wild three-day weekend that resulted in me crashing my car and spending a night in the drunk tank, after taking on three hicks at some cowboy bar out in Sparks. What the hell I was doing in Sparks I couldn't tell you. That's just how it went back then.

The first order of business was to touch base with Kelli's realtor friend, the sender of the infamous manila envelope. Annette Briggs was a former co-worker of Kelli's who'd moved to Bridgeport and started her own business. She was the one who told Kelli about the disappearance of Ted Parker, the envelope containing information about the incident.

Kelli had a whole network of friends and business acquaintances scattered around the state, and through them she compiled a lot of the information about the string of missing persons. I had to hand it to her, she'd done quite an impressive job putting it all together, like a regular private eye. But that was Kelli's thing, when she got onto something that hooked her interest she followed it through with relentless diligence. She could be a bulldog about it, and you damn well didn't want to get in her way once she got going.

We crossed the bridge over the Walker River at the east end of town and drove along the main drag. The sun hung low over the snowcapped mountains to the west and a stiff northerly breeze blew in a thick band of rain clouds. The streets were wet and the air temperature hovered in the low forties, promising a cold night ahead. Christmas decorations adorned the street lamps and storefronts, and smoke drifted from the chimneys of nearby homes, bringing the smell of burning firewood; the quintessential small town scene, deserving of its own picture postcard.

Bristlecone Realty was located at the west end of town, next to the Mono County Courthouse. We pulled up and I noticed a *closed* sign hanging in the window. "Wasn't she expecting you?" I said.

Kelli scrunched her face in thought. "Yes, she was," she replied.

We drove around to the rear of the building, found no vehicles back there. Kelli parked and got out, leaving the motor running. I fiddled with the radio while she went to the door and knocked, and a minute later she returned to the car.

"That's strange, Annie said she'd be here at least until five. I hope she's okay."

"Why don't you call her?"

Kelli took her cell phone out of the center console. "Hmm, it says I have three missed calls, over an hour ago. Did you hear the phone ring?"

"No, but the reception's been pretty bad. Maybe it rolled straight to voicemail."

She keyed over to her messages and put the phone to her ear. I turned the radio down and checked my phone for messages and email. Kelli finished listening and put her phone back in the console.

"Change of plan, Mason. Annie had to run up to Reno to help her daughter out. It's nothing serious, but she won't be back for a day or two. She feels bad about not reaching us. I'll call her later and let her know we're okay."

"So what do we do now?"

"She said we should go see Bob Jeffries, up at Twin Lakes."

I knew from reading the information provided by Annette that Twin Lakes was where Ted Parker went missing, but the name Bob Jeffries didn't ring a bell. I assumed he had something to do with the lodge where Parker was staying. I felt unsteady, like I was stumbling around in a dark room looking for the lights, and I wasn't sure what Kelli wanted from me. Do I lead, or do I follow? I was trying hard to go with the flow, but that really wasn't my nature, and the urge to take control was strong.

Take the next indicated step, Mason, and don't complicate things.

"What do you want to do?" I said flatly, keeping the expectation out of my voice.

Kelli thought for a minute. "Are you hungry?"

"Sure, I could eat."

"Why don't we do that, and then we'll find a place to stay. Once we get settled I'll call Annie and see what's up."

"Sounds like a plan, chief."

Kelli's eyes brightened and she let out a giggle, while I ignored too many questions floating around in my head. She pulled out onto Main Street and I turned up the radio, and listened to a country song I'd never heard before.

18

We ate a light meal at a café on Main Street and afterwards got a room at the Walker River Lodge, at the east end of town. After settling in, Kelli called Annie, but she couldn't reach her. She tried several more times over the next half hour, with the same result. Undaunted, she turned on her laptop and fired off an email to her friend.

Through all of this I lay on the bed reading a James Ellroy novel, but I was restless and had trouble concentrating. When Kelli said she had some work to take care of on her computer, I decided to go out for a walk. I put on a thermal under my flannel shirt and zipped up my heavy North Face jacket, added a beanie and some wool gloves, and I was ready to go. On my way out the door, Kelli asked me to bring her back a cup of coffee. I smiled, and stepped out into the cold.

IT WAS DUSK and the temperature had dropped considerably since we'd hit town. I walked west on Main Street, my mind a blank. Less than six hundred people lived in Bridgeport and it seemed every one of them was in for the night. A long haul trucker blew past me, likely on his way to Reno or parts further north, and a few minutes later a Forest Service truck came down Main and turned into an alley. After that the street was empty, and I found the solitude comforting. The café where we'd eaten earlier was closed and I didn't see anywhere else to get a coffee to go, so I continued on a few more blocks, to the Shell station located at the end of town. I wanted to buy a map anyway, scope out the lay of the land.

As I approached the station I saw an older model Ford pickup parked at the edge of the lot, near a couple of propane tanks. The truck was black and it had a camper shell on the back, and it was covered from end to end with a film of dirt and splattered mud. A jolt went through me at the sight of it, and instantly I was transported back to that lonely road in Bear Valley, the snowy night and the arm sticking out the window, waving Sam and me forward.

My breath came out in choppy plumes of steam, and I stepped a few feet away from the street corner and sat down on the curb. My reaction to the truck bothered me, and after a few minutes consideration I passed it off to some kind of subconscious trigger spurred by the mountains and the snow and the cold, and more importantly, my purpose in town.

While I sat there two cars and a semi passed by in quick succession, the draft blowing over me and infiltrating my clothing. I stood and shook my limbs to warm up, and walked across to the gas station. Closer to the truck I saw the camper shell was different from what I remembered, and even though it was old, the pickup wasn't *that* old. I mentally chided myself for being so jumpy.

The mind is a powerful thing, and while our memories can bring untold pleasure, they can also bring us pain, and the realization of that made me wonder if it wasn't best to let the past be. I'd spent a long time getting over what happened to Sam, and I failed to see what we could accomplish in Bridgeport that would have any real meaning in the grand scheme of things. Bring Sam's killer to justice? Man, that seemed so unlikely it was absurd.

Anyway, the point was moot. This was important to Kelli, and by extension it had to be important to me. I wondered if that made me cold or uncaring, that I had to *make* it important. Was it indicative of some deep character flaw? I pushed all that aside, figured there was no percentage in rehashing old stuff, and I entered the gas station mini-mart.

"CAN YOU TELL me how to get to the Twin Lakes?"

I stood at the counter with two coffees and a large bottle of water, and a couple of candy bars for my sweet tooth. I threw in a pack of gum and a protein bar for Kelli while I waited. The clerk had just finished helping a customer ahead of me. The owner of the Ford perhaps? I'd first noticed him while I was perusing the map stand; a guy about my height, bundled up in a threadbare black overcoat, one of those hunter's caps with the ear flaps pulled down low. His back was turned so I couldn't see his face, and when he walked out of the mini-mart I heard a slight scuffing sound, like something being dragged.

"Twin Lakes?" the clerk said.

He was an old guy wearing a hearing aid on his right ear, so I shifted to my left and spoke louder. "Yes. I have some business there tomorrow and I'm not sure where it is."

He reached for a small transistor radio on the counter, turned it off. "Sorry about that. So you're heading up to Twin Lakes are you?"

"Yes, tomorrow. How do I get there?"

The man gave me a friendly smile. "You take Twin Lakes Road, the one next to the station here, and follow it south. Now the road curves a bit, so be careful. Stay on it about thirteen miles or so to the first lake, a little farther to the second."

"Sounds easy enough," I said.

"Easy as pie, son."

The clerk gave out a full-throated laugh and he rang up my purchases, placed the items in a plastic bag and put the coffees in a cup holder. While he did this I looked out the front window of the mini-mart, saw the black Ford with the camper shell idling at Main Street. The truck seemed to linger there, exhaust billowing from the tailpipe, and a tingle went up my spine as those memories came back stronger than ever. The driver turned and stared at me as he drew down on a cigarette, and I tried to make out his features but the distance was too great. He took two more drags on the smoke and flicked it out the window, and my memories went into overdrive. The truck turned onto Main Street, trailing exhaust as black and foul as the thoughts in my mind.

"That there's the road."

"Huh?" I said, the clerk's words startling me.

"I saw you looking out at Twin Lakes Road. That's the one I was telling you about. It leads up to the lakes."

"Oh, yeah. Right," I mumbled, the distraction of the Ford lingering. I quickly forced my composure back into place, just so the clerk wouldn't think I was strange. He gave me the tally for my purchases and I handed over the money, and while he made change I asked him about Bob Jeffries.

"Ol' Bob runs the fishing lodge up on lake number two," the clerk said.

"Twin Lakes, right?"

"That's right. It's called the Twin Lakes Lodge formally, but most folks around here just call it the lodge. It's up there on the upper lake." The clerk studied me. "What's your business with Bob? You don't mind my asking."

"I don't mind. I'm up here with my girlfriend looking into that incident with Ted Parker. You heard of him?"

The clerk shook his head ruefully. "Yes, I know all about that. It's a heck of a thing, that young man turning up missing like that. I've lived here near thirty years and never heard of anything like it in this whole valley. I figured I'd left that sort of thing behind in the big city. Guess I was wrong about that."

"Was he from here?"

"He was from Tonopah, out in Nevada. He was here with a friend doing some fishing."

"Is that where it happened, up at the lodge?"

"No, that's where they were staying. The way I hear it, the two of them went for dinner at the roadhouse south of town. They got to drinking and such, and after a while Parker's friend hitched a ride back up to the lodge. There wasn't anything behind it, no trouble between the two, he was just ready to turn in for the night. When he woke up the next day, Parker was gone, and there's been no sign of him since."

"What happened to the friend?"

"He was pretty shook up by the whole thing, as you'd expect. He even stayed around town for a while to help out in the search. He's been back twice since, just looking around. Yes sir, he took it real hard."

The clerk's words troubled me, and I pictured Parker's friend, knowing exactly what he went through, each and every miserable step. Hopefully the kid would keep it together and not go down the rabbit hole like I did.

"What's your interest in all this anyway? You some kind of law enforcement?" The clerk looked at me curiously, and his face brightened. "Say, you aren't one of those private detectives, are you?"

"Oh no, nothing like that. Actually, I'm writing a book."

I have no idea where that came from, and the minute the words were out I regretted them. But it seemed to play well with the old guy, and I figured if Kelli and I needed a cover, this one was as good as any.

"It's about missing persons," I added. "More specifically, missing adults. You know, the ones whose pictures *don't* end up on milk cartons."

"You don't say? I suppose that's something most folks don't ever think about, grownups going missing. You've got yourself a publisher do you? Or you one of those freelance types?"

"Freelance, for now. But we'll see how it plays out."

"I see," the clerk said. "Well I wish you luck with it. I've always admired people who write books. It's not a skill I possess, but I sure enjoy reading them. My name's Hank by the way, Hank Newman." He offered his hand and I shook it.

"Mason Tanner. My girlfriend's name is Kelli Flynn. She's back at the motel. So what can you tell me about Bob Jeffries?"

"Well, let me see. I can tell you he's lived around these parts for a good while, close to twenty years, I suppose. He used to work for the State as a park ranger, but he's retired now. He's a nice fella too."

"How old is he?"

"Oh, I'd say Bob's got to be near seventy now. He keeps himself in good shape though, running that place of his up on the lake. He's got a nice little operation up there."

"He's a family man?"

"He was. His wife passed on some time ago. Bob never had any children that I know of, but he gets plenty of them staying at his place, especially in the summertime, when school's out." Hank paused a moment. "You sure ask a lot of questions, son."

He said it politely, the smile never leaving his face, but the point was made. "I suppose I do," I replied with a chuckle. "My father is a retired newspaper reporter and I guess some of that rubbed off on me. Anyway, I'm sorry if I bothered you, Hank."

Man, the lies were rolling off me now. Next thing you know, I'd be pulling a Jim Rockford and printing up bogus business cards to go along with my fake persona. I wasn't even sure the subterfuge was necessary, but by that point the die was cast. I'd have to be sure and bring Kelli up to speed on the book project. No sense in blowing our cover before we were finished here.

"It's no bother, Mason," Hank said. "But you might want to ease up on that a little. We're a small town and folks here are friendly, but we're also tight-knit, and what happened to that young man has got a lot of people feeling jumpy. I'd hate for you to get off on the wrong foot with anyone."

"Point taken, Hank, and I'll keep that in mind. And thanks for the information too, you've been a real help."

"It's been my pleasure. You take care now."

I left the mini-mart, feeling out of sorts. I didn't like to lie to people, yet here I was doing it wantonly. The scene with Hank Newman was illuminating, but equally troubling, and the unease over my purpose in town came roaring back. I was acutely aware that incrementally I'd moved closer to an emotional ledge I had no business being near.

I walked along Main Street, the cold seeping into my bones. Christ, it felt subzero, and no matter how fast I moved I couldn't get warm. After several minutes I saw the motel up ahead and I quickened my pace, eager to get out of the cold. Stepping off the curb at a street corner, I heard the sharp sound of an engine rev, followed by squealing tires, and I looked up in time to see the blur of a vehicle coming right at me. I froze, unsure if I should run forward or jump back, and when my brain clicked I ran, stumbling after three steps and dumping the coffee on the ground, followed by an awkward landing on my right hip against the curb. Rolling sideways, I caught a glimpse of the vehicle. It was the Ford pickup I'd seen at the Shell station.

The truck made a right turn and disappeared onto a side street, and I sat on the cold sidewalk catching my breath. It was full dark now, the street as quiet as a prayer, and I looked around for witnesses. There was no one about, and

I had the sudden feeling I'd been dropped into a *Twilight Zone* episode, one of those last man on earth stories. Well, except for the lunatic in the truck, that is.

I got to my feet and looked at the coffee soaking the ground. Kelli would have to go without. No way was I going back for two more. I tossed the trash in a nearby dumpster and started walking. My receding adrenaline kept the physical cold at bay, but a chill remained in my heart, along with a sobering thought. Was that guy *trying* to run me down?

19

I decided later that he wasn't, because to think otherwise was purely delusional paranoia and indicative of a mind gone off the rails, and as far as I knew, my mind was firmly attached and bedded in reality.

I told Kelli of my mishap, leaving out my misgivings over the driver's intent, and I drove the car back to the Shell station and replaced the spilled coffees with fresh ones. Hank Newman was surprised to see me, and I held off telling him what happened, simply said I'd tripped and dumped the coffees on the ground. He felt so bad about that he gave me the replacements for free. Nice old guy, that Hank Newman.

Back at the motel, Kelli and I settled in to drink our coffee, and I told her what I'd learned about Bob Jeffries and Ted Parker. When I was finished, she told me that she'd finally reached Annie by phone and that they'd made plans to get together on Wednesday. Annie was pressed for time so she didn't give Kelli much information, but she repeated her suggestion that we go see Jeffries, said he could fill in most of the details. Annie also said she had contact information for Brandon Moseley, should we decide to go see him at some point. Moseley was Parker's friend, the one who was there the night Parker disappeared. When I voiced reservations about traveling to Tonopah, Kelli seemed to withdraw, a chill settling between us. It bothered me, her shift in attitude and the vibe she put off, like I wasn't being a team player. What the hell did she expect of me?

I let it slide, deciding the best course was to shut my mouth and follow her lead. To a point that is. Hopefully I wouldn't reach it, the point where I couldn't do it anymore. Time would tell on that one.

After comparing notes we went out for some food. It was after seven and the pickings were slim in town, so we drove half an hour south and ate dinner at Nicely's in Lee Vining, overlooking Mono Lake. The road was clear and the driving easy, and we listened to music the whole way there. Kelli's pique over what happened earlier softened considerably, and by the time we got to the lake she was smiling outwardly and her eyes held a familiar playfulness I found comforting.

We had steak and mashed potatoes for dinner, and apple pie for dessert, and after our meal we sat at the bar and Kelli drank a glass of wine while I had coffee. Her drinking wasn't an issue for me, and I'll admit that I felt like joining her, but it was only a minor temptation. Kelli stopped with the one glass of wine. She was a lightweight anyway, and the alcohol seemed to mellow her, made her more reflective than usual. Back on the road to Bridgeport she turned the music off and looked at me for a long time.

"What?" I said.

She sighed in a curious way. "I don't know."

"What don't you know, Kelli?"

She sighed again. "I was thinking that you've never told me."

I reached over and turned the heater down; the car had turned uncomfortably hot. "What didn't I tell you?"

"About that night. In Bear Valley."

"I've told you. We haven't talked about it for a long time, but you know the story."

Kelli extended her arm and took my right hand in hers, held it with both of her hands. Her touch was soft and warm and I felt it travel up my arm and across my chest and down into my heart.

"I know we've talked about it, Mason, and yes, I can recite the story in my sleep. But you've never told me about *that* night, there at the store, after Sam was gone. I only realized the other day that I have no idea what happened to you then. Where you went, what you did. Maybe I'm being morbid, but I want to know."

I said nothing, silence stretched out between us like an enigma. I listened to the sound of the tires on the road, thought about the passage of time and what it does to our memories, the things we keep and those we discard, all of the stuff we *choose* to forget.

"It's okay, if you don't want to talk about it," Kelli said gently.

I collected my thoughts. Kelli waited me out. She was so good at that, her endless patience a virtue I could never achieve. When I was ready, I walked her through it, surprised at my clarity of mind, as if I could reach out and touch events exactly as they happened. Some things can never be forgotten.

"The kid working behind the counter that night was spooked by my erratic behavior, terrified really, and who can blame him? For a while there I was seriously unhinged. I found out later that his name was Tony French, and he was a student at Modesto Community College. He worked at the High Country Market part-time, weekends and during breaks at school. He claimed he never even saw Sam enter the store, let alone what might have happened to him. After getting nowhere with Tony, I called the sheriff in Angels Camp from the pay phone and told him about Sam. The dude gave me the runaround, some jive about waiting forty-eight hours before filing a report. He took my information and told me if Sam didn't turn up by morning I should call back and they'd send an officer out to see me.

"I hung up the phone feeling hopeless. Physically I was stuck there, since Sam had the car keys with him and it would be a few days before I remembered the spare. I asked Tony for a ride into town, but he just looked at me like I was crazy. Sam's car was unlocked, so at least I was able to get to my stuff, and I was contemplating if I'd freeze to death sleeping in it when Tony offered to let me stay inside the store for the night. He told me his uncle owned the place and he assured me it would be okay. I was reluctant to do it, but I really had no choice. Tony showed me a cot in the rear storeroom, gave me a spare key, and he closed up shop and split. Like a bat out of hell."

Kelli shook her head. "He let you sleep inside the store, but he wouldn't give you a ride?"

"Nuts, huh? Anyway, I clearly wasn't a robber, and once the kid figured out I wasn't drunk or high, I think he felt bad for me."

"But not bad enough to give you a ride."

"No. But it's ironic though, the way Sam and I encountered Gary and my wariness over his offer to us, and here I come into this kid's life and he's forced to make a similar decision based solely on his gut feeling."

"I can't imagine how hard that must have been for you," Kelli said, her face lit by the glow of the dashboard lights and the occasional passing vehicle.

"I searched for hours, until I got so cold I couldn't do it anymore. I must've walked a few miles, up and down the road, circles around the area, looking for some sign of what happened to Sam. But there was nothing, Kelli, absolutely nothing. No cars came by and the nearest houses were pretty far away, and it was so desolate and lonely it didn't seem real. I thought about calling someone, you or my parents or Sam's dad, but I couldn't, not at two in the morning, not without more information.

"I kept hoping he'd appear, as crazy as that sounds. I even left the car there for a few days instead of having it towed, in case Sam came back. You know, like a sign, something he'd recognize in case he'd gotten knocked on the head or something."

I took my hand from Kelli's and ran my fingers through my hair. The car was cold, and I turned the heat back up. We were almost to Bridgeport and I was ready to be done with it.

"Early the next day the owner showed up and I had a hell of a time explaining why I was sleeping in his storeroom. He actually pulled a gun and held me there until he called the sheriff and checked out my story. Can you believe that shit?"

Kelli reached over and touched the side of my face. "I'm so sorry, Mason."

She held her hand there, and when she took it away, I brought the story to an end. I was tired of talking and the rest of it she already knew. We pulled into the motel and parked the car, and inside our room we didn't speak. Kelli straightened her things and took a bath, and when she was done I took a shower.

We went to bed and made love, and I felt in Kelli a hunger that was new to me, an urgency to her lovemaking that was both thrilling and uncertain. Afterwards, I held Kelli in my arms as she slept, my thoughts drifting to many things, most of them good, some of them not. I felt both content and afraid; secure in my love for Kelli, yet wary of fate's willingness to take it all away. It was a long time before I finally shut my eyes.

20

I saw the Ford again the next day. I wasn't sure about it at first, but the pinched rear bumper on the right side convinced me. It was the same pickup that nearly ran me down the night before.

We were pulling up to Bob Jeffries's place at Twin Lakes when I first glimpsed the Ford, and it wasn't until later, after we'd introduced ourselves and Bob was showing us around, that I got a close enough look to know for certain. I asked Bob about the truck.

"It belongs to Garrett Knowles," he said.

"He's a guest?"

"No, we're closed this time of year. Garrett's a local fella, handyman of sorts. He helps me take care of the lodge."

"He lives here?"

"Most of the time."

I stared at the truck, long enough for Kelli to give me a questioning look, and I suppose something in my eyes connected the dots for her because she turned and stared too. Bob tilted his Stetson back and dabbed at his brow with a folded bandana. "You folks seem awfully interested in that truck over there," he said. "Anything I should know about it?"

I hesitated a moment, considering if I should mention the incident in town. "Not really," I replied casually, deciding to hold off until I had more information. "I'm just naturally the curious type."

"I suppose that's true, Mason," Bob said with a chuckle. "Hank Newman told me as much after your visit yesterday. I've got to say, you made quite an impression."

"A good one, I hope." My mind flashed on the thought of Hank calling Bob to fill him in; it was a small town indeed.

"He was surely taken, told me he'd never met an author before. So you're writing a book, are you?" Bob looked at me, his green eyes fixed unblinking on mine.

"Yeah, well about that," I said, my face heating up. "It's probably not nearly as glamorous as Hank might have put it."

When Kelli and I first approached Bob we passed ourselves off as a couple of vacationers curious about the lodge. It wasn't anything we'd worked out in advance, and I just kind of ran with it on the fly, unsure about using the book angle with Bob. Now I felt exposed.

"It's really just a hobby," I added, by way of explanation. "I've always been somewhat of a true crime buff."

"Is that so?" Bob replied. "I take it that's the real reason you're here. It's about that young man who went missing, isn't it?"

Bob's words were friendly and in them I sensed no challenge or judgment, and if he was offended by my changing story he didn't show it. "Yes," I said. "That's the reason we're here."

"Well then, why don't I show you the rest of the place, and afterwards I'll tell you what I know."

THE TWIN LAKES LODGE hugged the south shore of Upper Twin Lake. Its layout consisted of a rustic main lodge built of stone and heavy logs, with ten wood-framed cabins and a dozen campsites set about a lush forest of evergreen pine and cedar and black oak, the steep rise of the snow-covered mountains forming an impressive backdrop. There was a central pavilion with a huge stone fire pit and a raised wooden stage, and out on the lake a boat dock with a swimming platform and water slide. Beyond the dock, set back from the shoreline, was a boat shed and a small cabin where Bob told us Garrett Knowles lived. That's where the black Ford was parked.

Our tour of the property was enjoyable, the lodge reminding me of a summer camp I went to as a kid. Afterwards, Bob fixed us a lunch of tuna sandwiches and potato salad, with a bowl of sliced fruit and a pitcher of iced tea. We ate near the pavilion at a picnic table set under the shade of a massive oak tree. The sun was out and it was a beautiful day, and even though the air had a bite to it, it wasn't too cold.

The bucolic setting was incongruous to our purpose though, and when the discussion turned to Ted Parker, Bob Jeffries turned somber. "I've never had anything like that happen to one of my guests," he said.

"Did you know Parker?"

"I did. He's stayed here before."

"What about Brandon Moseley?" I said.

"I'd never met him. He's a nice kid though. He was very upset by what happened, as you can well imagine."

I shook my head knowingly. Yes, I *could* well imagine, indeed. All too well. The thought of Moseley's anguish over his friend's disappearance was a distraction I could do without. I glanced at Kelli, and she picked up the questioning then.

"How long had they been staying here?"

"They came in on Monday afternoon. Stayed in cabin number five."

"Were there other guests here at the time?"

"At the start of the week there were two groups camping, and one cabin rented. The campers pulled out on

Wednesday, the others stayed through the following weekend."

"And Parker disappeared on Thursday night?" Kelli said.

"That's the assumption," Bob replied. "He went out to dinner that night, and it was the last anyone saw of him."

"Do you know what happened to Parker's car?" I said. "Hank Newman told me that Brandon Moseley hitched a ride back up here from the roadhouse."

"It was found behind the restaurant with two flat tires."

"Two?"

"Yes, both front tires. There was nothing to indicate how they went flat. Parker had an Automobile Club account but no road service call was made."

"That seems significant to me," I said. "Could someone have tampered with the car?"

"I suppose it's possible, but there was no evidence of that." Bob turned and looked towards the lake. When he spoke, his words were restrained. "To be honest with you, there's been no evidence of anything at all. It's like that kid just walked off the map. Gone without a trace. It's all very disturbing."

Bob Jeffries was a big man, well over six feet tall, with broad shoulders and a stout physique, but he seemed much smaller then, as if the weight of Parker's fate bore down on him. After a few minutes he continued the story.

"Parker and Moseley were hanging out that night with some guys from Minden. They've all been checked out and cleared by the sheriff. They were part of a construction road crew working between here and Lee Vining, and they were easy enough to track down. That was about the only lead to go on, and when it didn't pan out, all that's left is, Ted Parker simply vanished. Hard as that is to believe."

As Bob spoke, I found it increasingly difficult to stay objective, to place myself in the role of interested bystander; I was too much a part of the story for that. I felt a strong urge to come clean with him about our true purpose for being there. I'd already badly fumbled the damn thing anyway, and to keep it up seemed counterproductive in too many ways. But I held off, intuition telling me that for now, the course we were on was the right one. I left my options open though, and I felt that soon enough I would tell Bob the truth. Something in his eyes told me he'd understand.

Bob told us what he knew about Ted Parker and he gave us a few more details about the night Parker disappeared, but the information was thin and didn't seem very useful at all. I suppose a private investigator could have made something of it, but for a couple of amateur sleuths it seemed like one big dead end.

After Bob was finished he offered to take us on a tour of nearby Bodie State Park. It had come up earlier in conversation that Bob had worked at the park for a number of years and he was pretty much an expert on the history of the town, and since he still knew many of the rangers working there, he promised us a behind-the-scenes tour. I'd heard of Bodie but had never been there, and being as I'm a huge history buff I agreed to it right away. Interestingly, Ted Parker and Brandon Moseley visited Bodie the day before Parker went missing. Was there a connection? Possibly. I figured at the very least, it wouldn't hurt to ask around and see who saw what.

Plans were made for the following day and once settled, Kelli and I thanked Bob for lunch and the information given, and we walked to our car. On the way, I looked towards the boat shed and the cabin where Garrett Knowles lived, and I noticed movement near the black Ford. I concentrated on it, saw a man who seemed to be staring back at us. A few seconds later the man turned abruptly from my gaze and slid behind a tree, caught in the act as it were. Pulling away in our car, I looked again in that direction, but there was no sign of the lurker to be found.

21

Bob Jeffries picked me up at nine o'clock on Wednesday morning. He arrived at the Walker River Lodge driving a late 70s GMC Jimmy outfitted for off-road use. He also brought a thermos of coffee and travel cups, and a couple of fat chorizo and egg burritos. The truck was in mint condition, and it was obvious from it, and our visit to the Twin Lakes Lodge, that Bob took pride in his possessions and he ran a tight ship.

Kelli begged off our excursion, deciding instead to hang around town until her friend Annette Briggs came back from Reno. Ghost towns really weren't her thing anyway, and history in general didn't thrill her. I was okay with it, as now I'd be able to selfishly explore to my heart's content.

The sky had cleared and the sun was out, and it looked to be a great day ahead. The temperature hovered in the high forties with no wind, and I dressed moderately and brought an extra flannel in my daypack, along with my wool gloves and knit cap. I don't like to dress too warmly, and I'd spent enough time outdoors to know that layering is the key. Bob had the heater running in the Jimmy and a Rodney Crowell tape playing when I hopped inside. That was a nice touch.

There are two ways to get to Bodie from Bridgeport, and we chose the southern route out U.S. 395. It took us about forty-five minutes to get there, with one stop along the way to see the ruins of Dog Town, the first gold mining camp in the Eastern Sierra. Back on the road, Bob gave me a thumbnail version of Bodie's history.

Gold was first discovered in the Bodie Hills in 1859, by a man named W. S. Bodey. The reason for the change in the town's spelling has been lost to history. Some people say it was an illiterate sign painter who was responsible, while others claim it was the citizens of Bodie themselves who chose to alter it. Bodey never had a say in the matter, as he died not long after his discovery, lost in a blizzard on his return from a supply run to nearby Monoville.

It took some time for Bodie to hit its stride, but by 1879 it was a certified boomtown, with a population of nearly ten thousand. The climate was horrible and the living conditions primitive, and it seemed every gambler, outlaw, con artist, and cutthroat in the western states gravitated there, earning Bodie the nickname of the *Wickedest Town in the West*.

A hundred million dollars in gold and silver was pulled out of the ground during the town's lifetime, and some people believe there's more to be had. Today, Bodie is a state park, and it's considered the finest example of a western ghost town to be found anywhere in the United States. It's kept in a state of arrested decay, the remaining structures left at the mercy of time and the elements. Simple repairs are made to keep the buildings standing, but no restoration takes place, and the town exists much as it did when the last residents moved away more than seventy years ago.

Later, while walking through Bodie, I was struck by a palpable sense of history in the air, like I'd stepped through a portal to another time and place. It's so quiet there you can close your eyes and almost hear the sounds of the old town come alive: the big stamps working in the Standard Mill; the boisterous crowds packing the saloons; the preachers in the pulpit condemning the evil taking root in the town and all the good citizens shouting *Amen!* and *Praise the Lord!*; the fire bell tolling the age of yet another poor soul sent off to meet his Maker.

Main Street beckons with its history of gunslingers and highwaymen, and the *Bad Man from Bodie*, perhaps a real person, or likely just a legend, but nonetheless symbolic of the random violence that seemed poised to erupt at a mere change in direction of the wind. The gambling dens and whorehouses are but ruins now, no longer enticing itinerant miners into drunken debauchery while fleecing them of their hard-earned wages, yet with a little imagination you can picture them as they stood, an oasis of pleasure amidst a vastly desolate landscape. A wicked town indeed, and living proof of a uniquely American time.

Bob turned the Jimmy off 395 and onto Bodie Road, a curving two-lane that snakes its way through a rocky canyon before daylighting into the gently rolling hills of the high desert. It's about thirteen miles to Bodie once you turn off the main highway, not a great distance if traveling by car. But thinking about horse-pulled wagons making the journey more than a hundred and thirty years ago brought to mind the story of the little girl, who upon hearing of her family's plans to move to the infamous mining town, wrote in her diary: *Goodbye God, I'm going to Bodie*. It was a sentiment that would resonate throughout the West.

The asphalt ran out and the last few miles were washboard dirt road, the Jimmy's stiff off-road suspension rattling my teeth. Nearing town, Bob told me that a number of rangers lived in the park year-round, taking up residence in several of the old homes restored to some semblance of inhabitability, but that was mostly the younger ones eager for adventure. During his time spent working at Bodie, Bob commuted from Bridgeport, though on occasion he too stayed overnight for an extended period. He described the soul-numbing solitude and extreme shifts in weather, and the odd sounds at night that might lead a more superstitious person to believe in ghosts. Bob Jeffries was an engaging conversationalist, and listening to him, I found myself eager to get to our destination.

We approached an unmanned guard shack at the park entrance, and beyond it a Ford F-250 four-wheel drive pickup was parked in the middle of the road, facing us. Bob pulled alongside the Ford and rolled his window down, cold immediately filling the cab of the Jimmy, the truck's heater pushing against it. "Howdy, Wes," Bob said to the man in the truck.

"Mornin', Bob. What brings you out today?" The man wore a heavy Carhartt jacket with a park ranger emblem stitched over the pocket. I noticed a military-style assault rifle set in a rack next to the passenger seat.

"Brought a friend out to see the town," Bob said.

The man's name was Wes Morris, and he was one of the full-time rangers who patrolled the park. After introductions and the exchange of pleasantries, Bob sipped his coffee while Wes appeared distracted by chatter coming over his radio. After a minute Wes turned the radio down and he looked at Bob with concern.

"He's been at it again."

Bob stared out the windshield, his expression steely. "When?"

"Over the weekend, and again yesterday. I found him wandering out by the cyanide pits. He seemed confused at first, but then he got hot and gave me some back talk. When he finally cleared out he wasn't too happy about it. That was over the weekend. When I saw him again yesterday in the same spot I was pretty well pissed off about it. I gave it to him hard, Bob. I hope you're okay with that."

Bob listened intently, the back of his neck turning a deep red against his crew cut. He seemed to work at containing a slow-burning rage, and I sensed that Bob

Jeffries might have a bit of a temper hidden beneath his casual demeanor.

"It's all right, Wes, he's got to learn. And you've got a job to do. Have you seen him around today?"

"No, but I suspect he'll show up eventually. I'll give you a call if he does."

"Thank you. We'll be seeing you."

Bob put the Jimmy in gear and rolled down the road, and Wes Morris went the other direction, out towards Bridgeport. I was curious about what I'd heard, but I didn't want to pry, so I sipped my coffee and listened to the tires crunch on the gravel road and the low thrum of the truck's heater. Bob pulled up to the visitor's lot and parked. His window was still down, and as soon as he killed the engine and the heater stopped, the cold took hold. Bob looked to his left, seemed to stare at something on the horizon. I leaned forward slightly, saw a black truck driving down a long, graded road, trailing dust. I was thinking that the truck looked familiar when I heard Bob mutter to himself.

"Goddamn him."

22

The truck came down the dirt road towards the visitor's parking lot. When I asked Bob where that road led to, he said it looped around to Bridgeport via Aurora Canyon. As the truck neared, I recognized it as Garrett Knowles's Ford. It veered off from us and parked a short distance away. Bob fitted his Stetson, told me to sit tight, and got out of the Jimmy.

He walked arrow-straight to the truck, and the man I assumed to be Garrett Knowles got out of the cab and waited by the front end. The truck's engine was still running, and from the open window of the Jimmy I heard the rough rumble of exhaust through a busted muffler, saw the smoke rise on the breeze and blow towards Garrett. Bob stopped and rested one hand on the hood of the truck, and he spoke to Garrett but the words were hard to make out. With his other hand, Bob gestured in an angry manner.

The scene as it unfolded intrigued me. In particular, Garrett Knowles held my attention. At one point he looked right at me, and I stared back, trying to fix his appearance in my mind. He wore a trucker cap pulled down low, his jeans faded and dirty, a flannel shirt buttoned to the collar. I noticed him favoring one leg, and it brought to mind the dragging sound I'd heard at the Shell station when the man in the black overcoat walked away. I thought maybe the distance was playing tricks on me, because Garrett's head appeared misshapen, and his skin had an unnatural look to it. And there was something weird about his teeth, he seemed to bare them in an odd way, like they were ill-fitting dentures or bad caps, something like that.

The thing between Bob and Garrett carried on for a full five minutes, and at one point the two of them had clearly started arguing. I thought about what Bob had told me, about Garrett being an employee of his, and found it very strange. I wondered about the real nature of their relationship, because what I witnessed seemed to imply something different. And what about what Wes Morris had said, about the person he'd found wandering off-limits in the park. Was it Garrett Knowles he was talking about?

I was figuring a way to ask Bob a few questions when the whole event abruptly ended. Garrett seemed to shut down completely, and I saw a dejected slump to his posture as he walked completely around his truck, clearly dragging his left leg, and got in the cab. He put the Ford in reverse and backed out farther than necessary, and he spun a wide turn, coming very close to the Jimmy on his way out. When he did, I made eye contact with Garrett, and I saw that his skin was pulled tight to his ears. And speaking of his ears, they appeared deformed, and I had the distinct impression I was looking at a burn victim. I stared at the Ford as it grew smaller on the road in front of a billowing trail of dust, an odd feeling gnawing at my gut.

I turned and watched Bob Jeffries walk purposefully towards our vehicle. He motioned me out as he went to the rear and opened the back of the Jimmy. I met him there, sorting my thoughts into questions that wouldn't sound intrusive. Bob seemed oblivious to the whole thing. "You might want to bring along your jacket," he said easily, his laid-back demeanor firmly in place. "The wind may pick up later."

"Good idea," I said. I reached for my daypack. "I'll bring this. It's got my camera and a couple of water bottles, and an extra shirt."

"It's a good day for pictures, that's for sure," Bob replied.

I waited for him to say something about Garrett, but it didn't seem to be coming. I struggled with my curiosity, and my place in things, and before I knew it I'd blurted it out.

"So that was Garrett?"

Bob seemed distracted, like he hadn't heard me.

"Knowles," I said. "The guy who works for you?"

"Yes, sure, that's Garrett all right." Bob mumbled his reply. He closed the back of the truck and smiled at me. "Let's get a move on, Mason, we're burning daylight here. I want to start off by introducing you to some of the folks who call Bodie home."

Bob Jeffries started on the dirt path leading down to the center of town, and I hurried a step behind him, my head filled with strange thoughts.

THE DAY TURNED out well, and the incident with Garrett faded as my interest was taken over by the charming allure of old Bodie. We spent nearly five hours exploring the remains of the once-thriving town, from the Standard Mill located on Bodie Bluff, to Boot Hill Cemetery down at the south end of town. The town sits at an elevation of nearly 8,400 feet, and Bodie Bluff, where most of the mines were located, rises to over 9,000 feet. The terrain is rocky and covered with sagebrush and bunchgrass, and there isn't a tree to be found anywhere, making lumber during the town's development a commodity nearly as valuable as the gold that was hauled out of the ground.

About a hundred buildings remain standing in Bodie, all in various states of disrepair, and peering through their windows or entering the ones open to the public offers a glimpse of time standing still. Many of the homes and businesses remain furnished as they once were, the possessions of long-forgotten inhabitants strewn about, cobwebbed and dust-covered in slow deterioration against the creep of time and the devastating effects of the elements. Ancient vehicles and broken-down wagons dot the landscape, with rusted-out mining equipment and indeterminate machinery left scattered in open fields and behind buildings and stacked in narrow alleyways. To some it may look like a huge junk yard, but to anyone with a sense of history, it's a veritable treasure trove of endless fascination.

Walking down Main Street, Bob described the pervasive vice rooted in a town comprised almost entirely of men; the sixty-five saloons and gambling houses, and countless brothels operating twenty-four hours a day, offering respite from the bone-crushing work of the mines and the harsh living conditions, and the constant boredom that came from the town's extreme isolation. His time spent conducting tours at the park had turned Bob Jeffries into a captivating host, and he spun tales of the kind you don't read about in history books. We continued north on Main Street and entered the site of the red-light district, where rows of one-room cribs once lined Bonanza Street. It was here that female companionship could be found from whores with colorful monikers such as *Madame Mustache*, *French Joe*, and *The Beautiful Doll*. A lot of money was made during Bodie's boom years, most of it by San Francisco mining speculators and Eastern big city investors, and what little of it came into the hands of the solitary prospector or impoverished mineworker inevitably fell into the pockets of the saloonkeepers and madams and cardsharps.

West of Bonanza Street are the ruins of Chinatown. Several hundred Chinese resided in Bodie, and like all western mining towns they were kept separate from the whites, left alone to practice their mysterious customs and traditions. They were shunned as second-class citizens, their sole purpose in life to service the needs of the town. The lure of vice extended into Chinatown as well, in the form of opium dens open to both Caucasian and Chinese alike, and prostitutes that could be had for a fraction of the cost of the trade over on Bonanza Street.

Our last hour was spent at the Standard Mill and the area around Bodie Bluff. At its peak the mill ran twenty stamps a day to crush and process the ore pulled out of the ground by the famed Standard Mine and the various other mining companies operating on the bluff. Little remains today of those operations, but evidence of their existence lies just below the surface, in the form of countless tunnels and drifts dug to depths ranging from several hundred to well over one thousand feet into the earth. Bob told of the treacherous nature of the surroundings, and we stayed on a very specific path in our exploration, the danger of falling into an unmarked shaft ever-present. We took the Jimmy high onto the bluff and I got some great shots of the town spread out below, and we drove down into the saddle between Standard Hill and Silver Hill and explored the old Bodie & Benton Railway depot.

Before heading back to Bridgeport, Bob parked the Jimmy near the peak of Bodie Bluff and we ate a late lunch. He'd packed some fried chicken and macaroni salad, and filled a cooler with iced tea, and after setting up two folding chairs we had ourselves a nice little picnic. Wes Morris drove by at one point and waved to us as he passed, and Bob told me that Bodie State Park was regularly patrolled by an armed park ranger. When I asked the reason for this, Bob said there were persistent problems with vandals and treasure seekers, and the protection of Bodie for future generations to enjoy was serious business.

It was at that point Garrett Knowles crept back into my mind, and the moment seemed ripe for delving into his doings at Bodie, and his seemingly unusual relationship with Bob. "You ever get anyone playing around out here?" I said, easing into it.

"Teenagers sometimes," Bob replied. "But they mostly stay down in town, like to get drunk and mess around in the cemetery. They dare each other to spend the night and we have to run them out before they freeze to death. Summertime isn't so bad, but all the same, we can't have them traipsing all over the place."

"I imagine those old mine shafts are a real concern, people falling into them."

Bob eyed me strangely. When he spoke, he looked away, out towards the railroad depot. "It's happened before," he said.

"Is that why Wes was so upset at Garrett? When he found him wandering around the cyanide pits?"

Bob just nodded, and drank his iced tea. I looked down at the Standard Mill, the gunmetal gray buildings and smaller outbuildings with their tin roofs and weathered wood siding bathed golden by the low afternoon sun. The temperature had dropped and snow covered the ground from a storm that had passed through recently. A sense of loneliness came over me, and I thought of the lure of gold and the lengths a man will go to seeking it. Intuitively, I knew I should stop prying, but curiosity had the better of me.

"I don't want to step out of line here, Bob, but I have to say, that scene with Garrett earlier was a little unusual. What's the story with that guy?"

"What do you mean?"

"The fact he's an employee of yours, yet watching your reaction to what Wes said, and later when you were talking to Garrett, seems to imply more."

Bob let out a chuckle. "Well you certainly are an inquisitive sort, Mason, no doubt about that. No wonder you're writing a book."

I felt my face flush, something in Bob's tone making me think he didn't believe the whole book story after all. "My mom is always saying the same thing," I replied, my mind distracted by the thought that maybe I should just level with Bob and be done with it.

"The truth is, Garrett is more than an employee of mine. His folks were close to me and my wife, and I served with his father in the Army. Ever since Art died in '75, I've taken Garrett under my wing. He was eleven then and his mother couldn't bear the load. She had three older sons and they were all trouble, so I stepped in to help out. Ellen, that's his mom, she was murdered when Garrett was in high school, and the killer was never found. Some folks suspected thugs from a Reno drug gang for the deed, as the oldest brother Steve was caught up in that sort of thing. I knew that if Garrett didn't get a solid male role model in his life, he'd become a casualty too."

Bob paused and finished his tea. A feeling gripped me, and while I wanted to hear more, at the same time I felt revulsion that seemed to boil up from deep inside me.

"I'd let Garrett help out at the lodge, and when things got out of hand at home I'd let him stay in one of the cabins if it wasn't being used, or else he'd stay with me and the wife."

"He's always worked there?"

"Off and on, ever since I bought the place. He never graduated high school, and it's hard for him to keep a job. He drifts around a lot, and he's gone for periods of time. But he eventually comes around and stays put for a while."

I thought about Garrett, wondered why I was so curious about him in the first place. I suppose it was because of what happened on Monday night, and the nagging feeling that it wasn't an accident. At the very least, I felt like I should tell Bob that Garrett had some seriously bad driving habits.

My thoughts drifted to Kelli, and I wondered how her day went with Annette Briggs. Hopefully she learned something useful, or at least enough to satisfy whatever it was inside her that needed answers. Honestly though, I felt like we were spinning our wheels, and a big part of me was ready to head back home and call the whole thing quits.

"You mentioned the old mine shafts around here," Bob said, pulling me back in. "The fact that people can fall into them. Well that's what happened to Garrett."

"Was he hurt badly?"

"He was tore up. Skull fracture, broken arm and ribs, shattered his left leg, knocked all his teeth out, cut all to hell. But that wasn't the worst of it. The fire did the most damage."

"Fire? Damn, Bob, what happened?"

"It was late October of last year. Garrett was out on the other side of the bluff here, where the Syndicate mines were located. He found his way down into one of the abandoned shafts and started exploring a drift. He had an old kerosene lamp he was using to light his way. Why he didn't use a damn flashlight, I'll never know. The drift pinched out and near the end there were some rotted planks covering up a dead shaft that went down about forty feet or so. Garrett got up on those planks and the bottom literally fell out from under him. He busted himself up bad on the way down, and when he bottomed out he hit a pool that had some kind of flammable in it, and that kerosene lamp ignited the whole works, lit Garrett up like a goddamn human wick."

I thought of Garrett's pulled-back skin and deformed ears. No wonder he looked like a Halloween mask. "How in the hell did he survive?"

"By pure luck, or the grace of God, if you believe in that sort of thing. He managed to roll out of the pool and onto a pile of shale, and he stripped off his shirt and used it to put out the flames. His face and arms took the brunt of it, and combined with all of his other injuries he was damn near dead. Before the fire burned itself out it generated enough smoke to send up a signal through the open shaft. Wes Morris happened to be driving past, this was about four o'clock in the afternoon, and he stopped to check it out. He heard Garrett down there moaning and he radioed for help. They were able to pull him out and airlift him to Reno."

"That's a horrible story," I said, trying to imagine the agony Garrett must have gone through recovering from something like that. "How long was he laid up in the hospital?"

"About six weeks, followed by months of rehab. He ended up with one leg shorter than the other, walks with a limp now, and damage from the skull fracture has really done a number on him. He hasn't been the same since. He gets angry easily, violent at times, and he's always agitated over some thing or another. It's like he can't settle down, can't hold still for one damn minute."

Bob paused a moment and looked off towards the setting sun, and he sighed deeply.

"I've often wondered if Garrett wouldn't have been better off dying down in that shaft. He's always been a strange sort, has a difficult personality, you might say. But after that accident he turned a bad corner, and whatever it was about him that put people off got magnified by a hundred, not to mention his appearance after all the skin grafts to repair the burn damage. Folks don't want to be near him, and I really can't say what kind of future Garrett has. It's hard for me to see it, you know?"

When Bob turned to look at me there was sadness in his eyes, deep worry lines creased into his weathered skin, and for the first time since I'd met him, he looked old to me. I didn't know what to say to him, or what to make of the story, or even the fact I was sitting there listening to it, being pulled into the life of Garrett Knowles. He had nothing to do with my purpose there, yet starting with the incident on Monday night he seemed to have become the focal point. Something about that bothered me, and it brought an unsettling feeling, almost like a premonition, of events being put into motion with me standing in the middle of it.

We packed up and hit the road back to Bridgeport. There was little talk on the way, and I dozed for part of the ride, images of Garrett on fire sticking in my head. When we got back to the motel Kelli came out to say hello, and Bob invited us to dinner at his place. We agreed to get together at five and waved goodbye. Watching Bob drive away, I was overcome by emotion, and I pulled Kelli close to me as we entered our room and shut the door.

23

I told Kelli of my premonition. She thought I was being silly, and the more I tried to explain it the more muddled my thoughts became, so I finally gave up and asked how her day went.

"Great," she said. "And yours?"

"Good. Bordering on great."

She nudged me. "Okay, smart aleck."

"Tell me about it," I said.

"First we drove down to Mammoth to see a client of Annie's, and we had lunch there in town. It was good to see her and catch up on things. Business is great and she seems happy. I always knew she had it in her, to strike out on her own and do well at it. On the way back we stopped to see some properties of hers. We also talked about Ted Parker."

"And?"

"She didn't have much to add, outside of what we've already learned. Parker was a good kid, known to a lot of people in town, and he minded his own business and never caused any trouble. Apparently he came here often to fish and backpack, and he was a pretty accomplished outdoorsman. He also did volunteer work at that ghost town you went to today."

"Bodie?"

"Yes. He was trying to get hired as a park ranger. Anyway, the word is, he came from a good home and got

125

along well with everyone. The consensus seems to be foul play, because Parker wasn't the type who'd take off without telling anyone."

"Was he still living at home?"

"Yes."

"What about a job?"

"For the last two years he worked at an auto parts store, and he went to community college."

"What about Moseley, did Annie have any information on him?"

"Pretty much the same story as Parker. Good kid, nice family, no red flags that anyone is talking about. Annie met him when he came into her office one day with a stack of flyers he'd made up, and he asked if she would put one in her window and hand them out. She gave me one."

Kelli reached for her purse, took out a folded piece of paper and handed it to me. I unfolded the flyer, saw the image of a man who could have been Sam Stoneman's double.

"Weird, huh?"

"More like creepy," I said.

"Look at the description."

I read the flyer. It described Sam almost exactly. I'd read similar flyers in the box of evidence back home, physical descriptions shared by the victims, further reinforcing the theory that all the cases were related.

"I went to see the sheriff here in town," Kelli said.

"How'd that go?"

"He was friendly enough, but he didn't have much information to give me. He said there was no clear evidence of foul play involved in Parker's disappearance, despite what people in town are saying, and there really isn't anything for him to investigate. He told me that in cases like this the family will sometimes hire a private investigator to try and locate the missing person."

I nodded at Kelli, thinking that maybe later we could take another run at the sheriff. "I think I'm going to come clean with Bob tonight," I said, shifting gears to something that had been on my mind all day. "About the book thing."

"Why?"

"It feels like the right thing to do."

Kelli considered this. "Maybe you're right. If he hears your story, he may tell us something he might not say otherwise."

I gave her a funny look. "What are you, *Columbo* now?"

She nudged me again, harder in the ribs. "Whatever you say, mister. Speaking of Bob, I heard a little piece of town gossip from Annie today."

"Yeah? So who's the postman sleeping with in this little burg?"

"Not *that* kind of gossip, Mason. It's about that guy who works for Bob."

"Garrett Knowles?"

"Yes."

"And?"

"And the word around town is Garrett was there the night Parker disappeared. There at the restaurant I mean."

"Really? Is anyone putting him together with Parker and Moseley?" I thought about what Bob told me, about Garrett's troubles getting along with people, and how his appearance drove them away.

"Annie didn't know anything about that. She'd only heard that Garrett was supposedly there that night, and later, no one saw him around for a while."

"What do you mean by a while?"

"A few days is what she heard."

"That's odd."

"And so is Garrett, from what Annie said. She told me some things, some of it pretty weird."

"Weird you say? Well listen to this."

I told Kelli what I'd learned from Bob Jeffries out at Bodie. When I got to the part about the mine shaft accident and the fire, she visibly shuddered, and she told me something that sent a chill right through me.

"I saw him, Mason."

"Who?"

"Garrett."

"What are you talking about, Kelli? When did you see him? And where?"

"This afternoon, after Annie and I got back to town. She dropped me off and I drove up to Bob's place. I thought you guys might be there."

"What time was this?"

"Around two, or a little after."

"What'd he do? I mean Garrett, how'd you run into him?"

"It was strange how it happened. I went up to the house and rang the bell. There was no answer, so I walked around the property looking for you. Later, when I was at my car getting ready to leave, I thought of putting a note on Bob's door. When I turned around to go do it, Garrett was standing behind me. Totally freaked me out."

"He was just standing there?"

"Yes, literally right behind me. I didn't even hear him walk up, and you know how quiet it is out there."

I felt anger at the thought of Garrett Knowles creeping up on Kelli. Added to his shitty driving habits, I was starting to dislike that dude in a big way.

"His face really looks bad," Kelli said. "He didn't say anything at first, he just stood there staring at me. Then he mumbled something I couldn't understand. He talks funny, with a heavy lisp, and he makes an odd whistling sound through his teeth."

"I saw him from a distance today, out at Bodie. I think he's got some bad dentures. Bob said Garrett lost all his teeth when he fell down that mine shaft."

Kelli shuddered again, hugging herself. "The strangest part was, he mentioned you by name."

"He what?"

"He said your name, like he knew you."

"Explain that to me."

"I asked him if Bob was around, and Garrett got very angry and went on a rant that made no sense. He kept mentioning his dad, and at the end of it he said your name."

"What did you say to him?"

"Nothing. I was too shocked. After he calmed down I asked him to tell Bob that I came by, and I got in my car and drove away. When I was leaving, I looked into my mirror, and I saw Garrett standing there still as can be, watching me. It looked like he was smiling."

I pictured the scene, feeling uneasy with it. "Well, I wouldn't give it too much thought," I said, deciding to play it casual and not rattle Kelli needlessly. "Bob told me that Garrett got messed up pretty bad when he bounced down that shaft. Mentally, I mean. Who knows what's floating around in that guy's head?"

"You're probably right," Kelli said. "But how did he know your name?"

"Bob must have mentioned it to him. Either that, or he's psychic." I gave her a deadpan expression. Kelli looked at me seriously, before breaking into a grin.

"Cut it out," she said playfully, tugging at my sleeve. After a moment she said, "I think we should drive out to Tonopah tomorrow and see Brandon Moseley, get his side of the story. We can also ask him about Garrett."

It took a split second for Kelli's words to register, and when they did, a doubtful feeling came over me. Kelli seemed to pick up on it. "We'll go home after that, I promise. Just one more thing and we'll be done here." She took my hand and squeezed it, and all resistance fell.

"Sure, I guess I can play detective for one more day. Or writer. Whichever works, right?"

Kelli smiled beautifully then, and her eyes brightened. "Thanks, Mason. I always knew you were all right."

It was getting late and Kelli went into the bathroom to get cleaned up. I considered joining her in the shower, but thoughts of her encounter with Garrett Knowles put a serious damper on my mood. While waiting for her to finish, I got a bottle of water and went outside for a walk. Our room was down at the end of the building, near a footbridge over the Walker River. I walked out to the middle of the bridge and listened to the water wend its way downstream. Patches of snow clung to the riverbank, wind rustling the bunchgrass and low bushes and barren trees that made up the landscape, and the smell of fire smoke from nearby houses mixed with that of wet earth, forming the unique scent of winter in the mountains.

I turned and looked across the street, at the old Victorian house opposite our motel. The desk clerk had told me some scenes from the movie *Out of the Past* were filmed there. It had been a while since I'd seen that noir classic, but I knew the plot well. Jeff Bailey was a man living a double life, here in Bridgeport. Through circumstances beyond his control, the past was about to catch up with him, and with it would come tragic consequences. Robert Mitchum played the role to perfection, setting the standard for the doomed film noir anti-hero. The stoicism with which he accepted his fate in the penultimate scene was haunting.

A strong sense of life imitating art came over me, and in some subliminal way, I saw my own past stalking me. I felt an increasing certainty that my time spent here would unleash forces beyond my control, and with them would come a day of reckoning.

24

We pulled up to the Twin Lakes Lodge a little earlier than expected. The sun had settled behind the mountains and dusk was upon us, stars just beginning to show themselves in the darkening sky. Bob wasn't in his house but the Jimmy was parked out back, so Kelli and I walked the property until we found him inside the boat shed. Garrett's truck wasn't around, and I wondered if he'd be joining us for dinner.

Bob said hello and asked us to wait for him out by the fire pit. On our way there we stopped by our car to get Kelli's jacket. The wind was up and the temperature was dropping quickly. Over at the camp pavilion Bob had a half-barrel barbecue fired up and meat on the grill, and a picnic table nearby with a spread of salad and baked beans and corn on the cob, and a basket of rolls along with a bowl of sliced fruit. Condiments and drinks in a bucket of ice rounded out the affair. The smell coming off the grill mixed with the scent of pine, and I realized how hungry I was.

"You think he'll be here?" Kelli said.

"Garrett?"

"Who else would I be talking about?"

I was about to say something smart when I saw Bob approaching. "We'll see," I whispered.

"You two ready for some grub?" Bob said eagerly.

"You bet, buddy," I answered. "Looks to me like you've got enough here to feed an army."

"Or a scout troop," Bob said with a laugh. "It's a bad habit of mine, making too much. Comes from running a place like this, always dealing with a lot of people."

"You do all this yourself?" Kelli said.

"Mostly. There's a gal who lives nearby and she helps out during the season. I asked her to come over and lend me a hand."

"Do we get to meet her?" I said.

"Not tonight. She had other plans."

"So it's just us for dinner?"

Bob held my eyes. "Yes, it'll just be the three of us." He went to the grill and started turning the meat, chicken and beef brisket. I gave Kelli a *hold steady* look, and went over to get us something to drink. The time for questions would come later.

DINNER WAS FANTASTIC and afterwards Bob served homemade ice cream for dessert along with strong coffee, a perfect combination. Later, we sat next to a roaring fire and shared stories about ourselves. Bob broke out a bottle of wine and he and Kelli partook. I was tempted to join them but did not, though I'll admit the pull was strong. I only felt that way occasionally, usually during times of discontent, and I was thankful for the ability to resist temptation.

Bob lit a pipe filled with sweet-smelling tobacco and it reminded me of my grandfather and evenings spent at his house in Long Beach, listening to stories of the Second World War and his service in the First Infantry Division, *The Big Red One*, and the liberation of Europe. They were good memories, and combined with the cold night air and the smell of the campfire, they put me in a very mellow mood.

After one particularly amusing story Bob told of an encounter he'd had with a bear up in Yosemite, the talk around the campfire trailed off. A hoot owl called from up in the trees and the sound of lake water rippling on the shore could be heard against the occasional gusts of wind. The cloudless sky was black as ink and there was no moon, and the stars clustered in their formations seemed close enough to touch. The mood was ripe for reflection, the beauty and simplicity of an evening spent in the mountains cutting away all of the endless chatter and white noise distractions we carry around inside us. I was building up to my confession. I wanted to clear the air with Bob, and maybe some part of me also believed what Kelli said was true, that in telling my story some key piece of information might come out. I collected my thoughts, saw Kelli look my way, anticipation written in her eyes.

"We haven't been completely honest with you, Bob," I said, jumping right into it. "Mostly it's me, but Kelli shares in it too." He looked at me blankly, albeit pleasantly, and I forged ahead. "I'm not really an author, and there's no book about missing persons. That was just something that came up randomly when I met Hank Newman. Why I continued to lie about it I can't say."

"Why are you here, Mason?"

"We're here because of information Kelli has gathered about the disappearance of Ted Parker, and others. And something that happened to me and a friend. A long time ago."

"What happened to your friend?"

"He disappeared."

"When?"

"1989."

I told Bob the story, taking my time with it. He asked no questions as I told it, and several times I sensed a deep recognition in his eyes that I found curious. When I was finished, Bob took a moment to stoke the campfire, and he said, "I'm sorry to hear about your friend, Mason. That sort of thing is never easy to live through. But what does your experience have to do with what happened here?"

"That was my doing," Kelli said. "Last year I read a newspaper article about a young man who went missing in Truckee some time ago. The article described other disappearances in the same area that appeared to be related, and the circumstances of those cases were very similar to what happened to Mason. I started digging deeper, and soon uncovered more disappearances connected in a way that led me to believe a single person might be responsible. When I found out about Ted Parker, it was another puzzle piece that fit, and I knew that we should come up here while it was still fresh and see what we could find out."

"Are the police aware of this?"

"No. This is something I've put together on my own. I do believe it warrants investigation though."

"What was his name, Mason's friend? And what was he to you?"

I felt a knot in my stomach. I hadn't anticipated this, and it was a direction I had no desire to go in. Fortunately, Kelli picked up on my signal.

"Sam Stoneman," she said. "We were all friends back in high school, in Costa Mesa." Kelli didn't miss a beat, her tone restrained, and I was thankful for her intuitiveness. "Sam's disappearance was devastating to those close to him. But the worst part has been not knowing with any certainty what really happened."

"How many others are missing?"

"Nineteen," Kelli said.

"That's a lot of people." Bob shifted in his chair as he relit his pipe. "And you believe the trail leads here, to my place?"

Kelli nodded while I considered the question. The trail led to that roadhouse south of town. But what if the information we'd been given was wrong, and Ted Parker really disappeared from here at the Twin Lakes Lodge? I made a mental note to explore that later with Kelli.

"I'm not sure what we think," I said. "Kelli feels strongly that all of the cases are related, and I'll admit, the information she's put together does a good job of supporting that idea. What I know is, the age and physical descriptions of all the victims match Sam's, and the time frame does too."

"Time frame?" Bob said.

"Each incident happened within a two month period, October to November. A lot of other details intersect as well. Kelli's actually plotted it on a map, and the trail literally leads here to Bridgeport."

Bob didn't respond, and it struck me that he could give Kelli a run for her money in the listening department. I was about to speak again when I was distracted by rustling in the bushes, and I sensed motion out of the corner of my eye. I looked in that direction but saw nothing. Bob and Kelli were refilling their glasses and they hadn't seemed to notice the sounds. I wondered where Garrett Knowles was, and thought maybe he was out there sneaking around, listening in. That seemed like something he would do.

"To be honest with you, I wasn't too keen on the idea of coming here in the first place. It's taken me a long time to get over what happened to Sam, and the sense that I'd failed him. It was a wound I didn't want to open."

"But you did come." Bob turned to Kelli. "How'd you talk him into it?"

"He's a good man. And sensible," she said, smiling warmly.

"You better watch yourself, Mason, this one here has got your number." Kelli blushed and she sipped her wine. "That Moseley fella's had a tough go of it too," Bob went on. "It was about like you said. He took a lot of blame on himself for not dragging Parker out of that restaurant. He and I talked about it a few times. I told him to go easy on the guilt, or else it'll eat you from the inside."

"So it's true he has no idea what might have happened?" Kelli said. "We were considering driving out to Tonopah to see him."

"None that he ever told me," Bob replied.

"Did you know Garrett Knowles was there that night, at the restaurant?" I said.

Bob drew down on his pipe thoughtfully, as if considering the veracity of my statement. "I hadn't heard that," he said evenly. "Who told you?"

"My friend, Annette Briggs," Kelli said.

"Ah, local realtor scuttlebutt." Bob's tone stayed even, yet I sensed the same tension as earlier in the day, when he seemed to do a slow burn over Garrett's presence out at Bodie. "People say a lot of things about Garrett. Most of it nonsense."

Kelli appeared ready to respond, but I cut her off with my eyes. I wanted to give Bob time to expand on his statement about Garrett, but before he did, the sound of movement returned in the bushes. This time Bob heard it and he sat upright. "Who's out there?" he said loudly. There was no response, and the movement stopped abruptly. "You're on private property. Make yourself heard."

A tense moment passed silently. Bob got up from his chair, set his pipe on the stone ledge fronting the fire pit and fitted his Stetson. The sound came back, indistinct now as it seemed to move away from us, towards the boat shed. Bob squinted in that direction, tightness in his jaw. He turned to us and spoke in a way that seemed forced. "I'm going to have a look. It's probably nothing, but all the same, you can't be too careful."

"Is Garrett staying here tonight?" I said.

Bob didn't answer. He'd already turned and walked away.

25

He returned ten minutes later, said he found nothing out of the ordinary on his walk to the boat shed, and he passed the sounds off to animals foraging in the brush. But something in his voice felt wrong, and I wondered if maybe Bob wasn't bullshitting us; I'd lay even money Garrett Knowles was out there somewhere.

Bob settled back into his chair and filled his wineglass, and relit his pipe. Once he got it going he took a few measured puffs, and he addressed the rumor we'd heard. He acknowledged that Garrett was working the week Parker disappeared, but he'd drifted off by Thursday morning and Bob didn't see him again until the following Tuesday. This was in keeping with the random nature of Garrett's employment, the way he would come and go without notice. He'd been like that ever since he was able to drive. Bob called it wanderlust, the way Garrett would take off for weeks at a time, never saying where he'd been when he returned. Bob knew that a lot of the time was spent out at Bodie, because he'd get the phone calls whenever Garrett did something wrong, and other times he was able to piece together Garrett's wanderings through small things that were said; trips to the Gold Country in the Western Sierra, Reno and Lake Tahoe, and Barker Ranch out in Death Valley, part of a weird fascination Garrett had with Charles Manson and his cult of followers.

While Bob may have expressed doubt about the rumor, I sensed it *was* possible that Garrett had been there the night Ted Parker disappeared. I thought about Garrett's difficult personality, and some strange ideas got into my head over that. Maybe he came into contact with Parker and Moseley. Maybe he knew something about what went down. Hell, maybe he was just a weird dude who gave people the creeps.

And what about the flat tires on Parker's car, how could that not be connected in some way to his disappearance? Maybe Garrett knew something about that. Considering the situation, I thought perhaps a meeting with the sheriff might be in order. I had no standing in the case, but if I told him about my past he might bring me into it. Kelli and I had never talked about that, the eventual step of involving the cops, but maybe now was the time to do exactly that.

The campfire danced and popped, sending smoke spiraling upward, and I stared into it, running through my mind all that had happened in the short time we'd been in Bridgeport. I felt a vague importance to it all, but couldn't quite put my finger on why. It was that premonition from before, coming back strong.

Kelli and Bob were talking about something and Kelli giggled in that silly way of hers, and I wondered if she might be a little tipsy. I eased my head back against my chair and shut my eyes, tried to visualize a blank sheet of paper, just to clear my mind. A few minutes later I excused myself to go to the bathroom. Bob told me to use the one inside his house, since the public restroom plumbing was turned off. I walked away slowly, my ears tuned and my senses alert.

I WAS INSIDE Bob Jeffries's house longer than expected. I'd gotten sidetracked looking at some photographs that caught my eye after I'd used the bathroom. They were arrayed on a wide mantle set over a stone fireplace in the living room. Bob's house was small but comfortable, very rustic and masculine, and like everything else associated with him, it was well-kept.

The lighting in the room was dim, so I turned up a wall sconce to better see. The photos were family shots, several of them featuring Bob and a woman I assumed to be his late wife. She was very pretty, her petite frame dwarfed by Bob's imposing stature. Most of the photographs looked to be 70s vintage, judging by the clothes and Bob's walrus mustache and shoulder-length hair, and the way Bob was posed exuded pride and confidence. They looked like a happy couple, and I wondered why they never had any children. Perhaps there was a story there.

Three specific photographs held me there longer than intended. The first one showed Bob and his wife, along with a second couple and a towheaded youngster smiling wide for the camera while holding a fishing rod in one hand and a large trout in the other. I immediately figured the kid to be Garrett Knowles, the other couple his parents. What were their names? I searched my memory until I came up with Art for the dad, but the mother's name evaded me. I focused on the kid, who was standing closer to Bob than the other man, and I noticed a distinct resemblance between the two of them. It seemed to me a cursory glance would lead most people to conclude the kid was Bob's. I held onto that thought, rolled it around my brain.

Curiosity aroused, I took the frame off the shelf and loosened the back, pulled the photograph out and turned it over. My assumption was validated by the inscription: *with Art, Ellen, and Garrett, Bass Lake, 1973*. I figured Garrett to be around nine years old and his father a couple of years away from death. Holding the photograph in my hand, I became self-conscious about what I was doing, and my heart beat fast at the realization I was invading Bob's personal life in a way that was unacceptable. I quickly reassembled the frame and placed it back on the mantle.

That's when I noticed the other two photographs, both of them featuring Bob and a grown man who might have been in his late twenties. The man was heavily bearded in both photos, with medium length hair under a ball cap. I compared these two photos to the one from '73, and there was no doubt in my mind that it was Garrett Knowles standing there with Bob Jeffries. Bob was bearded as well, and the resemblance between the two men was very strong.

There was a familiarity that nearly jumped off the print, and while the images could have matched thousands of bearded young men, the feeling that I knew *this* particular person was strong. But I'd never met Garrett, and what I saw out at Bodie was the burned-up version, so why the sense of knowing? I pictured Garrett without the beard, visualized the shape of his head and the structure of his face. His mouth was tight in one of the photos, but in the other he showed his crooked and brown teeth. I stared into his eyes, felt a stirring of recognition, fleeting but real. The more I concentrated on it the stronger it became, the awareness building quickly, to the point it literally jolted me.

"No way, it can't be," I said out loud, nearly shouting it.

My own words startled me, and I took in some deep breaths to quell the nervousness tightening my chest. I became aware of the time and how long I'd been gone, and suddenly I felt exposed. I snapped off the light and quickly stepped back into an adjacent hallway, scanning the room to make sure no one was watching me; I have no idea why that thought didn't occur to me while I was snooping. There was a bay window facing the lake, but it was very dark outside and the shades were drawn. Two smaller windows faced the pavilion and fire pit, too high up for anyone to look through unless they were standing on a ladder. Satisfied I hadn't been seen, I left the house and returned to the fire pit. When I got there, Kelli and Bob were gone.

26

I looked around the immediate area and saw no sign of them. An odd feeling tugged at me, an element of uncertainty in the air. I checked my watch and decided it was time to call it a night. While I had enjoyed my time with Bob Jeffries, there was an undercurrent present from the time we first met, most of it centered on Garrett Knowles. Connections were being made deep in my subconscious, facts intersecting in ways that didn't seem random, and I was ready to be done with it. I'd only known Bob for little more than a day, but it felt like I'd been pulled into his world for far longer than that. This trip was doing things to me, getting into my head in a way that was not good for me. This was the very reason I didn't want to come here in the first place, and now that I'd done my part and indulged Kelli, I only wanted to find her and leave.

Standing alone by the fire, I concentrated on my surroundings. Where could they be? Down by the lake? I moved in that direction, but as I neared, the only sounds I heard were the gentle lapping of water on the shore and the breeze passing through the tops of the trees. Irregularly spaced pole lamps cast murky light throughout the camp area, and I followed the lake, careful to keep clear of the rocks lining the shore. After a few minutes I cut to my left to pick up the trail leading to the boat shed. In the distance,

I saw the cabin where Garrett Knowles lived, but it was too dark to tell if the Ford was parked there.

The trail was familiar to me, though sparse light kept most of it in shadows. A halogen lamp mounted on a tall pine tree illuminated the area around the boat shed, and I used it to guide me forward. Anxiety crept up inside me, and while I wasn't necessarily worried about Kelli's safety, apprehension took hold; where the hell did they go? I called out for them several times, receiving no response.

Nearing the boat shed, I heard movement to the right of me, closer to the lakeshore, and I stopped and concentrated on it. It came again, the sound of something being dragged, and I thought of Garrett Knowles and his bum leg, and I wondered if he was out there creeping around in that way of his.

I came to a clearing in front of the shed, the area brightly lit from the halogen, and I heard a door open and slam shut in the near distance. I called out again for Bob and Kelli, but I knew they wouldn't answer. Across the lake I saw the lights of houses shimmering through the branches of the trees lining the far shoreline. It had turned much colder now, the air brittle with the bite of winter. The scene was beautiful, peaceful really, but my nerves pushed back with a deep sense of foreboding.

Noises came from inside the boat shed, things being dropped and moved around. Someone was busy in there, and I had a pretty good idea who it was. I felt tense but steady as I moved towards the door, one of those sliding types like you see on warehouses. Amber light seeped from the edges, and it made me think of whiskey, three fingers neat in the bottom of a glass. My mouth went dry and I craved that drink, the pull of it a lot stronger than earlier, when Bob broke out the bottle of wine. From inside the shed a transistor radio played, and I stood close to the doorjamb and listened to the rich baritone of a preacher sermonizing in the style of the Old Time Gospel Hour.

And I say to you my devoted flock, pray to the Lord for his forgiveness. Pray for him to drive away the sin that torments you, that burns inside you. For inside each one of us lives the heart of darkness. Inside each one of us festers temptation. Inside each one of us there is a wicked kind, the pure manifestation of all that is...

A surge of energy shot through me and my vision blurred, and I bent forward, hands on my knees, breathing deeply. I tuned out the preacher and turned within.

The wicked kind.

The phrase flipped a switch in me, illuminating a roomful of old stuff, an instant flashback slideshow of the worst night of my life. I could have turned and walked away. I *should* have turned and walked away. Kelli was not inside the boat shed.

But I didn't walk away. Like metal shavings drawn to a magnet, I felt powerless to move against whatever force held me in its sway. Fate was behind that door, and it would not be denied. In an absurd moment, I found myself praying silently for guidance as the radio preacher droned on.

Yes brothers and sisters, the wicked kind lives within you, tempting and taunting with the Devil's trickery, luring you from the righteous and leading you into the darkness. The wicked kind will break your spirit and cast your soul into the desert places, into the barren wastelands of Satan's playground. He who tempts the...

I stood upright and leaned my head back against the wood siding, closed my eyes and cleared my mind. Count to ten, exhale all the bad energy and focus only on the here and now. My resolve intact, I reached out and grabbed the wooden handle, and I slid the door open wide.

27

Garrett Knowles stood in front of me.

I knew it was him even though his back was turned. He wore a threadbare black overcoat that I'd seen once before, at the Shell station on the day I arrived in town. Garrett did not move or indicate any awareness of my presence. I paced my breathing to calm myself, unsure of what to do.

The preacher was building to his crescendo, riffing on the ways of evil and the path of righteousness, organ music swelling behind him as he prepared to deliver the money shot, when Garrett threw out his hand and turned the radio off violently. I noticed the hand sticking out from the too-long arm of the overcoat, the wrinkled skin and gnarled fingers, like the hand of a hundred-year-old man baked in an oven. I thought of the fire and dreaded seeing his face. Before I could make a move, Garrett spoke.

"Is that you, Mason?"

His voice was coarse, with a harsh sibilance to his speech. My heart thumped and I said the first thing that popped into my head. "You don't know me."

"Yes, I do."

"How, I've never met you."

"Are you sure?"

Garrett reached for a burning cigarette in a pie tin ashtray next to the radio. He inhaled deeply and held the smoke, and it triggered something in me. He let the smoke out slowly, enveloping his head in a cloud.

"They're not here."

"Who?"

"Who is it you're looking for?"

This guy was a real joker. I figured two can play at that game. "You're Garrett Knowles."

He made an odd clucking sound. "So what."

Garrett kept his back turned to me, and despite my trepidation over seeing his damaged face, I was in no mood for games. I would give him two minutes to face me or I was out of there. I glanced at my watch, and he said something that knocked me back.

"She's pretty."

"Who?"

"I like her."

"Who?" I repeated angrily.

"The girl."

"What girl, dammit!"

I was about to forcibly turn Garrett around when he lifted his head to the rafters and spread his arms, palms turned up, cigarette burning between two curled fingers. He sighed deeply, and when he spoke, his words were slowed down, like he was high on dope or something. "Kelli...I saw her today. She talked to me."

That sibilance was grating, the coarseness of tone almost indecent, and my head pounded as I pictured Garrett Knowles leering at Kelli like a punk. It triggered fury in me and I fought to control myself. Control was key. Lose it, and you're done.

I told Garrett he was an asshole for what he did to Kelli, made my voice low and mean, and I was about to say more when he spun around and screamed at me.

"I'm not an asshole!"

He dropped his cigarette and balled his clawed hands into fists, shaking them in front of him like some ham actor on stage. "I'm not an asshole," he said again, his chest heaving.

His face appeared unnatural in the light of a lamp on the workbench. It was an old miner's kerosene lamp, and seeing it brought the horrific image of Garrett on fire at the bottom of a mine shaft. Jesus, you'd think he'd have learned. He repeated that he was not an asshole, mumbling it like some weird mantra, staring at the floor with his shoulders slumped, the right lower than the left. Then he raised his head and looked at me, his eyes boring into mine with indeterminate emotion.

Garrett's face was so torn up it was impossible to discern anything about him. His grafted skin was red and waxy, his head lopsided and his nose crooked and half of normal size, his ears mere nubs below the wool cap he wore. His teeth were false and they stuck out too far and were too perfect for the rest of his face, and I suspected they were the reason he talked funny. But there was absolutely nothing funny about Garrett Knowles. He'd taken a hard ride down that mine shaft, and now I understood why Bob Jeffries thought Garrett should have died down in that hole.

"I wasn't there."

Garrett's voice was calm now, his eyes almost sleepy. "Where?" I said.

"The night Ted Parker died."

"You don't know that he's dead. No one knows that." *Except the killer*, I thought.

"You're wrong. I know things."

"What does that mean?"

"You shouldn't go there. He can't tell you anything."

"Go where?

"To Tonopah. Brandon knows nothing."

"You were listening to us tonight."

Garrett smiled, thin lips pulled back over horse teeth. "He was my friend."

"Who, Parker, or Moseley?"

"Both."

He tilted his head and looked at me in a curious way, and I wondered about his brain, how badly his wiring got messed up in the accident. He continued staring, saying nothing, the intensity of it making me look away. On the workbench I noticed crates filled with rusted tools and other artifacts I assumed were taken from Bodie. "You're not supposed to have those," I said, pointing to one of the crates.

"I can take what I want."

"Is that why you go there, to steal things?"

"It's not stealing. It's junk. No one cares."

"Where else do you go, when you leave here?"

"All over. My dad calls it wanderlust."

"Your father is dead," I said cruelly.

"You're wrong!"

"Bullshit. He's dead, and so is your mother."

"He's not dead!"

Garrett blew up, the heat of violence radiating from him. He held my eyes, and even though it was hard to look into his ruined face, I stared back at him, not giving an inch. It went on like that for a long minute, and when the moment passed, Garrett came back to earth, his voice calm again.

"I can help you."

"Help me with what? You make no sense."

"I can help you find your friend."

"What friend?"

"Do you ever wonder what happened to him?"

"You're crazy, man. You're fucked in the head."

"Do you wonder if he's dead?

"What the hell are you talking about?" I felt a thousand needles pricking my skin, the room closing in on me, tilting like some carnival ride.

"Do you wonder how he died?"

"Goddamn you and your bullshit games." I flexed my right arm, ready to blast this asshole in the face. Garrett moved a step away, and he sighed like a sympathetic parent.

"Sam Stoneman. He was your friend, and now he's gone. Do you remember?"

"Fuck you," I said, my breath hard in my chest. "You know nothing about Sam. You only know what you heard from crawling around in the bushes, watching us like a pervert."

"I know why you're here, and that you lied to Hank Newman. I know that Kelli is pretty. I also know that you went to Bodie with my dad."

"I told you, your father is dead. Are you stupid?"

Garrett laughed obscenely, exposing those ridiculous teeth, and he looked at me as if I was the pathetic one. "You know nothing," he said disdainfully.

I focused on his eyes. His melted face gave absolutely nothing away—how could it, when it wasn't even human—but his eyes told a different story. I recalled the photographs inside Bob's house, felt the pieces fall into place. It was the eyes. Despite the outside damage, the eyes had stayed the same. Goddamn, I *knew* those eyes. I knew them because I'd seen them before, long before tonight when I saw them in a photograph inside Bob Jeffries's house, and now standing here looking at the real thing. The preacher's sermon came to me, pounding into my brain.

The wicked kind.

My God, the truth was right in front of me. *Garrett was Gary*. He was the one who took Sam. A fevered heat came over me, and staring into those dead eyes, I saw the light of recognition come back, and in that moment we *both* knew the truth, and the die was cast.

"Do you want my help?"

Garrett's ugly voice broke the moment and I turned away from him, away from the pull of his evil aura. My head buzzed with confused disbelief, a crushing reality pressing down on me. "No," I said, turning to face him, forcing resolve back into my voice. "There's nothing I want from you."

"Why? Don't you want to know?"

"You're a bad person, Garrett. You make me sick just standing here." I was shaking now, overcome by blinding anger. I pointed my finger into Garrett's face. "You know nothing about Sam. And you stay away from Kelli, do you hear me. You stay away, or so help me God, I will put you in the ground."

"You don't know anything."

"Bullshit, Gary!"

The name wasn't a slip, but I got no reaction from it. I stepped back to clear some space between us, ready to do battle.

"Yeah, I know all right. Goddamn you, I know how you operate. I know all about you."

"You don't know me!" Garrett screamed, his entire body trembling as he wheezed deeply. "You don't know anything! I'm the one who knows."

I eased back another step. "I'm leaving now. I'm going to turn around and walk out of here. If you follow me, I will hurt you. Are you clear on that?"

He glared at me, his face a grotesque mask, and I felt an intense déjà vu; in that moment, I believed I could have choked Garrett Knowles to death and been justified in doing it.

I turned and braced myself for violence, but none came. I walked upright and steady towards the sliding door, my muscles coiled and ready to react, the urge to look behind me strong. I stepped through the opening and pulled the door shut, and the thought came screaming back that I'd just made the biggest mistake of my life.

28

After my encounter with Garrett in the boat shed things moved quickly. On my way back to the camp pavilion I intercepted Bob and Kelli. They'd been at a neighbor's house the entire time, but I tuned out their reasons why. I told Bob I wasn't feeling well and that it was time for us to leave, thanked him for his hospitality, and I ushered Kelli out of there like a man leaving a burning building.

Things got really strange when we passed the Shell station in town. As I turned right onto Main Street, I saw something to my left, in my peripheral vision. I braked and turned my head, but the angle was wrong, so I looked in my side mirror. I could have sworn I saw Garrett's truck parked at the back of the service station. The only way to know for sure would have been to back up for a better look, but I refused to do that. It was impossible for him to have gotten down the road ahead of us. But then I thought of Bear Valley and Gary's seeming ability to transport himself across great distances, and I hit the gas and peeled down Main Street, my mind hopelessly tangled.

Kelli knew something was wrong. I told her I was simply rattled by her wandering off, and I made up some lame story about being spooked by strange noises during my search for her and Bob. We made small talk on the way back to the motel, and thankfully Kelli didn't press me.

I never told her about my confrontation with Garrett, deciding that I needed to be sure of my suspicions. It was a huge leap to make, and as much as I felt in my gut that the burned-up mess I confronted in the boat shed at Twin Lakes was the same pitiless man who stood outside that phone booth in Bear Valley a lifetime ago, to prove it seemed impossible. But proof is what I needed, and from there I could move forward based on facts, not gut feelings. So now, in an ironic twist, I was the one keeping secrets.

Back at the motel we made our plans for the following day, and Kelli showered and got ready for bed. I followed her, taking a long and scalding shower, replaying the scene with Garrett in my mind. When I joined Kelli in bed she was already asleep, and I eased in beside her, overcome by exhaustion.

WE LEFT FOR Tonopah at sunrise the next morning.

From the moment I woke up I felt strung-out and emotionally fried, the coffee I drank to clear the cobwebs only making me jittery. Kelli seemed to go easy on me. If she was concerned about last night or my state of mind, she hid it well. By the time the car was packed and we were ready to leave I'd managed to come a few steps out of my funk, and I took a moment and walked out onto the bridge over the Walker River, just to take in some clean morning air. I reminded myself that life is what we make of it, and people like Garrett Knowles have no more power over us than what we choose to give them. When I got inside the car, Kelli was smiling beautifully, and she gave me a kiss that melted me with its tenderness.

Before leaving town we stopped to see the sheriff. I had a list of questions for him, about Garrett and the flat tires and a few other things, and I was hoping he'd be willing to talk. But the sheriff wasn't in when we got there, and rather than wait for him to show up, we decided to hit the road.

After leaving our contact information with the receptionist, we fueled up the car and left Bridgeport.

We drove south out of town and picked up Highway 120 near Mono Lake, took it to U.S. Route 6. It was two hundred miles to Tonopah and it took us about three hours to get there, with no stops along the way. With the directions Kelli got from Annette Briggs we found our way easily to the mobile home park where Brandon Moseley lived. I called several times on the drive to let Brandon know we were coming, but each time I got his voicemail. The park was east of town, old but not run-down, the surrounding desert lending an air of desperation to the whole affair. Tonopah seemed no different than any other desert mining town I'd been to, and I thought about places like Bodie, and wondered why it was that some towns lived and some towns died.

We pulled up a dusty lane and found trailer number nineteen near a small clubhouse with an empty swimming pool and a few tumbleweeds piled up against a wrought iron fence. I parked the car and we got out and stretched a bit, shaking out the road stiffness. We'd already worked out our approach and who would say what, and I felt pretty certain that none of it would go as planned.

Walking up the gravel path to the trailer, I took a quick look around. Quiet neighborhood, well-kept by trailer park standards, maybe fifty units in total. There was no one about, not even a barking dog to acknowledge our arrival. The sun rose to our left, casting a mid-morning glow over the park, and there was no breeze, the temperature in the low fifties.

At the front door I pulled open the crooked screen and held it while Kelli knocked. There was no answer. She knocked again, a little louder, and I went for the doorbell but saw there was none. After a minute we heard stirring from inside, the creak of the floor and the turning of a deadbolt. I shut the screen and we stepped back a little, about three feet from the front door. A young woman answered, her appearance disheveled. She looked at us with a face that seemed completely drained of emotion. Red eyes, pale skin, the slumped posture of defeat. She didn't speak upon opening the door, and I sensed immediately that something wasn't right with this picture.

"Hello," Kelli said.

The woman at the door stared unfocused. I wondered if maybe she was loaded, or coming down off a bad drunk. But something about her said that wasn't it, that she wasn't the type to be plastered at ten o'clock in the morning.

"Is Brandon Moseley home?" I said.

The woman did not speak. She looked at me now, her eyes coming into focus. I made a quick reassessment. She wasn't drunk or high, she was shell-shocked. I saw tears well up and her chest rise.

"Miss, is there something the matter?"

"Brandon? You want to see Brandon?"

"Yes," Kelli replied. "There's something we want to talk to him about. Does he live here?"

Tears falling now, the woman's whole body seeming to collapse upon itself. Her voice when it came seemed so small it stuck with me for a long time after.

"He did," the woman said.

Lived. Past tense. Shit, what now?

"When did he move?" Kelli said.

"He didn't."

Full-on crying now, the woman leaning against the doorjamb for support.

"Miss, what's wrong? Did something happen to Brandon?"

The woman looked at Kelli, her expression achingly forlorn. "Yes," she said. "He was killed, this morning. Out there on the street."

***

THE WOMAN WAS Moseley's sister. Her name was Rebecca, and this is what she told us:

At four-thirty that morning, Brandon had gotten up and prepared for his first day of work as an apprentice electrician. After too many dead-end jobs he was excited at the prospect of learning a trade and making some real money. He showered and dressed and woke his sister to say goodbye. She was pissed at him for doing it and told him to leave her alone. He walked across the four-lane highway fronting the trailer park, to the convenience store on the other side, where he would catch a ride to work from a friend. According to the clerk at the store, Brandon got a large coffee to go and walked outside with it. The clerk saw nothing after that.

Sometime later a passing motorist called 911 when he saw a body sticking out the front windshield of a late model Ford Taurus sedan parked down the street from the convenience store. It was Brandon Moseley. No one witnessed the accident, but a man pumping gas at the Mobil station just up the street saw a dark-colored truck, make and model unknown, peel rubber and drive very fast past the gas station. The man said he heard no braking or skidding before hearing a distinct thud and the sound of breaking glass, and when he stepped out into the street for a look, he knew something was wrong, so he called 911.

Rebecca was awakened briefly by the sirens, and she fell back asleep. Thirty minutes later a policeman knocked on her door, and after confirming that Brandon lived at that address, he asked her to make an identification. The police told her that Brandon was hit by a vehicle and he was dead by the time paramedics arrived. They had no other information, and there were no eyewitnesses to the accident.

After telling the story, Rebecca Moseley asked the reason for our visit. She had no visible reaction when I told her. I asked her if she knew Ted Parker and she said that she did. I was thinking of other questions to ask when Kelli gave me a look that said, *not now*. Kelli gave Rebecca our condolences, and we turned to leave. Rebecca said something and I looked at her.

"Excuse me?"

"Were you the one who called?" she said.

"When?"

"Last night, around eleven o'clock. I tend bar at the Mizpah Hotel and I got a call from a man asking if Brandon would be around today. When I asked the guy why he was calling me at work he said nothing, so I hung up on him."

"It wasn't me," I said.

"I didn't think so. The guy had a different voice. I just thought maybe you'd know about it."

"We're so sorry for your loss," Kelli said.

Rebecca closed the door. Kelli and I said nothing as we walked to our car, and we hardly spoke at all until we hit Goldfield an hour later. Driving through the desert, I thought about those calls I'd made to Moseley's cell phone. Calls to a dead man.

Part Three

Reckoning

29

Newport Beach, California
February 2010

L ife went on, and as the shock of Tonopah wore off and the events in Bridgeport faded into the background, the obligations and routines of day to day took over. One year was ending and a new one beginning, and once that page was turned we were off to the races. Kelli's workload increased dramatically, and she put in long hours at the office. The custom home project I'd started in the desert consumed nearly all of my time, and I made weekly trips to Palm Springs to oversee the work myself since my foreman, Mark Johnson, was sidelined with a bad back. Overnight our lives had turned hectic.

But even though it became exceedingly difficult to carve out time for ourselves, and stress reared its ugly head a little too often in the form of foul moods and a cold shoulder, I felt good about things. Our time spent in Bridgeport seemed to bring us together in a deeper way, and with it came a level of contentment I hadn't felt for a long time, despite the grab bag of feelings that came from dredging up all that old stuff.

We had a good, if not too busy holiday. On the week leading up to Christmas we visited Kelli's father in Grass Valley. Tom Flynn seemed to accept me in a way I'd never experienced before, or maybe his memory had slipped to the point he'd simply forgotten who I was. Nevertheless, we were up there for four days and it was a nice enough time, if you didn't look too far below the surface.

Christmas Eve was dinner with my sisters at the Cannery in Newport, followed by a nice visit at my mom's house and the exchange of gifts. Mom was supposed to be at dinner with us, but she bowed out at the last minute because she felt unwell. She claimed it was nothing serious, but sometimes it was hard to tell with her, as she could be pretty tight-lipped about stuff like that.

Christmas Day was reserved for my father, down at his place in Fallbrook. By the time we got there on Friday afternoon the party was in full swing, a houseful of people I didn't know. Dad barbecued and everyone brought a dish, and the spread of food and pastoral setting reminded me of Bob Jeffries's place.

After dinner and dessert and the opening of presents, Dad and I took a sunset walk to a small fishing pond on his property. We had a good talk and I felt very close to him, and even though he got a little preachy with me, I let him do it. At some point the conversation drifted to the concept of wickedness and its effect on the soul. Listening to Dad brought to mind the radio preacher's spiel and the boat shed and Garrett Knowles's burned face, and I took in what my father had to say, not because I desired a sermon that day, but because something deep inside me said it was important to listen.

We spent the night in Fallbrook, and after a hearty country breakfast the following morning, Kelli and I said our goodbyes and drove home. The whole next week leading up to the New Year was spent being lazy; reading and watching movies and making love. The weather was nice, unusually warm for December, and I got in some good surfing, and Kelli and I took a couple of bike rides up to Long Beach. We spent New Year's Eve with friends, and by the time Monday rolled around we were both rested and ready to get back to business.

About a week after we'd gotten home from Bridgeport, Kelli brought up the subject of her investigation into Sam's disappearance. It was the first time we'd talked about it since the long ride home from Tonopah, and to my surprise, she expressed ambivalence about moving forward with it. I took note of that warily, because Kelli wasn't the type of person who dropped something unfinished.

"I really appreciate you going through with it," she said to me one night after we'd finished an early dinner at home. A storm had blown in late that week and the wind drove steady rain against the side windows of the house. I'd made a nice fire and we'd settled in for an evening of reading and hanging out.

"I know how difficult it was for you," she added, her earnest expression taking on a golden hue in the firelight.

"You're welcome," I replied.

"That's it?"

"You need more?"

"Whatever, mister," she said playfully.

A minute passed between us, silent save for the sound of burning firewood and wind-driven rain, joined by the odd noises an old house makes as it stands up to inclement weather.

"I think maybe you were right, Mason," Kelli said.

"About what?"

"About leaving things alone. With Sam, and all that other stuff. Maybe it was a crazy idea to begin with. We have some good information, but I don't know how to make it work, or if we should even try. It just seems so random, so…"

She trailed off, frustration evident, and indecision too, very unusual for Kelli Flynn. She sighed with the weight of a heavy burden.

"I don't know if I'm expressing this right or if it makes any sense, but it's a feeling I've had ever since we got home."

Kelli turned and stared into the fireplace, as if in those flames hid the answers to the difficult parts of life, and if you looked long enough and hard enough they'd appear. Kelli wasn't often introspective—that was my domain—but on the occasions she turned within, she'd go deep, and stay down there for a long time. I sensed this was one of those times. I resisted the urge to coax it out of her, whatever she was feeling, and I waited for her to finish. When she did, I noticed a slight tremble in her voice, another little cue that all was not well.

"I can't get over it, Mason," she said softly. "The sense of trouble, or…no, that isn't it. It's more like this thing is moving around us, and if we're not careful it will swallow us, or step on us, or…this must sound really weird to you."

"No, it doesn't, Kelli. Keep going."

"Okay. Well, what it boils down to is letting the past go, and getting off this road before we get to a place that isn't good for us. What do you think about that? What I'm telling you."

What did I think about that? Man, was that a loaded question. I thought a lot, to be sure, but wasn't ready to share any of it.

I took measure of Kelli's mood, and her change of heart. Something had gotten to her, tamped down her enthusiasm to the point of giving up, made her fearful even. Maybe it was the harsh reality of Brandon Moseley's death, and the fact we'd stumbled upon it literally hours after it happened. I'd always felt that Kelli's investigation was abstract to her, more like a problem to be solved than anything else. It was like she'd found a loose thread and started pulling on it, and the unraveling became the goal, not necessarily *what* she was unraveling.

She wasn't there the night Sam disappeared, and to be a step removed from the reality of it was significant, especially twenty years on. To stand there and look into the eyes of the killer—to hear his words, to feel the funky, ominous vibe rolling off him like the decay of a red tide—was an experience Kelli knew nothing about. So my reaction upon discovering her investigation was completely genuine, and expected really, and Kelli would have no way of truly understanding why I didn't want to go anywhere near it.

But maybe now she did. Maybe now she saw the ugly truth of it. While Moseley's death may or may not have had anything to do with Ted Parker's disappearance, or Sam's or anyone else's, it provided a glimpse of life's brutality, and it directly touched Kelli and made it real for her. Believe me when I tell you that's a damn scary thing.

Anyway, it could be I was all wrong with my analysis, but nonetheless, something had made Kelli want to pull back, after she'd spent so long working on it. For my part, this new attitude fit in with my own agenda at that time, so I decided to go with it. I looked into her eyes, and said what she wanted to hear.

"You want to let it go, don't you?"

"For now, yes."

"Are you sure about that?"

"Yes, I am."

"But we can always come back to it later, right?"

"That's what I was thinking," she said.

And so we reached an agreement on the subject of Sam's disappearance, and for now it was to be put aside. But it continued to dangle out there, the ultimate loose end waiting to be clipped. For me anyway.

See, I knew differently. I knew things Kelli didn't know. And I held on to my belief that Garrett Knowles was indeed the man known to me as Gary, the one who took Sam. And I was also willing to believe that he was responsible for all of those other disappearances too. More than that, I believed that Garrett was responsible for Brandon Moseley's death, running him down like a dog in the street so that Kelli and I couldn't talk to him about what happened the night Ted Parker went missing.

I had another theory as well, that Garrett had flattened the tires on Parker's car as a means to offer help, to create the opportunity to do his dirty deeds. The same way he offered me and Sam a place to stay on that stormy night back in '89. Garrett was a real helpful dude, of that I was sure. But how to prove it? That was the problem I faced.

Kelli never knew about my feelings or my theories because I didn't tell her. I very quickly got over my guilt about that, knowing that when the time was right, I'd tell her all of it. But first I had work to do.

One day in January I took Kelli's box of information to my office, and I spent hours going through it, looking for some link between Garrett Knowles and the disappearances, something to use as a foothold for my own investigation. It was tedious work that yielded no results, and it soon became apparent that in order to do this right, I needed professional help from someone well-versed in this sort of thing. That's when I hired the private investigator.

I found him through Jerry Corbin, my dad's friend whose custom home I was building in Palm Springs. Jerry and I got to talking one day and he told me the story of his second wife and how she used to run around on him with some bodybuilder type, and Jerry was convinced they planned to fleece him for his sizable fortune, or worse, maybe knock him off for a big insurance payout. Well he turned the tables on the "vindictive bitch", as he called her, and he hired this detective to follow his wife and her dull-witted Adonis, and soon he had enough solid intel to leverage a no-strings divorce and a clean slate for his future. Ever since then Jerry had been shoveling work to his new detective friend on a regular basis.

That's how I found myself sitting in a coffee shop one Friday morning out on Highway 62 in the High Desert, waiting on some guy named Winston Styles. That's a helluva name for a private eye if you ask me. But Jerry Corbin said Winston was solid, and that was good enough for me. I'd hired Styles the week before, over the phone, and this was going to be our first face-to-face meeting. He promised me some good stuff on Garrett and I was anxious to get to it. We were meeting in Joshua Tree because Winston was there working a sting operation with his partner, something about a meth-dealing Marine from out in Twentynine Palms and a worker's comp claim filed against an auto repair shop owned by Styles's brother-in-law.

Yeah, this was going to be interesting.

30

Winston Styles leaned across the table, sliding his cup aside and slopping coffee everywhere. He drank a lot of it, black, cup after cup, and I wondered where it all went since he never once got up to use the restroom.

The guy looked nothing like I'd pictured him. For one, he was white. I'd assumed he was black from the way he sounded on the phone, and with a name like Styles, how could he not be? But he was a white dude, a deeply tanned and weathered white, like he spent a lot of time outdoors. His age was fifty-something and he was my height with a wiry build. His face was long with sharp features, and intense eyes that stayed on you, to the point of discomfort. He spoke in a clipped tone and he seemed wired, and I wondered how much of it was natural and how much the result of drinking a few gallons of java a day.

But Winston was a likable guy, and even though his manner was a little too frenetic for my tastes, I made adjustments for it. We were in a coffee shop fronting the highway, not far from the west entrance to Joshua Tree National Park. The place was done up in a seedy fifties motif, and combined with the bleak desert landscape and roiling black storm clouds that seemed to follow me from Palm Springs, where I'd spent the week working on Jerry Corbin's house, it lent the whole endeavor a hardboiled, noir-like edge. Like something out of a Billy Wilder movie.

Winston gave me a brief rundown of his investigation to date, then he got down to specifics.

"So this dude Garrett is a strange cat."

"Try talking to him," I said.

"I plan on it, in due time. For now I've been digging, mining data and putting this together." He slid a manila file folder stuffed thick with papers across the table, expertly missing the pool of spilled coffee. "Some late night reading material for you, Mason."

"What is it?"

"Let's call it a dossier on Knowles. You can dive into that later. For now I'll give you the highlights."

"Wow, all this already?" I thumbed lightly through the pages of information.

"I work fast," Winston replied. "You have to in this business, or you get left in the dust."

I closed the folder and put it aside. "Okay, shoot."

Winston slurped the last of his coffee, put the cup down and poured some more from the carafe on the table. The last trickle barely filled the cup, and he looked at me apologetically. "Sorry. I'll have the waitress bring some more."

"No worries, I've had enough. Tell me what you know."

"Well, like I said, your boy's a fucking weirdo, that's number one right there."

He pulled a narrow spiral-bound notebook from a well-worn leather satchel sitting next to him in the booth, and flipped through the pages.

"Let's see. Born October 9, 1964, makes him forty-five years old. He was born in Minden, Nevada, but raised until age nine in Coleville. That's in Cali by the way. From age nine he's lived in Bridgeport. He's a high school dropout, sophomore year, no work record to speak of, no arrests or serious trouble I've found so far." Winston flipped some pages. "Here's something interesting. Knowles has a sealed juvenile record. I'm still trying to get my hands on it, but I understand it has something to do with a kid he used to pal around with who ended up a paraplegic after a fall from a rock cliff up on the Walker River. The word I'm hearing is, the kid might've been pushed. By your friend Garrett."

"No shit?"

"Yeah, if it's true, that's some big shit right there. I'm turning up lots of behavior problems with your boy, anecdotal stuff, a lot of tales being told out of school. His name seems to show up in all the wrong places. Sometimes you've got to take that with a grain of salt, but you hear enough of it, patterns start developing."

"He's got a difficult personality. That's what Bob Jeffries told me."

"So I've heard. You know about the accident, right?"

"I've seen him, Winston. Even if Bob hadn't told me the story, it's obvious something really bad happened to the guy."

"Seriously, falling down a goddamn mine shaft, now that's what you call some shitty-ass luck right there."

"The worst," I said. "Have you been up there yet, to Bridgeport?"

"Not yet. I farmed all this initial legwork out to a guy I know from Reno. He's been working some things down in that area and he agreed to take up some slack for me until I finished this deal with my goddamn brother-in-law. Family, ain't they a bitch?"

Winston drained his cup, signaled the waitress for a refill.

"So anyway," he said, "I plan on being up there soon, maybe late next week. Boots on the ground, man, it's the only way to get it done."

I nodded and looked out the big window next to our booth as the waitress filled Winston's cup. A coyote trotted up and stopped outside, and it looked right at me. It was the strangest thing to see, right there on Highway 62, nine o'clock in the morning, truckers and vacationers and regular folks going about their day, and this coyote is staring at me like we know each other. Weird. I turned to say something to Winston about it, and when I looked back through the window the coyote was gone. Really weird.

"Now, about that list you asked me to look into."

He was talking about the map Kelli had put together, the one showing all of the towns where the young men disappeared. I'd made up a list and asked Winston to verify Garrett's presence on the dates given.

"What'd you find?"

"I can place Garrett in Coleville and Minden, but that's easy enough since he comes from there and still has relatives scattered about. I can also put him in Truckee and Placerville. Both times he was popped for speeding on the dates you gave me. The rest of it is going to take some time, and even then I probably won't come close to closing out the list. Is it really that important to you?"

"Yes, it is."

"Well then get ready to spend some coin, Mason, because we're in for the long haul. Information like you want can be had, but it's a tough nut to crack."

"Got it. Anything else?"

Winston drank some coffee, and he slid the cup to the side, slopping more of it on the table. He took a napkin and wiped clean the area in front of him, and motioned for the file folder. I handed it to him, and he flipped through it, pulling out a single sheet of paper. He set the paper on top of the file and slid it over to me.

"Check this out," he said.

I looked down at the paper. It was a copy of Garrett's birth certificate. Confused by its meaning, I looked at Winston. He put his finger on one part of the page, the line where normally the father's name is typed in, but it was blank. I asked him what it meant.

"I'm not sure. But I found out that Garrett's mother was not married at the time her son was born."

"Are you sure about that? I thought his dad's name was Art."

"The records don't lie, Mason. Maybe Art was the father, but on the day that form was made out he wasn't in the picture. At least not on paper. But you know who was?"

"Who?"

"Your buddy Jeffries."

"What do you mean by that?"

"It seems a handful of nosy-bodies up there in Bridgeport remember a time when Mr. Jeffries had a roving eye, and even though he was married for a long time, he never stopped playing the field. Talk is, he and Garrett's mother had a side thing going on."

"Is this talk reliable?"

"Reliable as gossip can be," Winston said. "Supposedly, when that dude Art went back to Vietnam for another tour, Bob remained stateside to comfort the lonely wife. Garrett's parents were either separated or not yet married when he was born. I still need to nail that one down. But either way, the birth certificate was left blank, and we're left with a mystery father."

"Are you saying Bob Jeffries is Garrett's father?"

Even as the words tumbled out of my mouth I was thinking about those photographs inside Bob's house, the physical similarities between him and Garrett, and the immediate feeling I'd had about that. I thought about Garrett standing in the boat shed, talking about his dad, and his angry, almost visceral reaction when I taunted him about his father being dead. It was an intriguing notion for sure, but I couldn't see what it had to do with Sam and all those others who disappeared.

"I don't know," Winston said. "Do you want me to follow through on that one?"

I thought about it. I wasn't concerned about the money it would cost. Business was good and I had plenty, and besides, Kelli on her own made more than we would ever need. Was it the best use of time? That was the question. This thing had gotten under my skin in a big way, and I wanted a quick, down and dirty investigation that would produce enough information for me to present to the cops. Which cops I didn't know. The FBI? Weren't they the ones who normally investigated serial killers? I shook those thoughts loose and answered the question.

"Look into everything. But I need it fast. Can you keep that other guy on the payroll?"

"Sure, whatever you need. Jerry says you're all right, Mason, and that I need to take good care of you."

"Thanks. And speaking of taking care of things." I slid a sealed envelope across the table. It contained Winston's retainer. "Is cash okay?

"Always."

"I put five in there."

"I only asked for three."

"Yeah, I know. But Jerry says you're all right, and that I need to take care of you." There was five thousand dollars in the envelope, and I planned on Winston Styles earning every penny of it.

"I like your style, Tanner."

"Back at you, Mr. Styles." I laughed. "You know, I thought for sure you were a black dude, with a name like that."

"Yeah, I get that a lot."

Winston put the cash-stuffed envelope in his leather satchel. I put the file folder on the seat next to me. Winston leaned forward, forearms on the table, hands clasped in front of him, and he stared at me with those eyes of his. It was unnerving, the intensity of it, and I imagined he could get plenty of information out of people simply by staring them down. I fidgeted, nervous about what was coming.

"What?" I said.

"You going to tell me what this is about?"

"Tell you what?"

"Why I'm looking into this guy Garrett Knowles. What's the play here?"

I thought of what I should say. I'm not sure where the reluctance came from, but it was there. Maybe it was because in the back of my mind I knew all of this sounded so damn crazy, the idea that one man could go undetected for so long, committing who knows how many crimes, murders if my theory was correct, and it was all tied to Sam, and now Kelli and I had stumbled onto it and it led to the crazy notion that somehow I was going to bring the killer to justice, a killer the cops didn't even know about. It was definitely crazy.

When I'd hired Winston I didn't give him a lot of information, simply told him that I wanted the background on a guy named Garrett Knowles. I told him about Bob Jeffries and the Twin Lakes Lodge, and about Garrett's parents and their connection to Bob, and that was pretty much it. And there was the list too, which on reflection seemed like an odd thing to ask about, not without some kind of backstory at least. But I was winging it when I first called Styles, just testing the waters, and besides, I'd never hired a detective before and wasn't sure how to go about it. For his part, Winston didn't ask me a whole lot of questions either. But now here we were, and *now* he wanted answers.

"This is like an attorney-client relationship, only different. I have to know what's going on. But unlike a dirtbag lawyer, who really doesn't care if you're guilty or not, I want the truth. You have to tell me if you did it, Mason. In a manner of speaking, of course."

He bored into me with those damn eyes, as another long minute ticked by.

"Come on, man, I'm not playing here. I need to know what I'm getting into, or else we'll have to part ways. Friend of Jerry's or not, I don't go into things blind."

I signaled the waitress for more coffee.

"Okay, Winston. Get yourself a cup and sit back. This may take a while."

HALF AN HOUR later I finished the story. I started with the night Sam disappeared and took it all the way up to Brandon Moseley's hit and run death in Tonopah. Winston went through three more cups of coffee during the telling, and at the end of it he finally got up to use the restroom. When he returned, he ran down what he considered the most salient parts of my story, including a few ideas on how we should move forward with the investigation. Then things got interesting.

Turns out in his previous life, Winston Styles was a police detective in San Francisco, and from the stories he told it sounded like he was a damn good one. He took early retirement after catching a bullet during a Chinatown shootout in '97. Winston killed the shooter but an accomplice got away, after gunning down a rookie patrol officer who'd literally stumbled into the alley where the shootout occurred. The officer died and his killer got away clean, and the case ate at Styles. See, he knew the rookie cop, the son of the detective who mentored Winston, taught him the ropes. Winston vowed to settle the score.

Fast forward two years and Winston was working as a bounty hunter for a Los Angeles bail bondsman. This was before he became a private investigator, something he did to stay sharp, as he put it, a way to stay in the game. He was down in Mexico chasing a pedophile bail-jumper when he got a line on the Chinatown cop killer. It was purely coincidental the way it happened, and it was an opportunity Styles wasn't going to pass up. He tracked the perp from Nogales to Ensenada, and he shot him dead in a rat-hole motel down on the waterfront. Winston offered no excuse for his vigilantism.

The takeaway? Winston Styles was hardcore.

I wasn't bothered by the story, and I felt no sense of moral outrage over this guy taking the law into his own hands. Winston seemed perfectly rational and clearheaded, exhibiting none of the hotheaded cop swagger we all know about. I'm usually a pretty good judge of character, and sitting there with Winston, the vibe was copacetic, and I felt good about having him on my team.

I thought of the boat shed, Garrett Knowles standing in front of me, and the feeling I'd had of wanting to reach out and choke him to death. If he proved to be Sam's killer, I absolutely believed I could go through with it. A disturbing thought came to me. What if the cops wouldn't investigate? What if too much time had passed? What if there was no justice for Sam, or the others? I knew beyond any doubt that I could not let that happen.

Winston and I parted company with a plan to meet again the following week. He needed a few days to wrap up the deal with his brother-in-law before heading up to Bridgeport. In the meantime, he would have his partner start running down my list, and begin the arduous task of verifying Garrett's whereabouts going back twenty years.

One angle Winston wanted to explore was the Brandon Moseley incident in Tonopah. He agreed with my gut feeling that Garrett might be involved, and he reasoned that if we could tie him to Moseley's death and effect an arrest that way, once Knowles was locked up he might break on the other stuff. From an investigative standpoint, what happened in Tonopah was the freshest crime we had to go on. That, and Parker's disappearance.

So that was the plan we worked out. I left my meeting with Winston Styles feeling good, energized about the direction things were taking. It felt like I'd moved one step closer to justice for Sam.

31

One week later I was back in Palm Springs when a strange incident occurred. It would prove to be the precursor to an escalating series of events over which I would have no control.

Mark Johnson had returned to work from his back injury, allowing me to spend more time at the office chasing other projects. I was still visiting the job site often, mostly to bullshit with Jerry Corbin, but also so Jerry could show me the latest of the changes he wanted made to the design of his house. He was doing a lot of that, and at the rate he was going, it'd be a miracle if the house ever got completed. Frustrating as it was, Jerry was paying the bills, on time, and he didn't seem to care about the final cost. Two months into the project and he'd already pushed me twenty percent over budget, with no end in sight.

Jerry was a cool old dude though, and I enjoyed my time with him. He seemed to have endless stories to tell, and in Jerry's world there was never a dull moment. When I told him how things went with Winston Styles, he lauded the detective again for saving his ass from that "vindictive bitch". Jerry laughed every time he called his ex-wife that, deriving great pleasure from the memory of her downfall.

I pulled up to the site on a Thursday morning in February. The Coachella Valley was unusually warm, and at ten o'clock the temperature was already eighty-five degrees and climbing. I looked to the west, at Mt. San Jacinto blanketed in snow, and I marveled at the fact a twelve minute ride up the Palm Springs Aerial Tram can result in a forty degree drop in temperature as you pass from the arid Sonoran Desert to the alpine forest more than eight thousand feet above. After watching the graceful flight of a red-tailed hawk soaring on the thermals, I grabbed my laptop and a bundle of blueprints and made my way to the small office trailer at the far corner of the two-acre site.

The concrete crew was making their final preparations for pouring the house slab, and I stopped to check out the work, irritation rising inside me. By now we should have been fully framed out, but Jerry's constant changes had seriously delayed the schedule, and I had to continually remind myself of the money I was making and not focus on the headaches of staying one step ahead of such a mercurial client.

Inside the office trailer I set up my computer and rolled out the drawings on a plan table, and I took a moment to consider Jerry and my dad as friends. They'd known each other for years, going back to my dad's time with Hughes Aircraft, but I knew nothing of their history and I was curious about it, mostly because they were about as different as two people can be. I could tell they were close though, and it brought to mind my friendship with Sam, and I wondered if Dad and Jerry were like that back in their younger days. After a few minutes my thoughts were interrupted when Mark Johnson entered the office.

"Good morning, boss," he said.

Mark was a big guy and he had an easy nature about him, and hard as I tried, in nearly six years I hadn't been able to break him of the habit of calling me *boss* all the time. Mark was from a small town in the San Joaquin Valley and that's how he was raised, real traditional about things like that. He was a workhorse too, and the most reliable foreman I'd ever known.

"Good to see you, Mark," I said, reaching out for his hand. "How's your back doing?"

"Better than it was. Working helps. Got to stay strong." He gave me what passed for a smile with him, kind of a half-grin that lasted about a nanosecond. Mark was all business and no bullshit.

"That's good to hear. So, bring me up to speed. Any surprises from good old Jerry this week?"

Mark updated me on the status of the project and we hammered out a two week look-ahead schedule that would see us through the start of framing. We went over a few different issues, talked about the hiring of some more help, and I told Mark about some of the other projects I was bidding. A few hours later we wrapped things up, and Mark followed me out to my truck.

"Say, boss, there's something I need to talk to you about," he said.

I put my laptop and a sheaf of documents on the seat, closed the door and faced Mark. "What is it?"

"I'm not sure exactly. It's a few things, actually, and they're kind of weird."

I smiled. "Just take it from the top, Mark."

"Sure, okay. Well, it started last week with a phone call, some guy asking for you. He wouldn't say what he wanted. When I asked him if it was about the project, he said 'what project?' I just assumed he was calling about the house, but when I told him about it he sounded completely clueless that you were even a builder. Weird, isn't it?"

"Sure sounds like it. So he had the number to the trailer here, but he had no idea where he was calling?"

"That's the second weird thing. He called me on my company phone."

"The cell?"

"Yes."

"What did he sound like?"

"Raspy voiced, like a guy who smokes too much. He had some kind of, what do you call it, a speech…ah, I can't think of the word. It's a—"

"Impediment," I said.

"That's it, a speech impediment. I guess that means he talks funny, right?"

A tingle rose inside me. "Yes, it does. What do you mean, funny?"

"He had a heavy lisp, and he kind of whistled when he talked. It was hard to understand him because the phone kept cutting in and out, sounded like he was talking through a tin can. When I asked him how he knew you he got real angry, said he knew things, and he kept repeating it. The guy made no sense."

The tingle spread, intensifying. "He said it to you like that, did he? That he knew things?"

"Yes, like it was supposed to mean something to me. I finally told him not to call me anymore, and that if he did there'd be trouble."

"And?"

"He called the next day. Twice the day after that. Each time I hung up on him. I wouldn't have answered the phone if I knew it was him, but the number was blocked. Finally he stopped calling."

"What else?"

"On Monday this week I saw a truck parked down there on the road." Mark pointed to the street that ended at Jerry's property. "I first noticed it in the morning around break time, and again at lunch. After that I made a point to keep watch on the street. Whoever it was, the guy stayed there all day, like he was staking us out."

"How do you know it was a man in the truck?"

"I could tell. It was either a man, or a really ugly woman."

"Why do you say that?"

"Something about his face didn't look right. It's a good distance down there, but my eyesight is pretty sharp. No, it was a man all right. I'm sure of it."

I thought it through. The construction site was the last open lot in a development off South Palm Canyon Drive, about four miles out of town, up on a hillside. It wasn't the kind of place you passed through on your way anywhere. A vehicle sitting at the end of the street could only be there for one purpose. I asked Mark to describe the truck.

"It was an old Ford. Black, covered with dirt."

I felt my head go light as the connection was made. Mark noticed my reaction right away.

"You okay, boss? You just went completely white."

I faked my way through it, clamping down on myself. "It's the heat. And too much coffee. Kind of hits you all at once." Mark nodded, but I could tell he was concerned. "Was there a camper shell on the truck?"

"Yes."

"Has he been back since Monday?"

"Not that I've seen. And I've been keeping a good eye out."

"Anything missing from the job site?"

"No, nothing like that. But it's strange, right? First the phone calls, then this guy checking us out. You think they're connected?"

"I doubt it," I said, keeping my tone steady. "But let's keep a close watch on things anyway. We don't want any trouble here."

"Sure thing, boss, I got you covered on that." Mark shuffled a bit, looking tense.

"What is it, Mark?"

"I, uh…I wanted to say I'm sorry."

"For what?"

"For not confronting the guy. I should have found out what he was doing here, shook him up a little. Maybe I could've found out if he was the one who called. I'm sorry I let you down on that one."

Mark's face turned red, a line of sweat beaded on his forehead, and I could tell he felt genuinely bad for what he perceived as a failure on his part.

"Ease up there, partner, okay? You didn't let me down. Your job is to take care of business *here*, not out on the street there, shaking people down. Got it, Mark?"

"Got it, boss."

"Good. And will you please stop calling me that?"

I smiled and Mark gave me one back, showing some teeth this time. He shook my hand and turned to go ramrod the concrete crew. I left the site, and driving down the winding road leading to town, I had a pretty good idea who was surveilling me, as improbable as it seemed. And even though four hundred miles separated Palm Springs from Bridgeport, to a man used to endless wandering in pursuit of his evil deeds, the distance was merely a drop in the bucket.

32

On my way back to Newport Beach I called Winston Styles for an update. He was in his car and our phone connection was bad, and I struggled through the conversation. During the time I was on the phone, Kelli called, and I switched over on the call waiting. She'd been up in Grass Valley all week tending to her father, and today she was supposed to drive home. I told her I'd get right back to her after I finished the call I had on the line. When I switched back over to Winston he was gone, so I hung up and called Kelli back. As the phone rang another call came in, and I saw on the caller ID that it was Larry Peters, but I didn't take it.

Kelli didn't answer, and I put the phone aside and considered some things. Was it true about Garrett Knowles? Was he really tailing me? Based on what Mark Johnson said, it seemed there could be no doubt. But how? And why? Maybe Winston's poking around had stirred up a hornet's nest. Maybe that was a good thing. Maybe the quickest way to bring this to an end was to flush that creep out into the open and force a confrontation, though the prospect of that seemed unreal, like something from a movie.

But this was real life, and even if Garrett wasn't responsible for all those abductions, I knew he was the one I first met at Val's Mountain Inn, the one who confronted me later that night behind the High Country Market. Yes, he was the one who looked at me with those dead eyes and spoke the words that haunted me for so long, and I knew beyond any doubt that he was the one who took Sam away from us, away from this world. Garrett was an evil bastard, of that I was sure. So yeah, anything was possible, even him driving all the way to Palm Springs to spy on me.

Kelli called back, the shrillness of the ringtone knifing through me. I took a moment to clear my mind of Garrett Knowles, made my voice pleasant when I answered.

"Hey, lady."

"Hello, Mason. How are you?"

"I'm fine. How's your dad?"

"He's doing better. His mind seems clearer at least. He even asked about you."

"Did he now?" I said in an exaggerated tone.

"Yes, he did, smart guy. In fact, he asked when you were coming up again."

"Get out."

"No, really, he did. Seems like you two are pretty tight now, buddy."

The lightness of the conversation counteracted the heavy thoughts crowding my mind. Kelli had that effect on me, like pulling the shades on a dark room, filling it with the brightness of day. God how I loved that woman.

"Are you on your way back?" I said.

"I'm leaving soon. But there was something I wanted to talk to you about. I was going to wait until I got home, but since I'm running late I figured I'd give you a call."

"What is it?"

"Well, I was thinking about Brandon Moseley, and what happened to him." She paused, and I wondered where this was going. I waited for her to continue, but she seemed stuck.

"Kelli?"

"Sorry about that, I'm trying to get my thoughts together. So anyway, I was thinking about Brandon, and that his death might be related to Ted Parker's disappearance."

I was driving through Beaumont and my speed had gone up over eighty, and I'd shot right past the 60 Freeway turnoff. "Shit!" I yelled into the phone.

"Mason! Is everything all right?"

"I'm okay, I missed my turnoff is all."

"Please, don't scare me like that."

"Sorry."

My ear got hot from having the phone pressed to it so I switched it to speaker mode and set it on the center console. "I put you on speaker," I said out loud. "What's this about, Kelli? I thought you were dropping all this." I felt foolish saying that, considering my own duplicity in hiring a damn private detective.

"I *was* dropping it, okay? But then I talked to the sheriff from Bridgeport and he—"

"Wait a minute, you called the sheriff?"

"He called me. Remember, we left him our phone number? Anyway, he didn't say why it took so long to call back. I mean seriously, it's been what, over two months since we were there? He didn't have much information, only that Ted Parker still hasn't been found and there are no solid leads."

"That was it? That's all he said?"

"Mostly, but he also said something about what happened in Tonopah. I can't remember exactly how he put it, but it was something along the lines of, once they identify the person who hit Moseley, it might lead to a break in Parker's case."

"He connected the two?"

"Pretty much. He was kind of vague about it, but his meaning was clear."

"Did he ask why you were interested in this in the first place?"

"No, he didn't."

"Don't you think that's kind of strange?"

"I suppose it is. I hadn't really thought of it. I know that he'd been talking to Bob Jeffries though, because he so much as said so."

"I suppose that was to be expected." I thought about Jeffries and the sheriff talking, and the implications of that. Coming up on Yucaipa, I decided to stay on Interstate 10 to the 57 Freeway, go home the long way. "So based on what the sheriff said, you're convinced Moseley's death is linked to Parker, is that it?"

"Yes, I think I am. It's ironic, don't you think? Him getting killed on the very day we went there to talk to him?"

I started to answer her when another call beeped in on the cell. I was going to ignore it until I saw it was Winston calling me back. I took the phone off speaker and put it to my ear. "Listen, Kelli, I've got another call coming in and I have to take it. Let's talk later. I've got some things to tell you."

"Okay, Mason. I'll see you tonight. I'll call you when I'm leaving Dad's place."

Kelli hung up, and as I switched over to Winston's call, I felt tension rise up my spine and grip the base of my neck like a vise.

"MASON, ARE YOU somewhere you can talk?"

"Give me a few minutes to get off the freeway."

"Check that. I'll stand by," Winston said.

I clicked off the line and tossed the phone on the passenger seat. I was tired of talking while driving. Exiting the freeway in Redlands, I pulled into the parking lot of a strip mall. My dashboard temperature gauge read eighty-two degrees outside, and I kept the engine on to run the air conditioner so I wouldn't suffocate in my truck. Love it or hate it, the one thing Southern California has going for it is the weather.

I dialed Winston's cell. "Styles," he said after three rings.

"It's me. Where are you?"

"In Tonopah. Listen, if you can't reach me by cell, call me at the Mizpah Hotel, room number ten. I'm registered under the name Stanley Jones. I'm—" I laughed out loud, cutting Winston off. "You find that amusing, do you?" he said.

"Sorry. It's not very original, that's all."

"Man, you really got a thing about names."

"So why the alias anyway?"

"Standard procedure."

"Are you concerned?"

"No, I'm careful. Now, back to business. Did you know about Garrett's mother being murdered?"

"Yes, Bob Jeffries told me about that, said Reno drug thugs were suspected, something about Garrett's older brothers being involved. What's the relevance?"

"Remember that sealed juvenile record I told you about? Turns out it has nothing to do with the kid who got paralyzed. By the way, his name is Greg Lockwood and he still lives in Bridgeport. I'm going to see him as soon as I'm finished here. He had some choice things to say about Knowles when we spoke on the phone earlier today."

"Impressive."

"Just doing my job, Mason, trying to earn all that long green you laid on me. So back to the mother. Now hold onto your seat, because this gets heavy, very heavy. Garrett killed her, that's what's in the juvie record. Can you believe that shit?"

I was stunned silent by the revelation. My mind went to that afternoon at Bodie, and Bob's telling of the story, not the slightest hint given that he was dishing pure bullshit. Unless he didn't know the truth. But I wouldn't bet on that horse no matter what the odds. Yeah, he knew all right, just like he knew who Garrett's real father was. Bob Jeffries was a man of many secrets, that much was clear. Winston asked if I was still there, his voice severing my thoughts.

"I'm here. Is there more?"

"Not much, but I'm working on it. This kind of information is sensitive as nitroglycerine. Sealed records are not to be fucked with. But I've got damn good sources, careful ones, and I'll get what I need. I know the brothers were involved in some way, but the deed was done by Garrett. It may have been accidental, but either way it's obviously significant. That's why he dropped out of high school."

"Did the thing with Lockwood happen before or after his mom's murder?"

"Before. Garrett was sixteen when he killed his mom, thirteen when he pushed Lockwood."

"You've confirmed that he did it? Pushed Lockwood I mean."

"Lockwood says he did."

"Damn, that Garrett's a real fine citizen, isn't he?" I said.

"The finest," Winston replied.

"So what happens next?"

"I'm meeting later with Moseley's sister. She works the bar here at the hotel, and I want to check some things related to the hit and run. I'm also trying to get some time with the sheriff here. My buddy from Reno knows the guy and he's run my bona fides by him, so hopefully I'll get some good intel. I hear they have a line on a suspect, and if our theory is correct, you know what that means. I'll find out for sure later. Then tomorrow I'm off to Bridgeport, and a face to face with the creep."

"Anything you want me to do?"

"No. Sit tight, and wait for me to call. I'm sending a package out overnight for you, a recap of the case to date."

"Got it."

"One more thing, Mason."

"What?"

"Stay frosty, because we're getting close, and if this dude Garrett is as bent as we think he is, things could get hot."

I was thinking that things were already hot, and I debated saying something about Palm Springs.

"Did you hear me?" Winston said.

"Yeah, sorry, I'm thinking about something."

"Is everything all right?"

"Sure, man, I'm cool."

"Well then why don't you sound like it?"

Damn, was this guy a mind reader? "I think he was here."

"Who?"

"Garrett Knowles."

"When?"

"Three days ago. In Palm Springs."

"Elaborate, please."

I gave Winston the details. When I finished, he said, "So, our friend is escalating. Interesting. This might actually work in our favor."

I went quiet, wondered how Garrett following me around could be considered a good thing. Then I got spooked, thinking Garrett's eyes were on me at that moment, and I slunk down low in my seat.

"You want a tail?" Winston said.

"Huh? What do you mean?"

"I can put my partner on you, see if Garrett shows up again. It might be good to pinpoint his whereabouts. Part of the reason I'm up here is to talk to him, but if he's down there, I'll have to make some adjustments."

I really didn't feel like having two people following me, and I told Winston that. We agreed that if Garrett turned up again we'd reconsider the idea. I clicked off the line, a heavy feeling descending upon me. Fear surrounded me like an invading army, death an arm's reach away, and I put the truck in gear and tore out of that parking lot like a man living on borrowed time.

33

I had just passed Anaheim Stadium when I remembered the call from Larry Peters, the one I didn't take. I dialed his cell and listened to it ring, trying to get plugged back into my day. I still had a lot of work to take care of and so far it felt like I'd accomplished nothing, having been completely sidetracked by all that business with Garrett Knowles. It was well after two and I hadn't even had lunch yet, and now I felt a headache coming on because of it.

"Mason, what's happening, dude?" Larry's big voice boomed on the line.

"Just getting back to you. I missed your call earlier. It's been a damn busy day, like you wouldn't believe. So, what's up? You ready to commit to the Palm Springs deal?"

"And turn into a damn lizard? I don't know if you've heard, but the desert is goddamn hot in the summer, and it's about a hundred miles on the wrong side of the ocean."

"You're a funny guy. So is that a yes?"

"It's a maybe, bordering on a possibility, edging towards sure, I'll help your sorry ass out, Mr. Big Time Contractor."

"Man, what the hell would I be without you, Big Larry?"

"Up shit creek, that's for sure. So anyway, the reason I called is, some freak was in here today looking for you."

"At the saloon? And what do you mean by freak?"

189

"Yeah, here at work. And by freak I mean some anti-social weasel walking around with a burned face and a bad attitude."

It was Garrett. First Palm Springs, and now Newport. What the hell was going on?

"Did he give you his name?"

"Yeah, he said it was Sam."

I felt a stabbing pain behind my right eye. "What time was this?"

"He was standing at the door when I opened at eleven. Can you believe that shit? He sat at the bar for an hour before he even said a word. When I asked if he wanted anything, he just grunted and shoved peanuts in his mouth. Finally he asked about you."

"What did he say?"

"Hell if I know. The dude talks all weird, and damn if I could understand half of what he said. He wanted to know where you lived, I got that much, and something about Bodie. Hey, isn't that a ghost town up north somewhere?"

"Yeah, it's near Bridgeport."

"So who the fuck is he anyway, some new contractor you hired?"

Larry laughed and I played dumb, said I had no idea who the guy was. "How long was he there?"

"I kicked him out about an hour ago."

"Huh? What do you mean by that?"

"I mean I grabbed the dude by the shirt collar and tossed his ass into the street."

"Damn, Larry, what happened?"

"I didn't like his attitude, and he was scaring away the customers. He smelled like a sack of shit, looked like it too. When I got on him about all the questions he was asking, the dude freaked on me, started getting all hyper and talking loud, stuttering like he was having a goddamn seizure. He kept telling me he knew things, like that was supposed to impress me. Man, I don't need that kind of shit here, so I tossed his ass."

"Did he take off then?"

"I haven't seen him around since. But you know what's really strange?"

"Stranger than what you just told me?"

"Ha! No shit, what can top that? But seriously, this is strange. When I got back inside after tossing the loser, there was a package on the bar, right where the dude was sitting."

"A package?"

"Yeah, about the size of a shoebox, wrapped in brown butcher paper. I never even saw him put it there."

"Then how do you know he did?"

"It had to be him, there was no one else sitting at the bar. Your name is written on it too, in a scrawl that could only come from a degenerate like that. Know things my ass. Now he knows not to come around here with his crazy bullshit. So what do you want me to do with this thing?"

"Hold onto it until I get there."

"Well hurry up, I have to split soon to meet a guy about a car I'm selling."

"Can you leave it for me?"

"Better not, shit disappears from this joint like you wouldn't believe."

"I'm on my way."

I hung up the phone as I merged onto the 55 Freeway in Santa Ana, and I hit the gas and got right on some guy's tail. He flipped me off and I swerved around him and accelerated, weaving through the traffic like your typical asshole driver, the whole time wondering what the hell it was that Garrett had left for me.

I HIT A WALL of traffic at Edinger Avenue and struggled through it until I got to MacArthur Boulevard, where I got off the freeway and made my way to Newport via surface streets. The drive was grueling and it seemed every street I turned onto was jammed for one reason or another, and by the time I made it to the peninsula it was almost four o'clock.

I parked my truck at the office and walked to the Balboa Saloon, a sense of urgency creeping up on me. The sun burned low and brilliant to the west, casting elongated shadows across my path, and the breeze had stiffened, dropping the temperature considerably. The air held faint stirrings of a change of weather; perhaps some rain heading our way? The line of cars waiting for the Balboa ferry stretched out onto Bay Avenue, and it seemed there were a lot of people on the street for a Thursday evening.

I pushed through the front door of the saloon and scanned the nearly empty room; a couple of guys shooting pool and one old-timer sitting at the bar, that was it. I didn't see Larry around, but down at the end of the room near a service entry I saw a familiar bartender talking on the telephone. He noticed me and waved, and I moved to the bar and sat on a stool, fighting off impatience fueled by a strong sense of outside forces closing in on me. I focused on my surroundings, once again gripped by the feeling of being watched. Paranoia is an insidious thing, and at that moment it was doing a real number on me.

After a few minutes the bartender walked over. His name was Chuck and he asked me if I wanted anything. I told him no, that I'd only come by to pick up something from Larry.

"You just missed him," Chuck said. "He had to scoot over to his pad and see some guy about that car he's selling."

"Did he say how long he'd be gone?"

"Man, you know Larry, that dude has no concept of time." Chuck slid a bowl of peanuts in front of me and he poured an iced tea.

"You didn't happen to see the guy who came in here earlier today, did you? The one who left a package with Larry."

"What time was it?"

"A few hours ago, something like that."

"I got here right before Larry took off." Chuck eyed me evenly. "Everything cool?"

"Yeah, everything's cool." I downed half my drink in one pull, pushed the glass across the bar. "I'm heading over to my office. When Larry gets back, will you tell him to call me?"

"Sure, Mason, I got you covered."

AT THE OFFICE I muddled through some work while waiting for Larry's call. But my mind was too clouded for work and I couldn't concentrate on anything, the day's events weighing so heavily on me it felt like my skull would crack. I called Kelli and Winston a few times but couldn't reach them, and by six o'clock Larry had not turned up and I felt like a bundle of loose ends.

Two unidentified calls came in on my cell phone and I ignored them both, and Mark Johnson called from Palm Springs. Jerry Corbin had come by and he was pitching a fit about some minor thing, and Mark asked if I could run out there tomorrow and deal with the guy. I listened without hearing and mumbled some response, then ended the call. I was preoccupied with thoughts of Kelli. It bothered me that I couldn't reach her, and I had to tamp down a lot of irrational thoughts taking root because of it.

I checked my watch incessantly, called Kelli and Winston some more, and grew increasingly more agitated while waiting for Larry to show up with Garrett's package. Just thinking about it blew my mind; Garrett, here in Newport Beach. It hardly seemed real. When I'd finally had enough of the waiting, I called the Balboa Saloon and got Chuck on the phone.

"He hasn't shown up yet," he said.

"Has he called you?"

"No. And he's supposed to work tonight. I gotta split and there's no one to cover things."

"I'm going over to his place right now. I'll tell him to get his ass over there when I see him."

"Thanks, Mason."

I hung up the phone, grabbed my jacket and went out to my truck. It was almost seven and rain had started falling, and like everything else that day, it felt wrong.

34

I left the peninsula and took Pacific Coast Highway north to Huntington Beach. I tried Kelli and Winston again on the cell and got nothing, and even though I'd be there in a few minutes, I called Larry too, but there was no answer. I was alternately pissed off and worried about Kelli going dark on me, the others I could deal with. I considered calling her dad but held off for now, telling myself that if I didn't hear from Kelli by nine, I'd make the call.

The rain was coming down steady now and I tuned in an all-news station on the radio for the weather forecast. While I was sitting at a light the report came on; heavy rain across Southern California, with snow at three thousand feet in the local mountains. The cold front was expected to move through quickly, working its way up the Eastern Sierra and dumping up to two feet of snow at Mammoth and Lake Tahoe. And earlier in the day it had been in the eighties. Talk about a change in the weather.

I thought about Sam and of our days spent skiing, and how a weather forecast like that one would've jazzed us to no end, with immediate plans made to drop everything so we could boogie up to the mountains and hit the powder. The thought brought a flood of memories and the memories brought me comfort, and I vowed to see this thing through, no matter where it took me, no matter what the cost. Sam deserved no less.

Coming up on the bridge crossing over the Santa Ana River, I saw two police cruisers with their lights flashing parked on the other side of PCH. I slowed and rolled down my window to see better, rain peppering my face. There were cars parked on the bridge and a knot of people looking over the railing. The scene registered in a bad way and foreboding seized me. I punched the accelerator and jerked my truck into the left lane, flipping a U-turn at Brookhurst Street through the red light, my heart jackhammering. Luckily there were no cars coming the other way, and I admonished myself for being so reckless.

But something was pulling me back, some unspoken thing beamed in from the fringes of the universe, something I felt as real as a cut to my skin; I had to see what happened on that bridge. I drove slowly past the scene, pulled over to the side of the street and hit my hazards. I left the motor running when I exited the truck, and I jogged to the bridge and joined the crowd looking over the side. There were maybe a dozen people standing around and a third police cruiser had rolled up. Cops were gathered down at the river—swollen fat with runoff from the storm—their flashlights beaming in all directions.

I couldn't see very well, so I moved in closer, next to a husky guy wearing a long overcoat. I tapped him on the shoulder to get his attention. "What's going on?" I said. The guy turned around and I about fell over.

It was Mike Cook.

Man, talk about a goddamn ghost from the past. I hadn't seen that guy in ages, at least since I'd gotten sober. I thought he'd died, could've sworn I'd heard that somewhere. Hell, he should have died, the kind of living he used to do. Yet here he was, alive and seemingly well, standing in front of me on Pacific Coast Highway, rain falling on top of us and bad vibes in the air.

In the time since our brawl at Blackie's by the Sea, I'd avoided Mike like an illness, because that's what he was, a toxic influence on every life he came into contact with. I'd heard bits and pieces about him before he finally dropped off the radar. I never wished Mike any ill will. God knows I contributed enough craziness of my own to our screwed-up friendship. But there was no place in my life for people like Mike Cook once I'd straightened myself out.

He didn't recognize me at first, then the light went on and he gave me a smothering hug, just like he used to do whenever he got liquored up. Thing is, with Mike you never knew if a haymaker was going to follow that hug, so you learned to be on your guard whenever he was around.

"Mason," he said, beaming. "Damn, it's been a long time, bud."

"Yeah, it has, Mike."

He didn't smell like booze, so at least he had that going for him, but still, I had no desire to catch up, and I only wanted to know what was going on under the bridge. But I was careful not to brush Mike off, at least until I found out if he was right in the head these days. Fortunately, he helped me out on that one, and he got straight to the point.

"Can you believe it? It's that bum Pete down there."

"Huh?"

"Pete. You know, that fisherman dude, the one who hangs out at the pier. I know you've seen him around. Everyone has."

"That's Pete?" I said, disbelieving.

"Hell yeah. Check it out."

Mike stepped aside and I moved past him and peered over the railing. A body floated face down at the point of the jetty, snagged on the rocks and bobbing in the current. The cops made a half-assed effort at retrieving it with some kind of long pole, looking pretty foolish in the process, and it might have been funny if not for the sad circumstances. I overheard some people talking next to me and they clearly mentioned Pete's name, and I leaned against the railing for support, my legs unsteady. Rain continued to fall and to the east, lightning flashed over Saddleback. The cops finally pulled the body in closer, and when they got it ashore there was no doubt about the man's identity. Pete the Fisherman. Poor old Pete, a guy who never seemed to catch a break in life. I wondered about that trouble he mentioned back in November, trouble down by the river. Jesus, Pete, what'd you get yourself into?

More cops arrived and they shuffled everyone off the bridge, and they closed the southbound lanes of PCH. I turned from the scene and jogged to my truck, hoping I wouldn't see Mike on the way. I still couldn't believe he was there, and I wondered if maybe I'd imagined the whole thing.

It was all so unreal. Hell, even the sudden rain was off-kilter. It felt like I'd stepped into a void, a black and uncertain place like I'd only experienced once before in my life. When I got to my truck the motor was still running, and I thought of the last time I left a truck running on the streets of Newport Beach, and that void opened up wide enough to swallow me whole.

35

Ten minutes later I pulled up to Larry Peters's house in Huntington Beach. The rain kept coming, lightning moving in closer, cracking the sky viciously, twisting my nerves like rusted wire. I sat in my truck alongside the curb, trying to get the image of Pete the Fisherman floating face down in the river out of my mind. But it was no good, I couldn't block it out. Rain fell through the branches of the jacaranda tree in the parkway, hitting the cab of my truck in an irregular *rat-tat-tat* pattern, sluicing down the windshield and weirdly reflecting the nearby street lamps. The more I dwelled on Pete the more unnerved I became, to the point my hand was shaking when I reached for my phone. I dialed Kelli's number, listened to it ring, praying that she'd answer.

But she didn't answer, the phone ringing straight to voicemail, and it took every bit of willpower to not scream into the damn thing and demand to know where she was and why she hadn't called. I gathered myself and left a reasonably calm message, tossed the phone aside and focused only on what was right in front of me. One step at a time. Take care of this thing first, then deal with the rest of it.

Larry lived a few blocks from downtown, near Manning Park, in a house he rented from a friend of his who'd hit it big during the dot-com bubble and got out before the meltdown. The friend owned a number of rental properties near the beach and he cut Larry a sweet deal on this one, payback for some jam Larry helped him out of back in the 80s. Larry kept vague on the details, but word on the street was the guy used to be a local coke kingpin, and when some heavy shit came down on him, Larry stepped in to help.

But those were the old days and Larry didn't mess with that stuff anymore, and his friend was a total straight-arrow now, Mr. High Roller with the fat portfolio, spreading it around to the little guys. The house was small, two bedrooms and a bath, with a detached garage that was bigger than the house itself. That's where Larry kept the old cars he restored and sold on a regular basis, a hobby of his that also turned a tidy profit.

The lights were off in both the house and the garage, and from where I sat in my truck it didn't look to me like Larry was home. I had to check it out anyway, and if he wasn't there, I'd regroup and wait for him to call. I zipped my jacket and reached for the door handle, and my cell phone rang. When I looked at the caller ID I saw it was Kelli.

"Where the hell have you been?" I nearly shouted into the phone.

"Mason?" It was a man's voice, feeble, and my heart dropped to my feet.

"Tom? Is that you?"

"Yes, it is. I saw that you called." It was Tom Flynn, Kelli's father. But why was he calling me on *her* phone?

"What's going on, Tom? I've been trying to reach Kelli for hours and she hasn't answered."

"What's that, you say you've been calling someone?"

Tom sounded completely confused and I wanted to reach through the phone and throttle him, but I checked myself; the man was sick in the head, and getting bent out of shape over it wasn't going to help. "How are you, Tom?"

I said casually, figuring I'd ease him into it. "Is everything okay up there?"

"Yes, I'm fine, Mason, and thanks for asking. Things are good here. Got a bit of weather blowing in. The TV man says it won't snow down here though."

"You had a good visit with Kelli?"

"Yes, I did. She's a fine one, isn't she? And she's been a lot of help to me too. Sometimes I can't think too clearly, my head gets fuzzy. Does that ever happen to you, Mason?"

A knife went through my heart. For all of our differences, Tom didn't deserve this, and I felt like an asshole for my harsh thoughts. "We all forget things," I said sympathetically. "It's good to have someone there to help out."

"Yes it is," he replied.

Lightning lit the sky, followed a few seconds later by the thunder. It was turning into a miserable night. I glanced back at the house. Still dark. Still no sign of Larry. "Can I talk to Kelli?" I said. "Is she there?"

"No, she's already left. She said she was driving somewhere. Bridgeport, I think." He paused, and I imagined him sorting it out. "Yes, that's the place. She went there to see someone she knows. But it's the damnedest thing, Mason, her phone is still here. Do you suppose she left it by mistake?"

"Bridgeport?" I said sharply. "Is that where she said she was going?"

"I believe it was. But what about the phone, what do I do with it?"

So that's why Kelli couldn't be reached. But surely she would have discovered by now that her phone was missing, so why hasn't she called me from a pay phone? And what the hell was she doing driving to Bridgeport anyway?

"Mason?"

"Hang onto it. When I see Kelli I'll let her know what happened."

"Sure. That sounds about right."

"When did she leave, Tom? Do you remember?" I winced for saying it like that, but Tom didn't seem to notice. Unfortunately, he couldn't get clear on the time either.

"I think it was after lunch. Or maybe it was dinner. I know we'd already eaten. I'm sorry, Mason, sometimes I can't think very clearly."

"That's okay, I understand." I thought about how shitty life turns out sometimes, and how there's not a damn thing you can do about it, and my heart ached for Kelli's father. "I'm hanging up now, Tom. If you hear from Kelli, will you tell her to call me, please?"

"Yes, I'll do that. Say, when're you coming back up here? I really enjoyed your last visit."

"Soon," I told him. "I had a good time too. You take care, okay?"

"I sure will. Goodbye, Mason."

I hung up and put the phone in the center console, and got out of the truck and started for Larry's house, not hesitating for a second to consider the situation with Kelli. Walking steadily to the front door, I kept my focus narrow and precise. Cold wind came in long waves, swaying the trees rhythmically, and the rain seemed to rise and fall on the wind. A cat came up on my right and brushed my leg, startling me, and I shooed it away not too gently. At least it wasn't a black cat. At the front porch I knocked on the door but got no answer, so I knocked again louder. No lights went on and no sound came from the house. The cat returned and I kneeled down to pet it. "Do you know where Larry is?" I said to the cat. It purred and wandered off.

I moved around to the garage. Larry's pickup wasn't parked in the driveway, and the alley was deserted, save for garbage cans set out in front of each of the garages lined up one side and down the other. The cat came back and brushed my leg again, and it took off for the far side of the garage, and I wondered if it belonged to Larry. The cat stood at the corner of the garage, meowing loudly, like it wanted me to follow. What the hell, I might as well follow the cat, as if this night couldn't get any weirder.

The cat squeezed through a partially open side door and into the darkened garage. I pushed the door all the way open and stepped inside too. The garage was big enough to fit several cars but only one was parked in it now, an early model Mustang I figured for the one Larry was selling. I flipped the light switch near the door and a strip of fluorescents flickered to life above a workbench along the far wall. Larry kept the garage tight; tools neatly hanging on a pegboard, rolling mechanic's toolbox buttoned up and pushed into a corner, workbench clean and free of clutter.

I'd been to Larry's house countless times and it was always neat and orderly. His tile work was the same way, and I marveled at how such a laid-back and seemingly carefree guy could be such a perfectionist about things. He certainly wasn't like that back in our Edgewood Apartment days. But then again, we were *all* young and dumb back then. I guess it's true what they say, that with age comes wisdom, or at the very least you learn the right and wrong of things.

Larry wasn't in the garage, and I'd about given up on finding him when the cat started meowing loudly over in the far corner, near a pile of old tarps. It jumped up on a nearby chair and seemed to beckon me, and I started that way, but after a step my eye caught something over on the workbench. I walked around the front end of the Mustang, the cat still on the chair in the opposite corner, meowing insistently.

"Hold on, dude," I said to the cat. "I'll be there in a minute." The cat didn't answer.

At the workbench I looked down at a box wrapped in butcher paper and tied haphazardly with twine. It was the size of a shoebox, my name written on it in a shaky scrawl.

My body stiffened and the cat hissed, and I reached for a socket wrench on the wall and threw it at the cat to shut it up. The wrench went high and bounced off the wall and onto the floor, and the cat leapt off the chair and darted out the door. I felt bad for the cat, but damn, enough of that already.

My hands shook as I reached for the box, and it was only then that I noticed the shape of the tarps in the corner, the ones the cat was so insistent about. I ignored the box and walked towards the tarps, which was really one large tarp crumpled over a chair. My heart thudded and a really bad feeling sliced through me. Thunder boomed from outside and the fluorescent lights flickered, and rain poured from the sky, pounding the roof of the garage. It wasn't until I'd gotten within a yard of the tarp that I noticed the pair of ancient Converse high tops I knew all too well from my frequent visits to the Balboa Saloon.

God help me.

My breath grew short and I had the immediate sensation of standing outside myself, watching from above. Bracing for a shock, I reached for the tarp, a feeling like spiders crawling up my skin. I had to do it but I was so damn afraid of it. Before another thought crossed my mind, I yanked the tarp free, and as it fell to the floor so too did I fall, deep within the void.

Larry Peters sat in the chair, looking naturally reposed, as if he'd been waiting there all evening for me to arrive. But there was nothing natural about the angle of his head, or the ugly bruises around his neck. Larry was dead, the life twisted out of him by a madman.

36

I called the cops from a nearby pay phone and got the hell out of Huntington Beach. I didn't use my cell phone for fear of them tracking me on it, and I was counting on no eyewitnesses to my visit, feeling pretty certain the bad weather had worked in my favor by providing some semblance of cover.

I knew I was skating on thin legal ice doing it that way, but felt there was no other choice. Kelli was still out there, seemingly on her way to Bridgeport, and something in my gut told me that was a bad thing. I had to get on top of the situation, and I couldn't afford to get tied up in some police investigation that might last all night.

So I phoned in an anonymous tip, apologized in a prayer to Larry for it, and drove straight home to sort it out. Passing back over the Santa Ana River, I saw no sign of police or bystanders, nothing to indicate that a man had died there that very night. It hardly seemed real, Larry and Pete both dead, seemingly within hours of each other. It never occurred to me that their deaths might be related.

Driving down the peninsula towards my house, I tried to get a grasp on the situation, a big picture view that might help bring some clarity to it. You can't explain crazy, I knew that all too well, but still, why did Garrett kill Larry? It made no sense. He'd already left the box for me, so why turn around and follow Larry home and take the man's life?

What did that accomplish? Was it because Larry tossed him out of the Balboa Saloon? I recalled the confrontation in the boat shed, how quickly Garrett's temper flared with the slightest provocation. Then I thought about our first encounter so long ago, the barely controlled rage simmering under the surface, the cold and lifeless way Gary looked at me as I got between him and Sam. I settled on the unpredictable nature of a criminally deranged mind as the reason. In other words, no reason at all for ending Larry Peters's life. At least none that any sane person could understand.

Once at home I opened the box. Inside was Sam's wallet and his car keys. I was surprisingly numb to it, as if I'd reached the point where nothing could shock me. I held the wallet in my hands, felt Sam's spirit in the leather. There was still money in it, and a picture of Kelli, and buried in the folds was a strip of paper from a fortune cookie.

Truth can be found in places least expected.

I wondered if Garrett had put it there to taunt me. But the yellowed paper and faded print told me no, this wasn't the work of his twisted mind, this was simply an artifact from long ago. I cried uncontrollably then, feeling completely helpless in the world, like every positive thing I'd done in my life since the dark days of 1989 was a lie. All I wanted was to climb inside a bottle, never to return.

I rode that wave until it passed, and upon regaining my composure I set my mind to work. Helplessness wasn't going to get it, and inebriation wasn't the answer. Decisive action was needed. I threw the box away, then thought better of it; evidence to be used later when I went to the cops. Recovering the torn pieces of butcher paper, I noticed something scribbled in grease pencil on the back side. I flattened the pieces and arranged them in order, studied the smudged and retarded writing, the arbitrary sentences, few of them legible.

Wickedly he passes through the shadows.
Death reveals the true nature of man.
Knowledge bestowed unto the seer is... something, a word I couldn't make out. It was all so random, the pure ramblings of a schizophrenic.

At the bottom of one piece of paper, separate from the rest of it and written in a smaller, neater hand, were these words: *now I take it all.*

I read it twice and felt fear. The third time I felt anger, and I knew with absolute certainty that Garrett Knowles was going to get a hell of a lot more than he bargained for. He would take nothing more from me. Or anyone else for that matter.

There came a knock on my front door. I ignored it at first, but then whoever it was knocked again, longer and more insistent. I looked through the peephole. It was raining like a bitch out there and someone was standing in it, a few feet from my porch wearing a yellow rain slicker with the hood pulled up, obscuring their face. Who the hell was this, and what did they want with me?

More knocks followed and I jerked the door open wide, ready to light into the fool, when I saw it was my neighbor, Leonard Hogan. I never liked that guy. He was your typical neighborhood troublemaker, always minding other people's business, constantly stirring up crap. Lately he'd been cozying up to me in an annoying way, and I was pretty sure he was angling for a discount on some home remodeling. Little did the asshole know I wouldn't build him a dog house, much less a room addition. And now he was at my front door, on a night I had nothing left in the tank, for anyone.

"Hello, Leonard," I said stiffly. Maybe if I threw off some real shitty body language he'd get the hint and leave me alone.

"Hi, Mason. Sorry to bother you," he replied. Real nice about it too.

"I'm a little busy here, is there something you need?"

He stayed back a few feet, keeping himself in the rain, even though I had a covered porch and he could have easily gotten out of it. Damn, he was a strange guy.

"I wanted to let you know that bum was hanging around here earlier today, and I had to run him off from your place."

"What bum?"

"You know, the one that hangs out by the Dory Fleet. I think his name is Pete."

"Pete the Fisherman, is that who you're talking about?"

"That's the one. He's a real piece of work, that guy. I caught him looking around your place. When I confronted him he started talking nonsense about how he had to see you. He was real agitated about it too."

"What did he say? Specifically."

"Well, let me think."

Finally Leonard stepped out of the rain, and he pulled his hood off. I waited for him to speak, my mind wandering.

"He kept mentioning a guy he saw, said he was burned, this guy, like from a fire or something. You know how that bum talks, all mushy-mouthed, with that heavy accent of his. You can't make out a thing he says."

"Stop calling him that," I said, anger heating my insides.

"Calling him what?" Leonard replied innocently.

"A bum. Stop calling Pete a bum."

"Well that's what he is. Why do you care what I call him anyway?"

"I just do, okay. Now get to your point, Leonard, or move on."

He set his jaw and glared at me. "Look, the guy was hanging around here acting suspicious, and I thought you wouldn't appreciate it. Someone's got to look out for things around here. Whole damn neighborhood goes to shit otherwise."

He challenged me with his eyes, his self-righteousness daring me to say something. I let it pass, and after an awkward few seconds he finished telling it.

"So anyway, he was going on about some guy named Larry and this other one that he said was burned, and he wanted to talk to you because he was worried about the guy named Larry. The bum…uh, sorry, I mean Pete. Pete said he was hiding from the burned one, because he'd seen something he shouldn't have, something having to do with Larry. Now does any of that make a bit of sense to you?"

"Is that it?"

"Yeah, I suppose it is. I just thought it was important, that's all. I'm sorry I bothered you, Mason."

I stood there in the open door, waiting for Leonard to get the hell off my porch. He pulled up his hood and turned to leave. I gave him three steps, and shouted after him. "He's dead, you know."

Leonard stopped and looked at me over his shoulder, rain pouring down on top of him. "Who?" he said.

"Pete. They found him a few hours ago, floating in the Santa Ana River."

"I didn't know."

"Of course you didn't. But look at the bright side, Leonard. Now there's one less bum for you to worry about."

I slammed the door and stumbled into the living room, my knees shaking at the implications of what I'd heard.

37

The door banged shut and my cell phone rang. I walked slowly to the coffee table and picked it up, ignoring the call when I saw the blocked number. But then a voice inside my head said to answer it, *now*. It was Kelli.

"Are you all right?" she said after my hello.

"Yeah, uh, I'm okay."

"You sound different. Are you sure you're okay?"

I was knocked off balance by what I'd heard about Pete and had completely forgotten about my worry over Kelli. Then it kicked in, and I felt the anger rise. "Dammit, Kelli, where the hell are you? Your dad said you were driving to Bridgeport."

"You talked to my dad?"

"I've been trying to reach you for hours. And out of the blue, Tom calls and says you left your phone at his house, and he tells me you took off for Bridgeport. I've been worried sick about you."

I tried to stem a flood of contradictory feelings. I wanted my point made, that what Kelli did was not acceptable, but I couldn't afford to lose control of the situation by being an asshole.

"I'm sorry, Mason. I got all the way to Truckee before I realized I didn't have my phone with me. I was going to stop and call you from a pay phone but the weather is horrible up here. I decided to drive on to Reno, hoping it would clear up, but it didn't. I finally stopped in Carson City and bought one of those disposable phones. I called you on it a few hours ago and you didn't answer. I'm sorry if I worried you."

I started to respond, but then remembered the calls that came in earlier, the ones that were blocked and that I'd ignored. It cooled my anger, and I decided to give up on whatever point I was trying to make about her dropping off the grid. Sure, I could have busted her for not leaving me a message, but the fight had left me, replaced now by concern. I looked at my watch, saw it was coming up on nine.

"Where are you now?" I said.

"I'm almost to Bridgeport."

"Listen, Kelli, I want you to turn around and go back, do you hear me? Get a room someplace and wait for the weather to clear, come home through Grass Valley, don't go anywhere near Bridgeport."

"What are you talking about, why would I do that?"

"I'll explain in a minute. But first, tell me why you're going there."

"Because Bob Jeffries asked me to."

"Why?"

"Because he has information about Ted Parker."

"He called you?"

"No, he sent me a text message."

"Was this before or after we spoke earlier today?"

"*After*," Kelli said, clearly agitated. "You know something, I don't like your implication."

"What implication?" I said lamely.

"Don't fuck with me, Mason."

Now she was pissed. Kelli never used that word. In fact, she rarely cursed at all, found it pretty abhorrent actually. I was losing her, time to pull back.

"Okay, never mind that, I'm a little stressed is all."

"You're forgiven," she said, but something in her voice told me I wasn't.

"So back to this thing with Bob, don't you think it's odd that he texted you, instead of calling?"

"I never even considered it. I get texts all the time, everyone does. It's a pretty standard way to communicate these days."

I ignored the clear sarcasm in her voice, chose to stay on point instead. "Did you call him back?"

"Yes, but I got his voicemail."

"So you haven't actually spoken to him?"

"No, Mason, I haven't." Kelli drew in an impatient sigh. "Why are you acting so weird about this? Driving through Bridgeport isn't that far out of my way, and if it wasn't for this crummy weather it would be no problem at all. Besides, I wanted to stop and see Annette. We've been talking about partnering on some deals and this seemed like a good opportunity to see the properties. I planned on calling you as soon as I got to her place, to let you know that I wouldn't be home until Saturday."

Kelli stopped speaking and my heart skipped about three beats. She said, "You know, Mason, I really didn't think I had to clear things in my life with you first."

She put a little something in that last part, a tone almost like contempt, and it pierced my heart. This was coming out all wrong and I had to find a way to turn it around. But my mind froze under the weight of all that had happened.

"Why all the questions about Bob?" Kelli said. "What's your concern, Mason? I thought he was our friend. We went to him for help and he treated us well, and now you're acting like he's up to something. Why?"

It came to me arrow-straight then, a full frontal blast of reality. It was all converging on Bridgeport, manipulated into being by Garrett Knowles as he moved his chess pieces into position for the final play. He was the one who texted Kelli, drawing her to him as the surest way to get at me.

Sure, it played. The spying in Palm Springs, killing Larry and Pete, leaving Sam's things for me with those screwy messages, and now this. I'd become his fixation, and now he was out to destroy me. I knew I had to get up to Bridgeport, put myself between Garrett and Kelli and stop the madness. But first I had to tell Kelli what we were up against.

"Mason, are you there? I asked you a question."

"I'm here. Listen, Kelli, things have happened today, bad things, and now I think you're in danger. This thing with Bob isn't what you think. We need to work this out, but first you've got to do what I say."

"That makes no sense. What danger? What is it you've gotten into, Mason?"

It came rushing out of me then, about Larry and Pete and the box containing Sam's wallet, and about Garrett's real identity, a flood of breathless words wrapped in my growing fear. Kelli was so quiet it felt like I was talking to myself.

"So you'll turn back," I said at the end of it. "You'll turn back and come home, right? Because it's too dangerous, Kelli, and Garrett is too unpredictable. I'm sure he texted you, not Bob. He wants you in Bridgeport for a reason. But you don't have to go. And even if it was Bob who contacted you we don't need whatever information he claims to have. I'll tell the cops about the box Garrett left for me, and through that they'll nail the bastard for killing Larry, and it'll be over, because the whole thing will unravel."

I paused and waited for Kelli's response, the silence on the line haunting.

"That's how we'll do it, Kelli. That's the right play. Okay? You got all that?"

A sense of desperation came over me. The line was too quiet, not even road noise in the background. "Kelli!" I shouted. "Talk to me, please!"

But I was shouting into a dead phone. The connection was lost.

38

It was simply a bad connection. A bad connection caused by lousy weather and a shitty disposable cell phone, nothing more than that. Garrett Knowles might be an evil bastard, but unless he could fly, there was no way for him to be anywhere near Kelli when the line went dead.

That's what I told myself.

But still the fear crept in, tried to gain a foothold within me. I fought against it, and set my mind to a plan of action. I felt certain that Garrett's next move would be in Bridgeport, that he would somehow get to Kelli in order to force a confrontation with me. It was the only thing that made sense, even though none of it made a damn bit of sense to anyone with a rational mind.

I called Winston Styles on his cell but did not reach him. Then I remembered the Mizpah Hotel and that ridiculous alias he was using, and when the hotel girl came on the line I asked her to connect me with Stanley Jones's room. After five rings Winston answered.

"Jones."

"It's me, Mason."

"I was about to call you."

"Where have you been, I've been trying to reach you."

"I've been out all day. My goddamn cell phone died and I don't have a charger for it, I left it at home. Can you believe that shit? I've been to three places looking for one and I've struck out all three times."

"Jesus, man, you guys and your phones."

"What's that?"

"Never mind. Listen, Garrett's out of his mind. He's been here today, in Newport Beach, and he's killed two people. Friends of mine. And now I think he's after Kelli."

"Your girlfriend?"

"Yes."

"Explain, please."

I gave him a quick rundown of the situation. As I spoke, I felt oddly detached from it, as if the events had happened a long time ago. Shock perhaps, or maybe some kind of post-traumatic stress thing going on. I felt very tired then, and I was glad as hell that I had Winston on my side, and that I wasn't going it alone.

"Christ," Winston said when I'd finished. "This fucker's nuttier than I imagined. First off, don't worry about the cops, phoning in that tip. We can smooth that one over later. I think that was good instinct on your part, playing it that way."

"Thanks. I still feel like shit about it."

"I know you do. But shake that loose right now and stay focused. Do you hear me?"

"Yes."

"Good. Now as far as Kelli is concerned, I don't want you worrying about her. As soon as I'm off the line I'm going to roll up the operation and hit the road to Bridgeport. I'm about finished here anyway. It's been less than a day and already I'm sick of the place."

"What about the weather? Kelli told me it's pretty bad."

"It's only raining here. I'll get some chains to deal with the snow. You don't worry about me, Mason, I'll make it there."

I had no doubt he would. "She's going to a friend's house," I told him. "But I don't have the address, or the phone number."

"Just give me the name, I'll figure out the rest."

"You can do that?"

"I'm a detective, Mason, I make my living at this stuff."

"Sorry, man." I gave Winston the information, including a description of Kelli and her car. Then he dropped a bomb on me.

"They nailed him, Mason. They've got an eyewitness, a woman who saw Garrett Knowles run down Brandon Moseley."

"You're bullshitting me."

"No, I'm not. It's still real fluid right now, and the witness is a little shaky, but I think it'll stick."

"What do you mean by shaky?"

"It's your typical meth-head situation, but she claims she's off the shit. I talked to the detective handling it and he says the girl's story is pretty solid. They've got her in custody on some warrants and she's trying to cut a deal."

"So what happens next?"

"The word I'm getting is, the detectives here are working with the sheriff in Bridgeport, and they may move on an arrest warrant tomorrow. So whatever fun and games Garrett has planned for you or Kelli or anyone else, he's going to have a helluva time doing it with the law crawling up his ass."

"You know this stuff better than I do, Winston, so tell me, when do we go to the cops with the other stuff, about Sam and the rest of them? And what about Larry, shouldn't I go down to the police station tonight and tell them what I know? Give them the box that Garrett left for me?"

"Let's wait on all that, let them get a net over Knowles up here first before we bring in the rest of it. I can run point on that, if you want me to. At least buffer the fallout from tonight and that thing with your friend."

"Absolutely," I said.

I thought of the way he put it, that *thing* with your friend. I guess Winston was pretty numb to this kind of stuff by now. Just another murder to him. Just another human being doing unspeakable things to another. Damn, what a world we lived in. What a wicked, cruel world we've made for ourselves.

"You still there, Mason?"

"Yeah, I'm here. I'm just thinking about all of this. It's like it's not even real, you know? Like it's some bad joke that's gone horribly wrong. You ever feel that way, Winston, about life? That it's all one big joke, one that was never funny to begin with?

"I used to," he said. "Now I accept it for what it is."

"Yeah? And what's that?"

"Life is cruel, Mason, and life is hard. But through the cruelty and into the hardness good is allowed to shine, and if we never had the bad, well then how the hell could we ever learn to appreciate the good?"

"Sounds simple."

"It can be, if you let it. Anyway, don't trip too hard on this my friend, we still have a ways to go."

"Sure, Styles, whatever you say. Just tell me one thing."

"What?"

"Tell me it'll all work out."

"It'll all work out, Mason."

I HUNG UP the phone feeling like a ship cut loose from its moorings. I was tired and hungry and flat worn-out, and I began the slow process of emptying my mind of all the troubling thoughts. In the old days I did it with booze, soaking my brain until I couldn't function anymore. And it worked too, for a while at least. The problem is, you always sober up, and when you do the bad stuff is still there, and the next time it takes even more booze to kill it, to make it go away for what seems like half the time. It's the ultimate losing battle, and it's the reason a lot of alcoholics end up drinking themselves to death; it becomes the only way to stop it.

I had an idea to go out and get some food, maybe walk along the beach to quell the noise in my head. But the rain kept coming, hard rain, the wind whipping it against the house, and for no particular reason I thought of that song by Jackson Browne, *Before the Deluge*, and I tried to remember the lyrics, something about troubled years that came before the deluge. Maybe this rain would wash it all clean.

The phone rang, the house line, and since I couldn't recall the damn song I answered the phone instead. It was Chuck, from the Balboa Saloon, calling to tell me about Larry. He was pretty distraught, his words coming out haltingly, and I acted shocked at the news, a guilty heat rising inside me. Chuck rambled on about this thing and that, and after a few minutes I hustled him off the phone, unable to listen any longer.

My appetite was gone but I made a sandwich anyway and forced it down, even though it tasted like cardboard. In quick succession three more calls came in, all about Larry. The word was hitting the street. One friend called to tell me about Pete, said the cops were treating it like any other random homeless person's death; just one more casualty of the streets. I finally turned the ringer off and stopped answering the phone altogether. It was getting to be too much of a drag.

At ten-thirty I took something to help me sleep. I didn't like to do that as it was a slippery slope in my sobriety, but that night I needed it. It was a prescription of Kelli's from a recent bout of insomnia, and even though the instructions said to take one, I took two, just to make sure the damn things worked. Stretching out on the couch, I waited for the pills to take me. Sleeping alone in the bed I shared with Kelli was not an option.

I thought of the dropped call from Kelli, the outright anger in her voice, and how it was so different from the conversation we'd had earlier in the day. It was like I'd spoken to two completely different people. Where did that come from? Maybe something had happened with her dad to cause her worry. I knew her father's condition weighed heavily on Kelli, though she was reluctant to talk about it. It was the same way when her mother was dying of cancer, and Kelli wouldn't talk about it to save her life. It was clear to me that Tom was in the early stages of Alzheimer's. I'd seen it before, with an Aunt on my mom's side. I knew there was a long, grim road ahead, and there would be no happy endings for Tom Flynn.

I tried to view the situation logically, remove emotion from the equation. I knew that Kelli would be safe at Annie's house, at least for tonight. Garrett couldn't possibly be in Bridgeport yet, and even if he was, Winston Styles, *Mr. Hardcore*, was on his way, so up yours Garrett Knowles; let's see you try and get one by that dude. Tomorrow I would regroup and decide on a course of action. Tonight I would let it all be.

As I started to drift off there was one thought that kept recurring, something one of the callers had said. It was my friend Evan Jenkins, and when he called to tell me about Larry he mentioned the police had a lead. It seems one of the neighbors saw a pickup truck parked outside Larry's house, and they reported it to the cops. Did they get a license plate? Evan wasn't sure, but he knew it was after seven o'clock when the truck was spotted.

I replayed the scene in my mind, wondering who saw me, *if* they saw me. When I finally slipped under the veil of sleep, I had visions of the police knocking down my front door, dragging me away for the murder of my friend.

I tried explaining it to them but they wouldn't listen. They said only a guilty man would leave his friend like that, like so much trash waiting out by the curb. They threw me in a tiny cell, and when the heavy steel door slammed shut it blocked out every bit of light in the world, and as the darkness enveloped me I slept the sleep of the dead.

39

The next day I woke up hard, groggy and out of sorts, like I was suffering from a bad hangover combined with jet lag. Rain lashed furiously at the house, and I wondered if it had stopped at all throughout the night. Sitting there in dawn's half-light, muted a dismal gray by the foul weather, I badly regretted my decision to take the sleeping pills. As much as I'd wanted the release that came from them, now there was a price to pay, and I considered how long it would take for the fog to lift in my brain. I tried to help the situation along with strong coffee, lots of it, but it barely helped. I wondered if this was how Tom Flynn felt on his worst days.

It was Friday, the twenty-sixth of February, a date that would live in infamy, to borrow one of history's most iconic phrases. At least for me it would, though at that precise moment I had not the slightest inkling of where the day would take me, premonition and intuition and good old common sense having abandoned me like a trio of fair-weathered friends. A lot had happened in twenty-four hours, and as I recounted it, I wasn't sure any of it was real.

Larry and Pete were dead, seemingly killed by Garrett Knowles, who was really a man known to me as Gary, a man who would travel great distances to heed his sick callings. Kelli and Winston were out there in the eye of the storm, Bridgeport, while here I was, befuddled and lost,

222

quite possibly the focus of a police investigation, or at the very least my pickup truck was, if the neighborhood peeper was to be believed.

But maybe his time frame was off, what then?

Maybe what he really saw was Garrett's truck. And maybe he even got the license plate number. Hell, maybe the cops were on to Garrett right now. That was a lot of maybes. A lot of conjecture.

More questions.

Where did Bob Jeffries fit in all this?

I was certain he did not text Kelli, as that was surely Garrett's doing. But Bob must figure in the picture somehow. Was he really Garrett's father? And if so, would he listen if I called him right now and told him the truth about his son? A chilling thought came to me. What if Bob already knew the truth? What if the bond he had with Garrett, whether it be paternal or otherwise, had led him to turn a blind eye to the whole thing? At the very least, I figured Bob Jeffries knew where some family skeletons were buried, and for that he could not be trusted.

Once I felt sufficiently awake and aware, I called Bristlecone Realty in order to reach Kelli. The information operator had no home listing for Annette Briggs, so her office was my only shot. I waited until after nine o'clock to make the call, hoping they'd be open by then. As the phone rang I thought about what Winston had said last night, and wondered if the sheriff had gotten a net over Garrett yet. Would the weather hamper them? The phone rang repeatedly before Annie's assistant answered. Her name was Denise and she told me that Annie wasn't expected in the office until later in the day because she was out with a friend looking at property.

I was incredulous at the news. Wasn't the weather bad up there? Well yes, Denise said, but Annie had taken advantage of a break in it, and besides, the roads were holding up well and Annie had an SUV built like a tank, and she was used to driving in the snow. What time did they leave? Denise wasn't sure, but she knew they planned on taking the entire morning, possibly well into lunch since they might go as far as Minden. When I asked about the friend, Denise confirmed it was Kelli.

Denise got suspicious then, about me and my questions, and she confronted me with it. When I explained who I was, she apologized for sounding a little harsh, but folks had been kind of jumpy in town ever since that young man went missing a few months ago, and well, most people just assume he's dead. And his poor friend was killed too, a hit and run out in Tonopah, and the word in town was that foul play was involved. Yes sir, Denise said, there were some strange doings lately and everyone was a little bit nervous about that.

My mind was already moving on to other things, so I quickly thanked Denise for the information and brought the call to an end. She gave me Annie's number and I asked her to pass a word along to Kelli for a callback.

I hung up the phone with a renewed feeling of desperation. There was no way to know how much of what I'd told Kelli had gotten through before the call dropped last night. I assumed she'd heard none of it, since she never called me back, and that she was oblivious to the threat Garrett posed. And now she was out there with Annette driving all over town, exposing herself to risk. I fought to keep my emotions in check as I dialed Annette Briggs's number. My heart thudded when the phone rang straight through to voicemail, and I sucked in a breath before leaving a message. Annie had never met me, so the last thing I wanted to do was leave some rattled, half-baked message on her cell phone. I calmly told her who I was and asked her to have Kelli call me as soon as possible.

Next I called Winston Styles. I was counting heavily on the detective as my insurance policy against whatever bad shit Garrett had in mind. But first I brewed some more coffee, filled my mug and took it and my cell phone over to the couch. Easing onto the cushions, I lay my head back and closed my eyes, hating the way I felt. I would have paid a king's ransom to have a clear head. Thunder rumbled outside my bay window and I heard the faint sound of waves crashing on the beach, and I wondered when the storm would pass. I gulped some coffee, and dialed Winston's number.

"Styles," he said upon answering.

"It's me," I replied. "Are you there?"

"Yes."

"How was the drive?"

"Lousy."

"So what's the situation?"

"I'm staying at the Walker River Lodge," he said. "Had a helluva time getting a room last night because I got here so late. The night clerk ran me through all kinds of bullshit, must've thought I was a creep or something. I don't get it, man, people are supposed to be friendly in these small goddamn towns."

Winston stopped talking and I had a bad feeling. Was something wrong on his end?

"Hey, Mason," he went on. "Did you know there's a house here they used in the movie *Out of the Past*? Seriously, I can see it from my room. Man, I love that flick. Bob Mitchum is the shit. You ever see that one?"

Winston was stalling with his small talk, and if I knew anything at all about him, it was that small talk wasn't his thing. Something was wrong.

"Cut to the chase, Winston, what happened?"

"I'm not sure. All I know is, the detective in Tonopah said they lost the girl."

"What do you mean, lost the girl? You mean the witness to the hit and run?"

"Yes. And by lost I mean they can't find her. They let her out of custody last night as a good faith gesture and she bailed. They're out there now looking for her, but she's in the wind."

"What does that mean?"

"It means it's going to take a little longer to grab Knowles. I was hoping they'd move on him today, but no dice now."

"Well that's fucking terrific. So now what?"

"It's your call. I can keep investigating Sam's disappearance, and the others, or pull the plug and wait for the cops to catch up with Knowles."

"And if they don't find the girl?"

"Then they have no case. Unless there's information I don't know about."

I lowered the phone and closed my eyes, my mind hopelessly fogged from the pills I took. I cursed my stupidity and wanted to lash out at someone or something. It was all turning out wrong and there was nothing I could do about it. I wanted to choke the woman who'd witnessed the murder of Brandon Moseley and ran like a scared little rabbit. Didn't she realize that she alone held the key to taking a murderer off the streets? How the hell could people be so goddamn selfish?

"Mason, are you there?"

I heard Winston's voice muffled from the phone I held next to my leg, and I put the phone to my ear. "Yeah, I'm still here," I said, my voice toneless.

"Look, this will work out. Catching bad guys is never a straight line, and all you can do is roll with the punches. Are you with me on that?"

"Thanks, Winston, I appreciate the sentiment, but right now my head feels like it's been stuck in a bucket of mud, and I'm not exactly tuned into positive vibrations, if you get my drift."

"What happened to your head?"

"Nothing, man. Just some sleeping pills I took doing a number on me."

"Sorry to hear that. Stay off the booze with those pills. I knew a cat popped a few of those one night and washed them down with some Johnnie Walker. He wasn't looking to do himself in, but it didn't matter. He still got a one-way ticket on the night train, straight to the Big Sleep."

"And this shit's supposed to make me feel better?"

"I'm only looking out for you, buddy. You're my client, Mason, and I take care of my people."

I was going to tell him about my alcoholism, and how if my sobriety could stand up to what happened last night, well there wasn't much chance of me chasing my sleeping pills with liquor. But I had neither the energy nor the desire to get into all that right now. "Thanks," was all I said. Then I thought of Larry and Pete the Fisherman.

"Maybe I need to go see the cops down here and tell them about Larry. I think they might be looking for me anyway." I told Winston what I'd learned from my friend, Evan Jenkins. "With that witness in Tonopah pulling her shit, maybe this is the best way to nab Garrett. He killed Larry, let's take him down for that."

"That's a possibility. But there are some holes we need to shore up first. I think it would go better if I was there with you, help lay out what went down. I'd hate for you to go in there in good faith and end up being the one they're looking at. I know how these guys think, Mason. Remember, I was one of them. Short of having an attorney there with you, you can't go wrong having an ex-cop on your side. I can reason with them if they start taking this in a bad direction. What do you say?"

"Whatever *you* say, Winston."

"I'll take that as a yes."

"Look, I'm gonna get off the line now and rest my head. I've downed more coffee than you on your best day, and I still feel like a goddamn zombie."

"Yeah, I guess I drink a lot of that shit, don't I. And the only worse coffee than what they got here is over in that shithole Tonopah. Jesus, what a dump that fucking place is."

"You're a riot, you know that, Styles?"

"That's what the guys on the force used to say."

"So listen, there's one more thing you need to know about."

I told him about Kelli and Annette and their plans for the day. Winston said he'd already driven by Annie's house last night and again early this morning, saw Kelli's car parked out front and lights on in the house. He'd wanted to make contact, but the circumstances were too sketchy, so he figured the best play was to keep a loose tail on Kelli until I had the chance to talk to her again and spell it all out.

"I'll keep an eye on things here. You rest up and get your head together. As far as you driving up here, that's a negative right now. The road's closed near Lee Vining, and no one knows when it'll be clear. I guess a snowplow went off the highway somewhere south of here and Caltrans can't keep up with what they've got running."

"That means you're stuck too," I said.

"Yes, I'm stuck too. Unless I go north and come home the long way. The road's clear to Reno. I suppose I could go east, back through Tonopah, but I really don't want to do that."

"Look, just keep an eye on Kelli, okay? That's all I ask."

"Consider it done."

"Thanks, Winston."

"You're welcome, amigo."

40

I was in a holding pattern.

I don't do holding patterns very well, never have, and it wasn't long before I was crawling the walls. I considered calling Annie again, but then I heard Kelli's words from last night, the ones about not needing my approval to do whatever the hell it was she wanted to do, so back off jack.

I decided to wait on the call, and trust that a bright and intuitive woman like Kelli Flynn could take care of herself. Besides, what was Garrett going to do, grab her right off the street? With Annie there? It wasn't likely. Also, I had Winston to watch over her, and with the bad weather and highway being closed, the odds of Garrett even making it through were slim. Unless he took the long way around. Yeah, I guess that was a possibility. Still, I figured that as long as Kelli stayed away from Bob Jeffries's place and stuck close to Annie, everything would be okay.

As for the situation with the cops, there was nothing they could use to hang Larry's murder on me. We were friends for a long time, a fact well known in our community, and there was never any trouble between us. We weren't involved in any dirty business either, so there was no double-cross angle for the cops to exploit. I got scared was all, and I'd acted irrationally, that's why I took off after finding Larry dead. They could try all they wanted to make more out of it, but it wouldn't stick. They could sweat me hard like some loser perp in one of those B-movie detective dramas, but they'd never hang Larry's murder on me.

As the gears turned in my brain the fog slowly lifted, and soon the picture became clearer. Take away the emotional component, the fear and anxiety, and all you're left with is a problem to solve. And solving problems is a lot like building a house, you start with a solid foundation and work up from there. I decided to start at the beginning, with Bob Jeffries. I figured it was time to call my good buddy and rattle his cage. The phone rang and I considered my approach. Do I play it all friendly and ease into my questions, or do I hit him between the eyes with the things Winston told me? Bob answered before I'd decided. Now it was time to go fishing.

"Hello," he said.

"Hello, Bob. It's Mason Tanner."

"Mason, how are you?"

"I'm good. How are things up there? I hear you're getting some snow."

"You can say that all right. It's settled down a bit this morning, but another front is moving in, looks to be worse than what we've already got. How are things down south?"

"Wet and windy. Cold too. It's been pretty miserable. But I'm sure it's nothing compared to what you're dealing with."

"I'd say so."

The conversation was inane, but a necessary precursor to whatever would follow. I had a feeling about Bob, a sense that his part in all this was much bigger than it seemed on the surface. Was he more than a mentor to a troubled young man? Of that I was sure. Did he play a role in Garrett's crimes? That was a question I couldn't begin to comprehend.

"So what's on your mind, Mason?" Bob's voice took on a subtle shift in tone. "I know folks are fond of talking about the weather and all, but I'm sure that's not the reason you called."

I chuckled, trying to make it sound funny, when in reality I felt heat rise up the back of my neck. I got up to open a window, the rush of cold air bracing. The rain had tapered off but the wind blew hard, funneling down my street like the cold blast from an open icebox.

"You're right," I said. "I didn't call to talk about the weather. But I am thinking of driving up there later today. I hear the highway is closed near Lee Vining."

"For now. They hope to have it cleared soon."

"That's good to hear. I was a little concerned about it."

"So what's bringing you up this way?"

"Well, Bob, that's the reason I'm calling. Kelli is up there."

"You don't say?" he replied, a genuine note of surprise in his voice.

"She arrived last night. She's up there visiting Annette Briggs, her realtor friend."

"Yes, I know Annie."

"They're talking about partnering on some deals."

"Well Annie is very successful, that's for sure. And admired around town."

"So you haven't heard from Kelli?"

"No. Should I have?"

I listened for signs of a tell, a hitch in his voice, something to indicate what hid below the surface. But he sounded like the same affable guy I'd come to know back in November. I wanted to ask him about Garrett, but I couldn't think of a reasonable way to do it. More than anything, I wanted to know if Garrett was in town, and if he'd been gone the last few days.

"I'm just trying to clear something up here. I seem to remember Kelli saying that you texted her recently, about that thing we were looking into back in November, the disappearance of that kid. But maybe I'm remembering it wrong."

"I didn't contact her," Bob said firmly, if not a little forcefully. "But about your visit earlier. There's been a man asking questions around town, about Ted Parker. He's some kind of private investigator out of Reno. You wouldn't know anything about that, would you, Mason?"

"No," I replied too quickly, the conversation evolving faster than my addled brain could absorb. "Kelli and I talked about doing that, but we never got around to it. Do you think Parker's family might've hired him?"

"I really couldn't say. But I've got nothing to hide, and neither does Garrett."

"Garrett? What's he got to do with it?"

"Nothing, Mason, nothing at all. But this investigator seems to think Garrett's got a great deal to do with it. I've never met the man myself, some friends of mine told me about him. From what I understand, he's been asking a lot of questions about Garrett. Some ugly things have been said, bringing my name into it as well. I'd sure hate to think you were behind it."

"Of course I'm not," I said, my tone defensive.

"That's good to hear. Because in my mind, Mason, that's about the lowest form of man there is, one who hires a snoop to dig into another man's past, asking a lot of questions that have no business being asked."

"Did he talk to him? Garrett I mean, did he talk to the investigator?"

"I don't know. I haven't seen much of Garrett lately."

"Is he there now," I said, a sudden boldness coming over me.

"No, Mason, he isn't."

There was distrust in Bob's voice now, and I decided to cut and run. "I'm sorry about all the questions, I'm just curious, that's all. The whole thing sounds so intriguing, private eyes and whatnot, like some kind of mystery novel. Anyway, I'll let you go now. I hope to be up there once the weather clears. Maybe we can get together for dinner or something."

"Sure, that would be nice," Bob replied, sounding like it would be anything *but* nice.

41

I had to get out of the house for a while, breathe in some clean air, feel the rain on my face. A funk slowly consumed me, and I had to get out from under it. I kept running scenarios through my mind, each one more frightening and confused than the last, and the conversation with Bob Jeffries only made it worse. I honestly couldn't tell if he was a good guy in all this, or if he was knee-deep in Garrett's twisted world.

I got dressed and stepped outside, started walking south on the bike path, my destination Seaside Donuts. I left my phone in the house, purposely putting a barrier between me and the situation, and I kept my field of vision very narrow, focusing only on the cold air seeping into my clothes, hoping the rain would start up again before I returned home.

At the donut shop I ordered a half-dozen of whatever looked good, and even though I was pissing coffee, I got a large to go, black, steaming hot. A vision hit me, the morning I bought coffee and food for Pete the Fisherman at this place, a morning that seemed so long ago.

Like another lifetime.

Like another man's lifetime.

I snuffed the vision, brutally stomping it like some hideous bug that needs killing. I couldn't mourn Pete right now. Maybe later, once the dust settled.

I left the donut shop, putting one foot in front of the other, refusing any and all thoughts but the trivial. I thought about how much energy it takes a man to walk out of a donut shop holding a cup of coffee and a sack of donuts he has no appetite for. I thought about where rain comes from. I thought about the wind and how it always blows down here on the coast, and how sailors have ridden that wind since before Christ was born, and once there was a time they thought the world was flat, and if they were not careful they would sail right through the firmament and fall into the abyss. What I didn't think about was Garrett Knowles, or what I was going to do next.

I made it to the pier and the rain came. Sitting on a bench, avoiding the spot where Pete sat last November, I ate a donut and drank some coffee. They brewed a damn fine cup at Seaside Donuts. I unzipped my jacket and took it off, and the flannel and the tee shirt underneath, let the rain hit my bare skin, the cold air wrapping itself around me. There were no people about, no one to intrude on my mindless respite from things over which I had no control.

I stayed that way for a long time, long enough to put my mind right. When I was ready, I stood and stretched, put my wet shirts on and zipped my jacket, tossed the donuts and coffee and started for home. When I got there I hung my jacket on the coat rack and put my wet clothes in the hamper. I took a very long and very hot shower, and after I'd dressed, the telephone rang. I answered it, and things started moving very quickly.

"MASON, IT'S CHUCK."

It was Chuck Wyatt, the bartender from the Balboa Saloon. "What's happening?" I said.

"You okay, you sound tired."

"I'm all right. Had a rough night is all."

"Yeah, same here. Thinking about Larry has fucked me, dude."

I did not reply. The wall clock said five after eleven. My watch said twelve after, and I wondered which one was right. I couldn't concentrate. "I don't know what to say, Chuck. It's a goddamn tragedy."

"It ain't right, man. It ain't right at all."

"No, it's not."

A long moment ensued, Chuck breathing on the line. Through the window I saw a police cruiser on my street, and it raised my hackles.

"So anyway," Chuck said, "the reason I called is to warn you."

"Warn me?"

"Yeah. I was talking to a friend of mine, works on the Huntington PD, and he said your truck was spotted at Larry's house last night."

"I sort of knew about that. Evan Jenkins told me a witness saw a pickup in front of Larry's. That's all he knew about it. Could've been mine I suppose, from when I went over there to see Larry. Is there a problem with the cops?"

"Not that I know of. My friend only mentioned they wanted to talk to you. I figured I should give you a heads up. I know how fucked cops can be."

"Including your friend?"

"Sure, he can be a real tool, but I've known him so long he lays off the tough guy crap when I'm around. Anyway, he knows that you and I are friends, and he thought he'd pass a word. You remember Todd Whitaker? That's the guy, my friend I mean."

"The name isn't ringing a bell. But thanks for calling me. There's really not much I can tell them though."

"I figured that. Anyway, take care, Mason. I'll be talking to you. I guess there'll be a funeral. For Larry I mean, sometime soon. Fuck I hate funerals. I gotta go, my old lady is yelling at me. See ya."

I hung up the phone and knew it was time to leave town. The last thing I could afford was to get wrapped up with the cops, not with Kelli still out there and Garrett circling like a shark. There would be time to square things later. Right now, I had too many loose ends to deal with.

It all centered on Bridgeport.

A plan quickly formed in my mind. I would borrow Mark Johnson's four-wheel drive Jeep, the one he'd outfitted extensively for off-road excursions, and one way or the other I'd get through the snow and make it to Bridgeport. Once there, I'd rendezvous with Kelli and Winston, and the three of us together would decide on the best way to end this thing once and for all. The cops and their questions would have to wait. I wasn't running, just taking a time out, putting some distance between me and the situation. A few days was all I needed, enough time to make sure Kelli was safe and Garrett Knowles was neutralized. In the meantime, maybe the cops in Tonopah would get their shit together and rope in Garrett for running down Brandon Moseley. If not, I'd burn that house down myself.

Feeling energized, I called Mark to set it up. He was unmarried and he lived out in North Tustin, in a small house near Peters Canyon. I explained the situation, leaving out my true purpose for going to Bridgeport, and Mark told me where to find the spare key for his Jeep. I thanked him and was about to hang up when he said, "Everything okay, boss?"

"Sure, why?"

"Your voice sounds funny."

"I'm all right, Mark. Just busy is all."

"The weather is pretty bad heading up north, you sure about driving?"

"I'll be okay. Thanks for the concern." I felt a flash of guilt for holding out on Mark. He was a damn good guy and he deserved the truth, but there was no way to lay all that on him now.

"I can go with you, if you like."

I was genuinely touched, and I felt pride well up at having such a fine man working for me. "Thanks, Mark, but I need you to hold down the fort here. I may be gone for a few days, and you know Jerry, he needs his TLC." Mark actually chuckled, and I did too, and I hung up the phone.

With the Jeep handled, I packed my bag and prepared to leave. I felt anxious the whole time, anticipating a call or a knock on the door from the cops. More than a few times I surreptitiously peered out the side windows of the house, on the lookout for anything out of the ordinary. The police cruiser I'd seen earlier had not returned, and the street was quiet. At noon I started getting nervous about the time, calculating how long it would take me to get to Tustin, switch vehicles, and make it to Bridgeport. I wouldn't get there before dark, that much was certain.

Before heading out, I called Winston and left him a message updating him on my plans. With that taken care of I was ready to go, and I took a last look around the house and wondered if I would ever see it again. I took in Kelli's essence, thought of all that had led me to this. I tried to feel Sam's presence but could not. Are you there my friend? Are *you* the unseen hand pushing me forward, giving me strength? Or is that God's work? Either way, I knew beyond any doubt what I had to do. I would succeed at this endeavor, or I would die trying.

42

I'd barely made it off the peninsula when I got a call from Jerry Corbin. I wasn't up to dealing with more bullshit, and as I stared at the phone I willed myself not to answer. But on the eighth ring I caved and hit the button, and immediately started scheming a way to end the call.

"Hello, Jerry."

"How are you, my friend?" Jerry replied jovially, like a guy without a care in the world.

"You caught me between it here, and I don't have a lot of time to talk."

"Now that's what I like to hear, keeping yourself busy, making scratch. But you're still keeping me at number one, right?"

"Right, buddy. Number one." I groaned inside. I liked Jerry, but right now he was bugging the shit out of me. I entered the 55 Freeway in Costa Mesa and gassed it, the rain coming down in sheets. "What's on your mind?" I said, hoping to nip the conversation quick.

"Well, I got to thinking about the house." Terrific, here it comes, more goddamn changes. "Maybe his and her baths would be kind of nice."

"Really, Jerry? You aren't even married. And given your track record, I think you'd want to keep it that way."

"Very true, Mason. But I'm eternally optimistic. And I'm a man who plans for the future, even when it comes to putting dual shitters in my new castle."

He gave out a huge laugh. I pulled the phone from my ear, took a deep breath. "We're just about ready to pour the slab," I said, using up the last of my patience. "This really isn't a good time to be changing things. Are you sure about this?"

"As sure as I ever am."

In other words, as soon as the changes were made, he'd change it back again. It was time to cut him short. "Look, can we talk about this later? Or if your mind is made up, go out and see Mark and tell him what you want done, he'll take care of it. I've got to jump now. I'm in the middle of something and I have to get to it."

"You okay?"

"I'm fine. Why do you ask?"

"Your voice, it sounds all wrong. Anything I can help you with?"

Crap, first Mark, and now Jerry, both of them seeing right through me like I was a piece of cheesecloth. Was I really that obvious? It made me feel good though, knowing that I had people in my life who cared.

"Thanks for asking, Jerry, but I'm all right. I've got business to take care of in Bridgeport and I'm pressed for time, that's all. I'm on my way up there now."

"You're driving?"

"Yes."

"Bad move, Mason. Haven't you heard the weather forecast? It's pure shit everywhere. Do you really have to leave today, like right now?"

"Yes, I do."

"Well let me fly you up there."

"Fly me? Since when do you fly?"

"Since I was a youngster." Jerry laughed. "Hell, son, I've been flying longer than you've been alive."

"No shit?" That Jerry Corbin, always full of surprises. "So what about a plane? Wait, don't tell me, you have one of those too."

"Two actually. One is up at Sun Valley, in Idaho. But I'm selling that bird."

"And the other?"

"That's Dottie, she's over at John Wayne."

"You named your airplane?"

"Oh yeah. After my first wife. I ever tell you about her? She was a cocktail waitress at the Cal-Neva Lodge when I met her, up there in Tahoe. Dean Martin was making eyes at her one night at the craps table, but she only had eyes for me, and I stole her away clean. That twerp Sinatra tried to make something of it, but I had six inches and fifty solid pounds on him, straightened his ass out real quick."

"That's a cool story, Jerry, but about the plane. What's the deal?"

"She's a nice little Citation, and she's fueled up and ready to go."

"You were planning a trip?"

"Not really. I just like to keep my options open. You never know when you might have to split town on short notice."

Jerry chuckled. Ain't *that* the truth, I thought.

"So turn yourself around and meet me at general aviation in one hour. I'll handle the rest. By the way, there's no inflight service on this ride, so bring your own refreshments."

I ran it through my mind. It was almost one o'clock, and I still hadn't switched vehicles. I was looking at seven hours on the road, probably more with the weather and highway conditions. "How long will it take to get there?"

"Ninety minutes tops."

"And the weather's not a problem?"

"Hell no, mate. I used to fly air rescue in the Tetons. Call me when we get a real storm. So what's it gonna be, Mason?"

"Let's do it. I'll see you in one hour."

WHILE WAITING FOR Jerry to arrive at the airport, I called Mark Johnson and informed him of my change in plans. I also told him to be ready for more changes coming on the house. Mark assured me he had things covered, and I knew that as far as my business was concerned, everything was in order.

All that other stuff?

Not so much. But at least I was working on it. Though the only thing I could see at the end of it was a huge question mark. I knew I couldn't afford to get ahead of myself; right now I simply had to *get* there, and hope the rest of it fell into place.

To that end I called Winston Styles, got his voicemail and updated him on the new plan. He would have to meet me in Bridgeport once we landed. I didn't know where that would be exactly, or if they even had an airport in town. Knowing Jerry, he'd probably put the plane down in an open field and call it a day.

I mused on the turn of events, starting back in November when I found that box of papers in Kelli's attic, and the unraveling of a mystery began. The improbability of it astounded me. Never could I have foreseen anything like this. But *this* is what it had become, and the true measure of a man is determined not by how he handles the circumstances of his life within the narrow confines of the predictable, but how he reacts to the unexpected. Does he rise to the occasion, or does he shrink back and fall under the weight of his fears. We all like to believe we'd be heroic if the time ever came for it. When the plane hits the tower, would we run *inside* to help?

Well I'm no different. And as I sat in the airport that day waiting for the other shoe to drop, I prayed that I had the right stuff.

43

Jerry arrived at John Wayne Airport focused and ready to go. He checked in with some people and worked out his preflight details, then went to the hanger to look over his plane. He returned a short while later and told me it was time to fly. The rain was really coming down, and Jerry had to repeatedly assure me it was no problem.

As I ran onto the tarmac my cell phone rang. I jogged to an overhang to get out of the rain and answered the phone. "Mason here," I said loudly.

"You okay? You sound winded."

"Winston? Is that you?"

It was difficult to hear with the rain hitting the tin overhang above me, and Jerry had started his plane and the sound funneled right at me. I turned and faced the corner of the building, trying to shield myself from the distractions.

"I got your message," Winston said. "When will you be here?"

I looked at my watch. "Around four o'clock. Can you pick me up?"

"Where?"

"Bryant Field." When Jerry arrived at the airport, the first thing I did was collar him and ask where the hell we were flying. "By the way, what's the weather like right now?"

"Cold as my ex-wife, but no snow. At least for now. They say more is coming though. Hopefully you guys can stay out of the soup."

"Yeah, hopefully."

"Listen, Mason, I've got two things to tell you, and you aren't going to like either one."

Jerry Corbin waved to me from the open cabin door of the plane. It was time to go. I swallowed a lump and braced myself. "Tell me."

"I lost Kelli." Winston waited before continuing. "I was tailing her and her friend, for most of the day. We were leaving Minden this afternoon and I got pulled over by the goddamn Highway Patrol. Can you believe that shit? I flipped out and gave the dude some grief, told him I was a private cop working a case and I couldn't afford to sit there by the side of the road while he wrote me some bullshit ticket. I told him lives were at stake if he didn't let me go."

"What'd he do?"

"He searched my car. Goddamn asshole. Kept me there forever while he dicked me hard, just to prove a point. By the time I got back on the road I couldn't pick them up. When I got to town I went straight to Annette's, but they weren't there. I'm sorry, Mason, I fucked this one up."

I checked my anger, knowing it wasn't Winston's fault. "It's okay, you couldn't help it. Have you been to Bob's place yet?"

"I just got back from there. Bob's not around, and if Garrett's in town, he's a ghost."

"Got it. So what's the other thing?"

"It's about Jeffries. My partner dug up some information. It seems Bob used to own a house in Bear Valley."

"In California?"

"Yes."

"When?"

"1989."

"Shit. He was there. When it happened."

"We'll never know for sure. The house was a rental property, and Jeffries sold it about ten years ago. It's probably the same house that dude Gary was planning to take you and Sam to."

"You mean Garrett. Garrett was planning to take us there."

"Yes, that's what I meant."

It troubled me to think of Bob's involvement in Garrett's deeds, but I suppose in some twisted way it made sense, if you believed that Jeffries was really Garrett's father. God what a mess. I had the sinking feeling that Winston and I would have to confront Bob at some point, that is, if we couldn't find Garrett first.

Find Garrett first.

I held that thought. Maybe that was the play, to physically detain Garrett Knowles and forcibly take him down south with us, deliver him to the Huntington Beach cops. I could give them the box from Larry's house and Winston could put the HB and Tonopah cops together on the Moseley hit and run, and that would be all she wrote.

I wondered if Winston had any official authority as a private detective in matters like this. Could he actually arrest someone if it came down to it? Would we get in legal trouble if we grabbed Garrett and did what had to be done? I'd have to ask Winston about those things as soon as I hit Bridgeport. Right now I had to go.

"I gotta split. The pilot is shitting his pants waiting for me."

"Go, get a move on. I'll keep watch here."

"Keep an eye on Jeffries. He's the key to this thing. If for some reason we get crossed up, I'll make my way to the Walker River Lodge. You're still there, right?"

"Yes."

"What name did you use this time?"

"You'll love this. I actually used my real name. But it's not what you think."

"Huh?" I looked at Jerry, signaled I was almost done. "Your name isn't Winston Styles?"

"Close. It's Hiram Styles. Winston is my middle name."

"You're kidding me."

"I wish I was. Can you believe a horseshit name like that? Christ, my old man was a goddamn ballbuster. It was his idea, you know, hanging a tag like that on me. I mean that name's all right for the 1800s, but come on, I ain't that old."

Winston's humor was a welcome relief, and I was damn glad to have him on my side. Before hanging up, I had one more thing to tell him. "Hey listen, Hiram, go easy on yourself about losing Kelli. I couldn't do this without you."

"Thanks, Mason. Oh, and fuck you."

WE TOUCHED DOWN in Bridgeport at a quarter to four. Outside of a little turbulence leaving the Los Angeles basin, the flight was easy and thoroughly uneventful, and I think Jerry was disappointed he didn't get to show off some of his more extreme piloting skills. I was good with that, the smooth flight giving me a chance to rest and recharge my batteries.

Jerry's plane was first class all the way, plush and expertly appointed. Aside from a short siesta I took in the back, I spent the flight in the cockpit listening to Jerry yammer on about all kinds of stuff. I did a lot of nodding and chuckling at appropriate times, not really tracking the narrative too well, but thankful nonetheless for the distraction from my more troubling thoughts. Namely, what the hell was going to happen when we landed and it was time to put some kind of plan into action?

Finding Kelli was priority one, and after that I could see us going straight to Bob Jeffries and bracing him for information. I mean lean on the guy hard. And if Garrett was around we could throw the two of them in a room and go full-on Gitmo on their asses. Beat the goddamn truth out of them and let the chips fall where they will. I felt an increasing animosity towards Bob, borne out of my suspicion that he did indeed have a part in all this.

On our approach I saw the airport was located at the east side of town, adjacent to the Bridgeport Reservoir. The Walker River Lodge was next door, which would make things easy for me if Winston got delayed for some reason.

Jerry taxied the plane and right away we were buffeted by wind. I hadn't felt it coming in, but now that we'd landed there was no denying it. Heavy cloud cover obscured the twilight and the Bridgeport Reservoir was blanketed in snow, and before Jerry had fully stopped the plane snow flurries hit the windshield. It looked like we'd made it under the wire.

"You going to be all right going home?" I said.

Jerry gave me a Cheshire cat's grin. "You don't worry about me, Mason, I'll be fine."

"Good. I can't afford to lose my number one, best client ever."

"Aren't you a card. But wish me luck, because this bird's heading to Reno."

"No shit?"

"Hell yes, buddy. I'm feeling lucky tonight."

I grabbed my duffel bag and geared up for the weather, and in a few minutes I was ready to roll. Jerry came around and opened the cabin door. Wind blasted through, the air unbearably cold. Before I stepped out, Jerry took hold of my arm. When he spoke it was loud and in my ear.

"Listen, Mason, I'm not feeling too good about what you're doing here. I got a sense about it. You sure you don't want to let me in on it?"

He looked into my eyes and held them. His were blue and direct, with a take-no-prisoners light in them.

"You don't have to say anything if you don't want to."

It hung there between us, and though I was tempted to spill it, I held out, and kept my business my own. "No," I said. "I can't, Jerry, not now."

"I understand. Hell, I've been on a few secret missions myself." Jerry seemed to think for a few seconds. "Are you heeled?"

"Am I what?"

"A gun, do you have one?"

"No, I don't. Why?"

"Hold on." He disappeared into the rear of the plane.

I turned and looked out at the runway and the surrounding area. I didn't see any vehicles, and it occurred to me I'd never asked Winston what he was driving. This could get real interesting. Jerry returned and he pressed something into my palm.

"It's only a twenty-two, but you've got ten rounds there and you aim it right, it'll get the job done. I thought I had the Sig on board, but no dice."

I looked down at the black gun in my hand, at the name etched on the side. It was a Walther P22, a sharp looking piece. Too bad I had zero experience with guns. I was about to give it back when I thought otherwise. Better to keep it. Maybe Winston could give me a quick primer on its use before I actually had to shoot somebody.

"Thanks, Jerry," I said. "You know, this elevates the contractor-client relationship to a whole new level."

"You bet it does. By the way, you know how to use one of those?"

"Uh, no. Is it complicated?"

"Not if I show you some things."

Jerry proceeded to show me the basics of the handgun, where the safety was, how to insert the magazine and operate the slide and chamber a round. "Piece of cake," he said after finishing the demonstration.

It was at that moment I realized something that had eluded me for a long time. I'd always thought Jerry Corbin reminded me of someone, but I could never pin it down. Now I knew. Jerry looked exactly like Hemingway, circa the years right before he lost his marbles and did the Dutch up at his place in Idaho. Imagine that, Papa's doppelgänger instructing me in the use of a firearm. Weird.

"I'd better scoot," Jerry said. "Weather's turning shitty and I've got a hot date with a craps table."

I shoved the gun in the back of my jeans, like I'd seen on television about a million times, but it didn't fit too well and was uncomfortable. Funny how they never show *that* on those programs. I gave Jerry a crisp salute before jump off. Then I thought of something. "By the way, Jerry, how'd you make your money anyway?"

"Your old man never told you?"

"Naw, we never talked much about it."

Jerry smiled that cat's grin. "Oh, a little of this, a little of that. But that's a story for another day. Tell you what, as soon as you get back from this little mission of yours, call me up and we'll go have a few. I'll tell you all about it."

"But I don't drink."

"Then I'll buy you a lemonade. Adios, Mason."

I stepped off onto the tarmac and Jerry pulled the cabin door shut. I walked in the direction of the Walker River, the lights of town shimmering beyond. After a minute I turned and watched the plane liftoff and bank sharply to the west, and when it was out of sight I took a look around. The snow fell steadily and the wind gusted from the east, and picking out Winston's vehicle wasn't a problem since there were absolutely no vehicles to be found anywhere in the vicinity. Something must have held him up. At least the motel was close by. It would be brutal to be outdoors any longer than necessary. I situated my duffel bag more securely, tucked the pistol inside it so the damn thing wouldn't fall down my pants. I took one last look around, saw nothing there for me, and started jogging towards the river.

44

The room was two doors down from the one Kelli and I stayed in back in November. Winston wasn't there but his stuff was. Clothes hung haphazardly in the closet, several drawers filled to overflowing, an open leather satchel and papers stacked on the table, next to a bottle of Knob Creek and a short glass. But of course, what private dick doesn't keep a bottle of hooch with him?

The coffee pot was half-full and there were Styrofoam cups scattered about; Styles keeping himself jacked on caffeine for the business at hand. But where was he? Calls to his cell phone went unanswered, and I'd received no messages from him, not even a note pinned to the door. At least he'd arranged my arrival with the motel clerk, so there was minimal fuss involved securing a key to the room.

I sat at the table and leafed through the papers. Detailed reports in Winston's neat and compact handwriting. He wrote well, concise and to the point, with a nice narrative quality to his work. I put the reports aside and looked at another document. It was a fax copy of the title report for Bob Jeffries's house in Bear Valley. I felt a tingle move from my hand and up through my arm, goose bumps rising on my flesh. I closed my eyes and thought back, focusing through the prism of all that I'd learned. The implications of this new information were daunting, to say the least.

I quickly snapped out of it, and looked at the bottle of bourbon sitting on the table. I felt no pull from it. I considered those times when I did, what it was that made liquor so enticing. Oblivion? Release? Or was it cowardice? Booze and smokes, a heartbreak combination if ever there was one.

Back to the business at hand.

My mind jumped to all sorts of things, scattered, disarrayed. Yeah, that's some kind of plan you got there, Mason, sitting by yourself in a motel room cut off from your people, grasping at the inconsequential as a means of distraction. I looked at my watch. Coming up on five o'clock. It was dark outside and through the open curtain I saw snow flurries dancing in the dim light from some nearby fixture. The outline of the *Out of the Past* house sat perfectly framed in my view through the window. What would Robert Mitchum do right now? He'd probably kick someone's ass, just for the simple pleasure of doing it, then he'd get down to business.

I decided to give it until six o'clock, and if I didn't make contact with Kelli or Winston by then, I'd go to Bob's place and kick things up a notch. Maybe Jerry's pistol would come in handy for that. I stowed my gear and charged my cell phone, and stretched out on the bed. The wind shook the front window and from where I lay, the old house across the street was blocked from view. Cold seeped in through a bad front door seal, the window faring as poorly. The weather was a bitch, and I had a sinking feeling she was going to have her way with me tonight.

At some point I drifted off. My ringing cell phone woke me. I recognized the number as Annette Briggs's real estate office. "Mason Tanner," I said, springing up out of the bed.

"Mr. Tanner, this is Denise, from Bristlecone Realty."

"Hello, Denise."

"I'm sorry to bother you like this, but I'm very concerned. You see, Mr. Tanner, it's been—"

"Call me Mason, please."

"Yes, well I'm worried because they haven't returned yet," Denise said.

"Kelli and Annie?"

"Yes."

"Have you spoken to them today?"

"Not since this afternoon, when Annie called to arrange some business matters. She sounded upset. When I asked her if anything was the matter, she said she thought she was being followed."

"By who?"

"She wouldn't say. Right away she started downplaying the whole thing."

"But you didn't believe her?"

"No."

"Why?"

Denise did not respond. I leaned against the table, my hand resting inches from the Knob Creek. Very subliminal. I jerked away from it and pulled a chair around and sat down, elbows on my knees, a rapid sensation coming over me.

"Tell me, Denise. I'm here in town now, to find Kelli. I have my own concerns about this, so please, tell me what you know."

There was a sigh, and a moment's hesitation. "Annie was seeing a man. He's a realtor from Carson City. They were engaged actually, but only for a short time. He was abusive to her. I don't mean physically, but verbally and mentally hurtful. He's a petty little man who's possessive and distrustful, and he didn't take the breakup very well. Annie has been convinced for some time that this man from Carson City has been following her, or that he hired someone to do it. She's grown quite paranoid about it."

The information about Annette's love life was an interesting footnote, but one I deemed irrelevant to the case. As for someone following her, that was clearly

Winston Styles, at least as far as today was concerned. But then again, maybe it was Garrett doing the following. I forced my mind to view this new development logically; getting emotionally wound up would net me exactly zero. The takeaway was this: Kelli and Annette were unaccounted for, and time was the critical factor now.

"Anyway, Mr. Tanner, I didn't mean to bother you about all this. I only called to see if you'd heard anything from your girlfriend. I'm about to close the office for the day and well, it's all a little too unsettling."

"I understand, Denise. But let's not get carried away here, I'm sure Annie and Kelli are fine. They've known each other for a long time and it's likely they got sidetracked is all, reminiscing about the old days."

"I hope you're right."

"Let's you and I stay in touch. We hear anything, we'll let the other know, okay?"

"Sure, I'll do that. Thank you, Mr. Tanner, thank you so much for listening. Goodnight now."

"Goodnight, Denise."

I hung up the phone, and prepared to leave.

45

There was no way to get a rental car in town, so I called Hank Newman at the Shell station. I had no idea if the old guy still worked there, or if he'd even remember me, but it was worth a try. Outside of Denise over at Bristlecone Realty, I literally had nowhere else to turn, and there was no way I'd call her for a ride, not in her rattled state. Annie wasn't answering her phone and Winston was still missing in action, and even though I desperately needed his advice and expertise, there was no time to wait. So I was forced to improvise, and I settled on the only course of action available. I decided to go up to Twin Lakes and confront Bob Jeffries. It was time to shake the family tree and see what fell out.

If Garrett was there I'd invite him to the party as well. And if he didn't want to join? Well fuck him, he was going to anyway. I'm not a violent man by any stretch, unless I'm fueled by booze, but it had been a long time since I'd let liquor trigger that part of me, to the point I now considered myself to be thoroughly non-confrontational in all aspects of my life. But not today.

Today I would revert to my bad old days, in all their ignominious glory. Today I would go hard on Bob and Garrett and any other damn person who'd endeavor to stand in my way. Today I was seeking truth, and I'd find that truth regardless of the consequences.

I picked up the Walther and aimed it two-handed at my reflection in the mirror, counted off four shots, all zeroed-out center body mass. Even though I knew jack shit about guns, I would become a shooter today, if shooting is what it took to get the job done. I stuck the pistol in my waistband at the small of my back, fiddled with it until it felt right, and put a leather belt on and cinched it tight; a little added security for my piece.

When I was ready to go, I scribbled a note to Winston, and I left the room and started walking.

THE PHONE LINE at the Shell station was busy when I called, and since I was too wound up to wait for it to clear, I walked there instead. Fortunately, Hank was still working there. Unfortunately, his shift didn't start until six-thirty, so I had some time to kill before he arrived. I ate a couple of overcooked hot dogs and a bag of Fritos, standing outside in the cold to do it. The weather was fierce, but I was prepared for it. I'd layered my clothes and insulated myself with waterproof gear, and felt sufficiently protected should the temperature drop to single digits. After wolfing the food I went back inside for a large cup of black coffee, and since it was only a few minutes until Hank's shift, I lingered in the back of the mini-mart to drink it.

Newman showed up on time. Man, you gotta love those old guys, prompt in a way today's generation didn't understand. I waited for Hank to get settled and for the mini-mart to clear out, then I sidled up to the counter, and when I spoke I made sure to do it loud and towards his hearing aid.

"Remember me?"

Hank hesitated before smiling wide. "Sure, I remember you, son. You're that author fella, the one who's writing a book about missing people. Mason, that's the name, right? How's that book going, by the way?"

Score one for the old man. It was good to see he apparently still believed my cover story. That told me Bob Jeffries had not spoken to Newman, or if he had, he didn't reveal the truth of my business in Bridgeport.

"The book's moving along," I said. "And yes, the name's Mason Tanner. Thanks for remembering."

"That's no problem at all. You're an easy fella to remember, being as you're the first author I ever met. So what brings you to town? You following up on some leads?"

"Yeah, something like that," I said, my mind distracted by how I should go about asking Hank for a ride out to Bob's place, in a way that didn't sound suspicious.

"Boy, that's sure something else about what happened to Parker's friend out there in Tonopah. The sheriff was talking the other day about how some foul play might be involved in all that. He wasn't at liberty to say more, but I got the sense they were looking at someone here in town for it. Hey, maybe you can put that in your book."

I nodded and sipped my coffee, figured I'd let Hank ramble for a bit, see how things stood from his perspective.

"You know, there's been a man poking around town. Private detective is what I heard, asking a lot of questions about Bob Jeffries and that fella Knowles, the one who works out there at the lodge. Some right real intrigue going on, especially for a bitty little place like we got here."

Hank gave me a look, like maybe he thought I was involved in all that detective business. I kept my face blank, and decided to go for broke. Enough with the scheming.

"Say, Hank, I need a ride somewhere. You think you can handle that for me?"

IT WAS ONLY fifteen miles to Bob's place. Hank Newman talked enough for twice that distance. Yakking my ear off about this thing and that, most of it centered on my book, forcing me to lie repeatedly to the old guy, to the point I wanted to scream out the truth.

I couldn't complain though, about all that talking. Without Hank's help I'd be hoofing it to Twin Lakes, and freezing my ass off in the process. The intensity of the storm had increased rapidly, yet despite the worsening road conditions, Hank drove it expertly, his restored vintage Delta 88 outfitted with new snow tires. It was an old man's car and it looked ridiculous with those tires on it, but it was obvious Hank took a lot of pride in it.

There was a Sinatra disc in the player, the one where Frank's face is all painted up like a clown on the album cover, and a few times Hank hummed along to the tunes. He didn't seem to be in any hurry to get back to the Shell station. He'd locked up the mini-mart and left his customers to fend for themselves with the self-serve pumps. I found out later that Hank Newman owned that Shell station, and furthermore, he was a very wealthy man. Yet he worked regular shifts there with his other employees. I found that information fascinating.

At Twin Lakes, swirling snow blew fast across the road and Hank's dashboard thermometer read twenty degrees. Out on the lake, whitecaps were visible, and the trees lining the shore bowed severely against the stiff wind. Pulling up the driveway to the lodge, I saw a large *for sale* sign posted.

"I see Bob's finally got the sign up," Hank said.

"He's selling the place?" I replied, despite the clear evidence in front of me. I did a double take at the name on the sign: Bristlecone Realty. My mind raced. Was this one of the stops Annie and Kelli made today, looking at properties?

"Yes, he is, unfortunately. I heard he made the decision fairly recently. It sure surprised folks in town. Bob's been a fixture here for a long time."

"You have any idea why he's doing it?"

"None at all. But I'm sure Bob's got his reasons."

I'm sure he does. Like maybe my investigation. Is the heat getting too much for you Bob? Strange men in town asking their strange questions, digging through Garrett's life, and yours too, the net closing as the past finally catches up with you? I felt jacked on adrenaline, and I was ready to get into this thing *right now*.

"You can let me out here," I told Hank.

"You sure about that? It doesn't appear Bob is home. It's mighty cold to be waiting for him."

"Oh, trust me, Bob is expecting me."

"Suit yourself. You take care now, you hear?"

"You too. And thanks for the lift."

"It was my pleasure. You'll send me a copy when it's finished? Your book I mean."

"Sure, Hank. I'll even sign it for you."

Hank Newman lit up like a kid at Christmas. He turned his Oldsmobile easily and cruised down the road back to town, leaving me to the business at hand.

I SITUATED MY clothes to block out the cold, and trudged up the road to Bob's house. Images from my past visit to this place hit me from all sides. I felt nervous but not scared, my steps determined and my will strong. This would play out the way it was meant to be. The important thing is, I was taking action. I checked my phone for missed calls or messages, found nothing there. I was alone in this.

Up the curving drive I went, to Bob's rustic mountain home, the snow past my shins and the wind gusting. Lights burned where I remembered them and the pavilion lay deserted, the grounds barren and white and a little bit sad in their emptiness. I could not see the boat shed or Garrett's cabin, and I wondered where he was.

Are you out there creep?

Are you listening to the radio preacher spew his gas?

Well get ready, because here I come. Get ready to pay for your sins. Get ready to answer for all that you've done, the lives that you've ruined. You think you know things? Well you don't know the hell that's about to descend upon you this day.

I made it to the house and stopped to listen. There were no sounds or signs of movement, and I could very well have been the last man standing, for in the fishbowl of the Twin Lakes Lodge I was truly alone. I made one lap around the house, taking my time with it, walking as stealthily as possible so as not to give myself away. When I came back around to the front of the house I took another lap.

Satisfied by what I'd found, I grew bolder and looked for a way inside. I was pretty sure Bob was not in the house, and I was beginning to wonder if he was even on the property. I still had the grounds to cover, and all those cabins and the boat shed, but a search of the house first seemed prudent. The front and side doors were locked, but the back door was not, and I let myself into a small mudroom that led directly into the living room.

I made a thorough search of the house and found it empty. The heater was on and there was food out in the kitchen, so it seemed likely Bob was around somewhere, or had been recently. I stopped in the living room to look at the photographs on the mantle, just to reaffirm what I already knew. But the pictures of Garrett were gone. Interesting. House for sale, incriminating pictures taken down. Bob was circling the wagons.

I took my cell phone out of my pocket but there was no signal. I tried Bob's landline and got no dial tone. It raised an alarm in me; was it because of the foul weather, or some more nefarious reason? Anxiety hit me and I regulated my breathing to control it.

It was time to search the grounds. But first I mapped it out in my mind, taking it one step at a time, visualizing what I had to do. When I was ready, I went to the back door, stopping abruptly when I heard a sound coming from outside the house. I tried to place it but could not. I heard it again, more clearly now, the sound of a vehicle approaching. I moved to the bay window facing the lake, looked out at the driveway leading off the main road, but blowing snow and frost on the glass made it difficult to see anything.

I figured if someone was out there they'd likely come to the house first, probably the front door. I made my way to the mudroom, my ears tuned to new sounds, but there was only the wind and the slight ticking of the house's heating system at work. I slipped out the door and around the corner of the house, keeping myself pressed against it. I felt the gun at the small of my back, decided maybe now was the time to use it. I reached around and took hold of it, held it down against my leg, something else I'd seen on cop shows.

Nearing the front of the house, I swung wide to get a vantage point on the front door. A stand of pines stopped short of the house, shrubs filling the spaces between the trees, and I stepped into the cover of the bushes. Inching my way forward, I got to where I could see the front door clearly. A man stood there looking through the window, his back turned to me. He wore a black overcoat and a hunter's cap pulled low, and like a blast of electricity to my brain it registered.

It was Garrett Knowles.

I remembered that coat and hat from my first visit to Bridgeport, at the Shell station, right before that son of a bitch tried to run me down.

I froze in place and composed myself, focusing on my strategy. I knew I couldn't rush him because he'd hear me and have a chance to react. But I wasn't sure I could cover the distance slowly without him hearing me anyway. I had the gun though, which meant I had the advantage. Unless he had one too. Yeah, I guess that was a possibility.

Screw it. I started moving. One step forward, followed by another, until I was on him. He never even heard me. I had the fucker. I stuck the barrel against the base of his skull and pressed it hard, made my voice menacing.

"What's up, asshole?"

46

The man turned and I backed up. He growled in a voice that put mine to shame. "Put the goddamn gun down, for Christ's sake."

Shit, it was Winston Styles. I moved back a few more steps, still holding the weapon in both hands, pointed at the only person who could help me. I froze in that position until my brain clicked. Winston laughed at me. "You know, if you're gonna go Rambo on a guy, it helps to release the safety."

My face burned and I tilted the Walther, saw he was right. "Sorry. I guess I got a little ahead of myself. Where the hell have you been?"

"Is the house open? You been inside?"

"Yeah, I was in there when you pulled up. Why?"

"Let's go inside and talk. Get the fuck out of this weather."

INSIDE THE HOUSE, Winston went to work brewing up some coffee. He made himself right at home, like any good cop would. We kept all the lights off but one and drew the shades. When the coffee was ready, Winston filled a large ceramic mug and we sat down in the living room. I passed on the java; I was keyed up enough without pumping my system full of caffeine.

"How'd you find me?" I said.

"The note you left at the motel."

"Tell me what's going on."

"You're not gonna like it, Mason."

"That's the second time you've said that today. Tell me."

"Okay. Annette Briggs is in the hospital, Kelli is missing, and I wrecked my car."

"Shit, Winston, what the hell happened?"

"I was trying to pick up their trail, driving all over this damn valley from here out to Mono Lake and back. Can't even tell you how many miles I drove. Then I caught something on the scanner."

"Scanner?"

"Police scanner. I take one with me wherever I go. So anyway, I hear some chatter about an accident over at Conway Summit, a car off the side of the road. I had a feeling about it, so I hotfooted it over there."

"What time was this?"

"Sometime after three. When I got there I saw Annette's car in a deep ravine, and a wrecker on site trying to pull it back up on the road. Annette was already gone in the ambulance. I collared a highway patrolman and got the details. Annette's car was pushed, Mason. At least that's what the patrolman said. The rear end was smashed, and the CHP called in the sheriff because of their suspicions."

"What about Kelli?"

Winston held my eyes. "She wasn't there."

"What does that mean?"

"They only pulled one person from the wreckage."

"So she walked out of there."

"No way, Mason. And even if she did, where would she go in this storm?" I went silent, tried to comprehend the situation. Winston drank some coffee. "It had to be Garrett," he said. "I figure he rammed the car and forced it off the road, grabbed Kelli and split. Bold. Bold and crazy.

The fucking guy's circling the bowl. We've got to find him."

"Yes, we do," I said, my words sounding hollow. I looked at Winston. "I was worried when you didn't show up at the airfield. Figured I was in this alone."

"Sorry about that." He slurped more coffee, managing not to spill any. "I tried calling you from the accident scene but my phone reception was for shit. After that I had more pressing matters to deal with."

"Such as?"

"Such as *my* goddamn car going off the road."

"What the hell happened?"

"I was on my way back to town, took my eyes off the road for one stinking second. When I looked up, Bambi was standing in the middle of the highway."

"Bambi?"

"Yeah, man, a fucking deer. Can you believe it? I swerved to miss the damn thing and spun out, rolled the car into a ditch."

"Are you okay?"

"I'm an ex-cop, Mason. I've rolled a few vehicles in my day."

"Sorry. So what happened after that?"

"I thumbed a ride to the motel from a truck driver, froze my ass off waiting. The car had a broken rear axle so I left it there. Man, my partner is going to be pissed about the car." Winston got up for more coffee.

"How'd you get here?" I said.

"It was in your note, about getting a ride from the gas station dude. I figured I could tap the old guy for my own lift. Oh, he was happy as all get-out to oblige, once I told him I was your publisher, that is."

"Huh?"

"I had to think quick, and he kept yammering about the book you're writing, so I put two and two together and it equaled instant credibility with Mr. Newman." Winston swigged his coffee. "That's a sweet ride he's got, by the way. Maybe I'll replace the Crown Vic with something like that when I finally get off this piece of shit case of yours."

A thought came to me and I voiced it.

"Look, Winston, it's only a matter of time before Hank Newman gets curious as hell about what's going on up here. I mean he's a nice guy and all, but come on, driving both of us? That's got to rate some major suspicion at some point. He calls the sheriff, we might get snagged dealing with a lot of bullshit."

"True. That's a good point." Winston drained his mug and set it on the table. "You ready?"

"For what?"

"For finding a crazy man."

GARRETT WAS NOT on the property, but Bob Jeffries was.

We found him in the boat shed and he was in a bad way. He was sitting on the dirty floor, leaning sideways against the wall, wedged next to a tool bench. At first glance Bob appeared to be sleeping, just taking a load off, but then I saw the pool of blood beneath him and his arms held tight to his stomach. He'd been knifed repeatedly, and he was literally holding his guts in.

I kneeled down and looked into Bob's eyes, at the life draining out of them, and I saw our chances slipping away. Winston made a quick search of the shed, and he came over and stood at my shoulder. When I glanced up, he nodded towards Bob; *go on*, it said, this one is yours.

Turning to face the dying man, I knew we had little time. He seemed to recognize me, a momentary light coming to his eyes, before the light receded back under heavy lids. I had the distinct thought that I should get help for Bob first, but I ignored that thought. I needed answers, and the way I figured it, Bob Jeffries owed me.

"Who did this to you?" I said. His eyes widened with awareness, but he said nothing. "Kelli is missing, Bob, and I believe Garrett is responsible. Tell me what you know."

"I'm sorry," he muttered.

"For what?"

"For what he became."

"Garrett?"

"Yes."

"He's your son, isn't he?"

"I don't know."

"Bullshit you don't know!"

I inhaled hard through my nose, pure anger rising inside me. Bob's eyes locked on mine, and in them I saw ambiguity. He wheezed horribly but still he held my eyes.

"Look at me, Mason. I'm a dead man, why would I lie to you?"

He gurgled and let out a hacking cough, closing his eyes. He opened them and stared at a point beyond my shoulder.

"I honestly don't know. I loved Ellen, but she was married to Art, and she was involved with other men, not just me. I treated him as my son."

I stared at Bob, my mind awash in conflict. None of this fit with my narrative. I wanted absolutes, not half-truths and outright lies. I wanted Bob to be guilty, of *something*.

"Did you know about him, about the killing? Because he *is* the one, and don't you try and tell me different. He's the evil son of a bitch who took my friend, and the others."

Bob gazed at me vacantly. "No," he said. "I didn't know."

"Bullshit! You damn well knew. Garrett and his goddamn wanderlust, disappearing for weeks at a time. Tell me, Bob, did he ever leave at the end of the season? Say October or November? Every fucking year. You knew, damn you, you had to know."

"No, Mason, I did not."

I wanted to beat the truth out of him, beat him savagely before his split-open guts took him. I felt dizzy and closed my eyes, saw bursts of light, hopelessness consuming me. Winston took hold of my collar and pulled me to my feet. "Go outside, Mason."

"Fuck it, I'm not done with him. I have to know about Kelli."

"Go outside. I'll take it from here."

The cold determination in Winston's eyes shocked me sober, and I gave in to it, turning slowly to leave the boat shed.

Ten minutes later Winston approached the clearing where I stood. I was staring across the lake at the houses on the far shore, tripping on the fact that all this was going down, life and death in their own backyard, and those people had not a clue. It came to me that if you shook out all the dark places on a typical night in America, you'd be shocked at the things you'd find, the things we pretend don't exist; pain inflicted wantonly, greed and criminal hubris, pure meanness brought forth from a rotten core. It was a hard world out there, and tonight was the hardest.

"She's at Bodie. Garrett has her. We've got to move, now."

"And Bob?"

"He's dead. And don't you spend one goddamn minute thinking about that, you hear me? He dealt the play a long time ago when he covered up for that murdering son of his."

"Tell me."

"Get in the damn truck, Mason, I'll tell you on the way."

47

We took Bob Jeffries's four-wheel drive Jimmy, seeing how he wasn't going to need it anymore, and we raided his house for whatever else we deemed useful. I had mixed feelings about that, but figured Winston was right, Bob had dealt the play and there wasn't much point in dwelling on it. We said little during our preparations, the heaviness of the boat shed settling between us, and I let hang my questions until we were clear of Twin Lakes.

Winston stripped off his black overcoat, the one that might've gotten him killed if I'd known how to use a pistol, and he replaced it with a more appropriate snow jacket from Bob's closet. It fit too large but it would do. He also took some heavy gloves and a wool cap. Once sufficiently protected, Winston signaled it was time to go.

I took the wheel since I knew the way to Bodie. The storm had worsened, and with each ratcheting notch of intensity our chances of finding Kelli diminished by equal measure. On the road, Winston broke it down for me.

Bob Jeffries had made no deathbed confessions, at least regarding his knowledge and culpability in Garrett's crimes. He stuck to his story about Garrett's parentage, and all he would say about the rest of it was that Garrett had it rough in life and he was a difficult person, and if he murdered all those people it was only because he was sick from damaged brain wiring that went undiagnosed for far too long, and the fall down the mineshaft and subsequent fire only made a bad situation worse.

Winston believed Bob Jeffries knew full well the truth of the matter regarding Garrett and his murderous deeds, but he'd been denying it for so long he came to believe fiction over truth, and he was prepared to die with that belief. Winston had seen it countless times with battered spouses and career criminals, a pathological inability to admit the truth if it spit in your eye.

Bob confirmed it was Garrett who'd knifed him, said it happened when Garrett returned to the lodge with his truck smashed. Bob knew something was going on when he saw Garrett moving through the boat shed collecting ropes and lamps and other gear that he used on his excursions to the restricted areas of Bodie. Garrett refused Bob's questions, about the truck or anything else, and the situation escalated badly. Bob demanded answers and he got physical about it, and Garrett turned violent.

Jeffries had no idea it involved Kelli until after he'd been attacked, and Garrett started railing on about wickedness and righteousness and all the things he knew. He let it slip about the pretty girl he'd hidden in a place she'd never be found. Bob implored Garrett to tell him the truth, but the son he'd denied to the bitter end responded by leaving his father to die alone on a dirty floor in an old wooden boat shed.

I wanted to hate Bob Jeffries, but could not. I wanted to believe him guilty as an accomplice to murder, but could not. Everything I knew was wrong, and I wondered if the truth even mattered anymore. I looked at Winston. "Did you do it?"

"Do what? Kill him?"

I didn't answer. The storm was really raging now, the goddamn storm of the century. How the hell would we make it to Bodie?

"Christ, Mason, is that what you think of me? After all this?"

I turned and stared at the man I'd hired to help me. "You did it before, in Mexico."

"That was different."

"Was it?"

"Goddamn right it was. Besides, Jeffries didn't need killing from me. His lunatic offspring took care of that on his own."

"I'm not blaming you if you did. This thing's really got my head turned around."

"Well I didn't, so stop with all that thinking. You've got to keep your head on straight, Mason, because this shit's likely gonna get wet."

"Wet?"

"Bloody. Goddamn down and dirty, and bloody as hell."

I said nothing more about it. We drove on, the Jimmy holding steady despite the road conditions, the highway deserted on a night when sensible people were bundled safe inside their homes, drinking hot chocolate by a roaring fire, watching reruns on the tube with their loved ones by their side.

"Listen, Mason, we have to get something clear here," Winston said after a while. "When we track this asshole down, our focus is on Kelli. We find her and get her to a safe place, you got it? We're not going to spend two seconds exposing ourselves to harm by trying to bring Knowles in. What's the point in that? If the right play is to put him down, we take it."

I set my jaw. Winston went on.

"Look, I know you want justice for your friend Sam. If we can get at the truth and make that happen, great. But I'm telling you, I've seen this play out before. It's entirely possible Garrett never cops to his crimes. They can nail him for Larry's murder, and maybe Moseley's, but there's a better than even chance none of the other stuff ever comes out. He gets the right lawyer, the right judge full of liberal compassion, and he spends the rest of his days in a psych ward instead of some hardcore hellhole like Pelican Bay where the fucker belongs. And forget the death penalty. California's lost its balls on that one. Ain't never gonna happen. You get my drift?"

THE GOING WAS slow on U.S. 395, and by the time we'd reached Willow Springs I'd slowed the Jimmy to a crawl so I wouldn't miss the turnoff. The highway sign came into view and I turned onto the paved road heading eastward, through the curving, rocky canyon leading to Bodie. It was difficult going, the road hard to make out in the furious blowing snow, and I had the defroster on full in an effort to keep the windshield clear.

"What do you know about this place?" Winston said.

"The history?"

"Save the history, I mean the layout."

I gave it to him, feeling certain the storm would obliterate any landmarks or sense of direction once we got there. I also told Winston about Wes Morris and the park rangers who lived in the town.

"Shit, you mean people actually stay out here?"

"Some do," I said.

"Hopefully this storm drove them all out."

"Hopefully."

"So how does Garrett manage to skulk around the place with people there all the time?"

"I have no idea. But he's been doing it for a long time, so whatever his technique is, he's perfected it.

I suspected that Garrett was holed up somewhere on Bodie Bluff, in the vicinity of the old mines. The Standard Mill was another likely spot, and Winston suggested we search there first and work our way outward.

Once we cleared the narrow confines of the canyon visibility improved slightly, though the storm raged undiminished. I thought of Kelli and what was happening to her, where she was, if she was even still alive. I'd been blocking all of that from my mind in an effort to stay focused, and now I indulged my worst fears. Anxiety spiked and I gripped the steering wheel, fought to keep my vision clear of the blood pounding in my head. It had been twenty-four hours since I'd last spoken to Kelli, since the broken cell phone connection that triggered so much fear in me. I prayed that she was all right, that despite whatever Garrett had done to her, she was not in any pain, that she had some way to allay her fears and know that I would move heaven and earth to find her. I gripped the wheel tighter.

"Ease up there, Mason," Winston said. "I know you're sick with worry, but you've got to keep a lid on that, focus only on the here and now, on what's right there in front of you. Do you read me on that?"

"I'll be okay. Don't worry about me."

"Good."

We came to the end of the paved road. From this point it was three miles of unpaved washboard road to the old town. I slowed at the transition, unsure about getting stuck. A hundred yards further along I saw what appeared to be vehicle headlights in the distance. I stopped the Jimmy and leaned forward, my face inches from the windshield, concentrating through the darkness. A truck came bouncing up the road, the headlights throwing jerky light.

"We've got visitors," I said.

"I see it. Sit tight, let's see where this goes."

The truck came within fifty feet and stopped, throwing a blinding spotlight on us, and I instinctively raised my hand to shield my eyes. I recognized the vehicle, and I turned to Winston. "It's that park ranger I told you about."

"You think he'll let us by?"

"No."

Wes Morris made no move to exit his vehicle. We sat there, the two trucks separated by blowing snow and blinding light. The Jimmy idled roughly and the heater blew air, and after a few minutes sitting there I'd had enough.

"I'll talk to him. Maybe he'll remember me," I said, exiting the Jimmy.

Outside the truck the wind blew fast across the unprotected terrain, snow flying in all directions, more than a foot of it on the ground. It was so cold your skin hurt, and every exhale shot a plume of steam. My ears felt clogged and everywhere I looked was blurred and indistinct, and I knew that a person left outside and unprepared in this weather wouldn't last an hour, if that. They were truly the worst circumstances imaginable, and I cursed Garrett Knowles for all the misery he'd put upon me.

I walked forward, waving my arms, hoping Wes Morris would recognize me. I glanced back at Winston, but I couldn't see him through the snow flurries and the glare of the spotlight coming off the Jimmy's windshield. When I turned back I saw Wes step from the truck and walk slowly towards me, his right hand resting on the butt of his holstered pistol. He shouted at me as he neared.

"This is Wes Morris with the park service. Hold your hands up so I can see them, and state your purpose."

I raised my arms high in the air so there would be no confusing my intentions. When Wes got closer, I pulled my hood down and took off my beanie so I'd be more recognizable. "Hey, Wes," I said loudly. "It's Mason Tanner. We met last November, when I was here with Bob Jeffries." He didn't seem to remember, so I stepped in closer. "I've got a man named Winston Styles with me. He's a private investigator and a former cop. We need your help, Wes. Some bad shit's going down in Bodie and people are in danger."

We stood maybe ten feet apart now, and still Wes did not recognize me.

"No one's here. We cleared out all the park employees because of the storm. What's this danger you're talking about?"

Wes unsnapped his holster and pulled his weapon, kept it pointed down against his leg. Time stretched out and I wondered if I had it in me to shoot him if that's what it took to save Kelli. But there was no way I'd get to my pistol before Wes raised his and took me out.

"Well, what is it? Tell me now or get back in your truck and leave. This is state property and it's restricted."

When I turned to look at Winston again, a series of loud pops rang out, sounding like gunfire, and I dropped to the ground and rolled sideways. I looked towards Wes, saw him lying face down in the snow. The shots continued rapidly, pinging off Wes's truck and stitching the ground in front of me, and I curled into a ball, praying I wouldn't be hit.

The firing stopped as suddenly as it had started, replaced by the distant echo of a vehicle driving away. Winston sprinted past me, and I put on my wool cap and hood and followed. Coming up on Winston's shoulder, I saw him roll Wes Morris over onto his back, at least two exit wounds visible.

"He's alive, but I've got to get him out of this cold or he's done."

"Garrett," I said, the freezing air jackhammering in my chest.

"Son of a bitch!" Winston yelled. "How the fuck did he hit anything in this blizzard."

"What do I do?"

"You go, now. Find Kelli. Once I get this guy taken care of, I'm right behind you."

I stared back at Winston. His eyes bored into mine.

"You can do this, Mason. Stick to our plan. Search the mill first, then the bluff, just like we talked about. I've got to save this guy, and Kelli's a goner if you don't step up right now. Do you read me on that?"

"Yes, I read you loud and clear."

"Good. Then get the fuck out of here!"

48

I eased the Jimmy around Winston kneeling at Wes
Morris's side, administering whatever aid he could. I had
no idea what he planned to do. Radio for help? Or maybe
he'd haul the wounded ranger into town, to whatever
medical facility they had there.

No matter, I was alone now, and it was up to me to see
this through. Maybe Winston would return in time to help
me, though it wasn't likely. I looked into the rearview
mirror, saw only blowing snow and eerie shadows. I felt
my pulse in my ears, an otherworldly sensation coming
over me. Jerry's pistol dug into my lower back, a physical
reminder of what lay ahead.

I chanced greater speed on the unpaved road, the heavy
thrum of the tires in deep snow marking my progress. The
dashboard thermometer read seventeen degrees outside, the
clock nine-thirty. Everything about what I prepared to do
reeked of impossibility, a task so daunting it felt like a
dream. But it was no dream. Kelli was out there
somewhere, in a wide expanse of barren terrain abandoned
to time for longer than I'd been alive. I wondered about the
ghosts of Bodie, what *they* thought of all this dirty business
playing itself out in their town.

The thought came to me that all of this could be a waste
of valuable time, and it was entirely possible Kelli wasn't
even here, that she was held captive in some other remote

place, or worse, dead and gone already. Sure, Garrett was just fucked enough in the head to do that, lure us out here on a fool's errand. Maybe after shooting Wes Morris down in cold blood, he split town via Aurora Canyon, leaving me to search in vain. Sure, it played, and I could see Garrett's final words to Bob Jeffries as nothing more than a red herring, and a sharp stick in the eye for whatever warped grievances guided Garrett in the killing of the man who was most likely his own father.

I yelled out in the cab of the Jimmy, my voice booming in my ears, smacking the steering wheel hard with the heel of my hand and cursing the twisted machinations of Garrett Knowles. I forced myself to focus only on the task at hand. Finding Kelli was the only thing that mattered. Everything else didn't exist. She was here, she had to be.

At the entrance to the park I continued straight ahead, rather than make a left turn and follow the road to the visitor's parking lot. Today I was not a visitor, and I was no tourist either. Today I was a desperate man fighting desperate circumstances. Faint tire marks lay exposed in the freshly fallen snow, going off in random directions, and there was no way to know who made them. Garrett could be anywhere. Stick to the plan, so if Winston comes back, he'll have a starting point. I headed straight for the Standard Mill.

Visibility extended only as far as the beam from the truck's headlights, and obstacles seemed to jump out randomly into my field of vision; old cars and mining equipment, lean-to structures standing up to their umpteenth blizzard, wooden poles from long-abandoned transmission lines. I tried to orient myself but everything blended together in a blur of blowing snow and blackness. At Bodie Creek the Jimmy bottomed out and got stuck, and I fought to stay calm as I rocked the truck to free it from the gully, all the while calculating how long it would take me to walk the remaining distance if it came down to it.

After a few minutes I freed the truck and bounced up the other side of the creek, and I punched the accelerator, heading straight across a debris field.

I heard a loud pop, followed by another, and a sick feeling twisted my guts; Garrett was shooting at me. I gassed it and went for broke, and within seconds I realized it wasn't gunfire I'd heard, but blown tires from driving through all that debris. I kept going, determined to make it to the mill. The steering wheel jerked and the front end wobbled badly, and I knew I was riding on the rims, but I pushed on. I came to one of the main roads in the town, wide and flat and clear, and I remembered it as Green Street. I took it at a good speed to the next clear road, hung a left and up ahead saw the gate to the Standard Mill. Without a thought I plowed through the heavy steel gate, the sound of scraping metal and breaking glass piercing the cab. The headlights snuffed out and darkness enveloped me, and I skidded the Jimmy to a stop.

I checked my clothes to make sure everything was zipped and secure against the cold, grabbed a heavy flashlight from the seat next to me, and I stepped out of the vehicle. The Jimmy was a mess. Tires blown and headlights gone, front end smashed, barbed wire twisted up in the rear axle; no way was I driving out of here. I focused on finding Kelli. Without her, I didn't care about making it out of that place.

I made my way to the main structure of the mill. Despite my layers of clothing, cold seeped in from everywhere, and I forced quick motion in order to keep blood flowing. At a speed short of running, I worked my way up the slope to the back of the mill. No lights were visible from inside as I stumbled around the perimeter looking for a way in. If Garrett had come here, he surely would have left some sign. He'd only had about a ten minute head start after shooting down Wes Morris, and it didn't seem likely he could cover his tracks so well. But there was nothing to indicate anyone had been up here since the storm began. Several times I probed the near distance with the flashlight, looking for Garrett's truck, but all that came back was driving snow that seemed to dance and glow in all directions.

I heard a faint noise, like a door being slammed shut repeatedly, and I worked my way towards the sound, my sense of direction turned completely upside down. I kept the building close at my side as I traversed unsteady ground, my left hand brushing it like a bug's antenna, my only tether to anything real. For everything beyond was a mass of swirling confusion, and I knew that any effort to search beyond the mill would be fruitless, and deadly.

I made it to the banging door, the wind blowing it on its hinges, and I pulled it open, wedging a rock against it. Once inside, my senses responded to a different kind of disorientation, that of a dark and unfamiliar room. I had no idea what the layout was. Back in December, Bob and I had only toured a small portion of the mill, and those memories were faded now and useless to me. I walked slowly, using my light sparingly so as not to tip-off Garrett.

I came to the room that once housed the huge stamps used to crushed the ore the miners pulled out of the ground. I knew this room because I'd been here with Bob, but that fact was no help to me now. I searched among the accouterments and detritus of a bygone industry, and at the point I felt my resolve hopelessly slip, I heard sounds incongruous to those of an old building and the storm pounding against it. Down a narrow corridor I followed the sounds, muffled and indistinct, yet genuine and separate from everything else. I reached the end of the corridor and there on the floor, cut into the heavily warped planks, I saw a trapdoor.

Dim light seeped from the edges and sounds came from below. I knelt down and placed my ear to the floor, felt heat rise through the cracks in the boards. I sat back and leaned my head against the wall of the corridor, took some time to think it through. I had to go down there, but I needed to shore up my nerve first. I pictured war movies I'd seen as a kid, the ones featuring tunnel rats who blindly descended into the unknown; I'd always gotten the willies at the mere thought of doing something like that. Jesus, this is what it came down to?

I tested the trapdoor, pulling it up easily. Heat rushed out and light glowed from deep down a narrow shaft, a rickety wooden ladder extending towards the light. The sounds had stopped and I quickly set the wood cover back into place. It was a blind entry, no way around that. I took in some deep breaths to steady myself, secured my pistol and shut off the flashlight, tucked it into an inside pocket. As I raised the trapdoor again, a thought came to me. I lowered the wood cover and stood up, and I made my way back outside, into the storm.

49

It was a desperate gambit, but the only thing that made sense given the circumstances I faced. I reasoned that if Winston managed to make it back here, he would surely lose valuable time searching for me. Unless I pointed him in the right direction.

I returned to the disabled Jimmy for the things I'd need. There was a jerry can filled with gasoline strapped to the back of the truck, and I took it from the metal rack and set it on the ground, and inside the glove box I found a lighter. Bob had an old blanket rolled up in the rear cargo area and I set it on top of the gas can. I turned and surveyed my surroundings, found it right there in front of me. I took my things and made my way to the house thirty yards distant.

It was a neat old place, one of the most intact structures in the town, and I really hated what I was about to do to it. I set my things on the porch and kicked the front door. I had to hit it several times with my heavy boot to break the hasp, to the point my knee ached, but finally it gave way. I went inside, and in the back room I found a wrought iron bed with a sagging mattress. I soaked the blanket in gasoline and shoved it under the bed, took a narrow stick and dipped it in the gas can and torched it. Waving the burning stick over the gas-soaked blanket ignited the vapors, and the mattress caught fire quickly. I stared at it for a long minute, felt the heat on my face, and I turned and exited the house. I doused the area around the porch with the remaining fuel and lit it up, took several steps back and wondered how long it would burn. Hopefully long enough for Winston to see it. I became entranced by the flames, fascinated by all those dancing yellow fingers and roiling black smoke surrounded by blowing snow. I snapped out of it, turned and faced the Standard Mill, set my path and took off.

I came to the stamp room from a different side of the building now, a more direct route in line with my flaming beacon. I shortened my steps, hoping the fresh tracks in the snow would be obvious to Winston on his return. I had no time to leave breadcrumbs for the guy, and I was counting on him being sharp enough to figure it out.

This new route took me straight to the big room that led onto the shaft. To gain entry I broke out a narrow window, as the only door on that side of the building was bolted too securely for me to kick in. I risked the sound of shattering glass, and it took a few seconds to clear the jagged frame so I wouldn't cut myself going in. The window was high off the ground, so I dragged a partially crushed steel drum over and stepped up on it, and pulled myself in through the opening. I came down awkwardly, landing backwards on a wide tool bench covered with broken glass, and I steadied myself to keep from rolling off. Careful not to cut myself, I dropped onto my feet, holding still to look and listen. The wind howled outside, making odd whistling sounds as it gained entry through the seams of the corrugated metal siding of the ancient mill. I felt for my gun, found it there at the small of my back, but when I went for my flashlight it was gone. I looked around the immediate area but could not find it, and I chose to go on without it. I began the slow walk towards the shaft.

Moving forward on sensory perception, my eyes adjusted gradually to the darkness. I prayed that my beacon of fire was still burning and that Winston Styles was on his way. When I got to the shaft I kneeled down to listen. Nothing had changed, and I realized again that all of this could be a waste of time, and once I'd explored whatever was down there it would be too late for Kelli. I had to chance it though, and I decided the percentages favored this spot as Garrett's hiding place.

Bulky clothes restricted my movement, so I stripped off my jacket and flannel, leaving only my long sleeved shirt and tee shirt underneath. I stretched my arms and legs, preparing myself to go down, and once ready, I pulled the wood cover and shoved it out of my way. Peering at the glow of light below, I couldn't gauge the distance; twenty, thirty feet, maybe more? The ladder looked intact as far as I could see, but I had no way of knowing if it would carry my weight. I screwed up my courage, and lowered myself down onto the first rung and started my descent.

Midway down, one of the rungs gave way and I dropped roughly, swinging sideways and scraping my face against the side of the shaft. I wedged myself there and regained control. The shaft was maybe four feet square and shored with rough-hewn planks, a musty smell rising with the warm air, and I wondered if the heat was a natural occurrence or the result of something burning down there. There was no smoke though, or the smell of it, so I quickly discounted fire as the source. I resumed my descent, listening intently for sounds of movement below. With each step down I ignored the ringing in my ears and the tightening in my chest, the smell of fear rising from my clothing. The top of the shaft grew smaller and panic set in, and I fought against it mightily. My arms ached from holding onto the ladder and my right knee burned from kicking in that door, and I focused on the pain to keep my mind clear of everything else.

Finally I hit bottom. The shaft brought me to an anteroom of sorts, with tunnels going off in three directions, dim electric bulbs strung overhead. Where did the power come from? The tunnels were quiet, not even the sound of the wind way down here in the ground, and I began to doubt that Garrett was here at all. Keeping my focus, I forged ahead, moving into the middle tunnel. I eased the Walther from my waistband and released the safety. Fifty feet in, the tunnel doglegged and brought me to a dead end, and I backtracked out of it and wondered why someone had strung lights there in the first place. I chose the tunnel to my right next, and moved into it without hesitation.

After a few steps I thought of Winston and of breadcrumbs, and I turned back and dropped my beanie and gloves on the ground at the mouth of the tunnel. I moved forward slowly, listening with every step. Up ahead, the overhead bulbs veered to the left and disappeared into a blind, and when I got there I stopped and listened. Sounds came to me now, dripping water and a low grade humming, shuffling and movement.

I moved forward a little at a time, hugging the wall, to the point I chanced a better look. Two quick steps out, and a large room at the end of the tunnel came into view. I stepped back into the shadows and considered my approach. I could creep into the room and try to get the drop on Garrett, or just banzai the distance and hope for the best. It was maybe sixty feet to the room, a distance I could sprint in seconds. Either way was risky. I opted for stealth and started moving, holding the pistol down at my side, two-handed so it wouldn't get knocked loose if I was ambushed.

Nearing the end of the tunnel, the layout of the room became clearer. The bulk of it seemed to extend to my left, leaving what appeared to be an unlighted alcove to the right. I chose that as my point of entry, shifting my position in the tunnel. The urge to run came back strong and I ignored it, walking steadily until I reached the alcove. I slipped into it and pointed the pistol in front of me, quickly scanning the room. It was empty of people but full of junk. Several tables piled with mine artifacts, more of it strewn on the floor. In the back of the room there was a cot and evidence of inhabitation. My heart sank with the realization that Kelli was not here. I lowered my weapon and stepped out of the alcove, and when I did there was the sound of movement behind me, and I realized the mistake I'd made. I turned and raised my pistol, and Garrett Knowles came flying down on top of me.

50

I had just enough time to turn sideways and take the impact of Garrett's landing on my right shoulder, and as my knees buckled we both tumbled forward, the Walther falling out of my hand. I tried to gain position, but Garrett was on me so fast the move was futile. He didn't speak as he came at me, a look of blind hatred in his eyes, and I knew this would be a fight to the death.

We rolled on the uneven wood floor, across debris strewn about, Garrett going viciously for my neck with his shriveled and clawed hands. I pushed him away and reached for a steel rod lying next to me, jabbed the end of it hard into Garrett's chest, forcing him off me. On my feet quickly, swinging the metal rod wildly, I made contact and heard him wail. I went for his head and he threw up his arms to protect himself, and I knew it hurt like hell each time that rod slammed into him.

He seemed to sway like he was going down, and I chanced a look around for my pistol. That was my second mistake, for in an instant Garrett was back on me, throwing solid punches to my face, each one like a heavy mallet swung with precision. I felt my nose go and my eyes watered, and I swung the steel rod feebly, trying to gain some separation. Hammering blows hit me all over and my face exploded as I tried in vain to cover up.

Garrett stopped punching and he stepped back a few feet, grabbing tools and metal parts from the table next to him and throwing them at me like they were baseballs. I shrank back to fend off the assault, the ridiculousness of it filling me with blinding anger. I charged Garrett and hoisted him off his feet, pushed him headlong onto the table. We rolled over the top and onto the floor, white-hot pain piercing my side, Garrett pulling a jagged piece of rusted metal from inside me. Before he could stick me again I got to my feet and I yanked him up and threw a forearm to his chin. I heard a sharp crack and I gave him another one hard in the mouth, and I threw fists to his face, blow after blow, and at some point the bones in my left hand shattered but I kept at it. Blood oozed from my side and ran down my leg, the pain incredible, but in the pain my fury grew.

Garrett fell onto his ass and he sat there staring at me through bloodied eyes, his false teeth gone and a gaping hole left in their place, looking inhuman in the dim light of the room. He began to laugh, a maniacal, obscene laugh, and he let out a banshee wail and rose to his feet, coming at me so fast I had no time to react. Garrett tackled me and went for my throat, the wound in my side shot through with pain, my head throbbing from my battered nose. He choked me and I grasped at his hands, but he was a strong son of a bitch and his hands felt fused to my neck. I thought of Larry and the last seconds of his life, and I simply could not believe it was going to end like this. As my head got lighter and my vision blurred, I prayed for Kelli and I prayed that Winston would find her and finish the job that I'd started.

Saliva dripped from Garrett's mouth hole and onto my face and his funk consumed me, and I focused on that hideous face and I refused to die. I flailed my arms until I felt an object next to me and I grabbed it, swinging it into the side of Garrett's head. It wasn't enough so I swung harder. Garrett finally loosened his grip, howling as he reached for his face. I rolled over and gagged, then I vomited, shafts of light slicing my head as I fought for oxygen. I stood woozily and Garrett came at me again, kicking me high in the chest, and as I fell onto my back he straddled me and raised a huge chunk of metal high over his head, poised to bash my skull in with it.

I heard my name then, echoing in the tunnel, and I wondered if it was the Angels calling me home. I looked sideways through the slit of my swollen eye, and I saw not Angels coming for me, but Winston Styles entering the room from the tunnel. He stopped and planted his feet and raised his pistol two-handed, and I tried to tell him not to shoot because I didn't know about Kelli yet, but my voice wouldn't come. Tears filled my eyes and I reached out my hand and tried to scream as Garrett raised the chunk of metal higher. Winston had only one play to make and he took it, firing repeatedly into Garrett's back, the rounds going straight through and blood raining down on me, and as Garrett fell over the chunk of metal in his hands fell, and I turned from it but it landed on me anyway. Garrett toppled over dead, and God how I wanted to be dead too, for in that moment I knew that the only person who meant anything at all to me in this goddamn wicked world was lost with the last gasps of breath from a man I used to know as Gary, from a long time ago.

51

San Francisco, California
Autumn 2012

It was late afternoon when I let myself into my small apartment on Lombard Street. It's a nice place on Russian Hill, just up from Jones and a little south of the crooked part that draws all the tourists. The apartment building three doors down from me, at 900 Lombard, stood in for Jimmy Stewart's pad in the movie *Vertigo*. I think of that often, whenever I pass by the place.

You see, I relate to Stewart's character in that classic film. A lot. Scottie Ferguson's haunting decline after witnessing Madeleine Elster throw herself from the bell tower hits very close to home for me. So close in fact, it's the reason I left Orange County and moved four hundred miles up the coast. Too many memories. Too damn many unavoidable memories.

Rest assured, picking an apartment so close to that iconic film location was purely coincidental, and unlike Scottie, I'd long ago stopped seeking out reminders of the past. But whether you seek them out or not, in time those memories *will* find you.

I may as well tell you now that Kelli was never found. Garrett Knowles died without revealing her whereabouts. He was dead before he hit the ground, according to the coroner. I'd say Winston was a pretty damn good shot that day, which is probably a good thing for me, because had he not come along when he did and blasted that murdering son of a bitch to hell and gone, I'd likely not be here now telling you this story. I didn't blame Winston for shooting Garrett and thereby insuring Kelli's demise. He was faced with an impossible choice, and he took the only clear option available to him. Yet despite Winston's jaded and hardened views on crime and punishment, I knew he anguished greatly over his decision.

I spent two weeks in Bridgeport after that horrible day in the Standard Mill; five days in the hospital recovering from my wounds, the remainder a continuous film loop nightmare of days bleeding into nights, piling one on top of another until I literally lost track of them. A thorough search was made of Bodie and not a single shred of evidence was found to locate Kelli. If Garrett had truly taken her there, and not buried her in some godforsaken spot between Bodie and Mono Lake, then she has become part of the town's history, taking up residence amongst the spirits of the past. But there's another way of looking at it; Kelli is with Sam now, and in the deepest part of my soul I always believed that's where she belonged.

I was in the air when Annette Briggs's car went off the road. If I had arrived an hour or two earlier things might have turned out differently. I'd be a complete liar if I told you I never spent any time obsessing over that one. A witness later came forward and said he saw a black Ford pickup truck with a camper shell speed up and slam into Annie's Range Rover, sending it over the side of the highway. Annie confirmed as much when she came out of her coma. She'd suffered numerous broken bones and a skull fracture in the accident, and she had no recollection of anything outside of the initial impact and her car going through the guardrail. Annie was inconsolable when she heard about Kelli, and in the past two years I've been to

Bridgeport three different times, just to sit with her and let her know it would be all right.

Despite the eyewitness, there was no conclusive proof that it was Garrett Knowles who pushed the car off the road. No license plate was noted, no description of the driver gleaned. Unofficially, the sheriff believed as I did, that it was indeed Knowles who was responsible. How and when he got to Kelli remained a mystery, as the position of Annette's car when it came to rest indicated that it would have taken an incredible effort for Garrett to get down the slope and somehow remove Kelli from the scene.

Wes Morris fared about as well as Annie did from the whole sorry mess. He took three bullets that night, two of them going clean through. The third lodged near his heart and for a while it didn't look like he'd make it. For some reason, Wes wasn't wearing his flak jacket that night. He finally pulled through, and after a lengthy convalescence he took an early retirement from the Park Service.

After I'd left Winston at Wes Morris's side, he did what he could to stabilize the ranger. And then Winston took a big risk. He moved Wes into the ranger's truck, blasted the heater and bundled him up against the cold, and he radioed for help. He identified himself to the dispatcher and laid out the situation: one officer was down and civilians were at risk somewhere in Bodie, most likely at the Standard Mill. He told them to send law enforcement and emergency services immediately, and he signed off and came to save me. My beacon of fire worked, guiding Winston straight to me. He followed my tracks in the snow, and he even saw my breadcrumbs. I guess from that standpoint, I did something right that day.

In the days and weeks and months after the events that took place in Bodie, I went through every known stage of grief, and once the process was complete I went through them again. Somehow, miraculously, I stayed sober throughout the healing. But I knew that to fall into a bottle would give Garrett Knowles the ultimate victory. He'd already taken so much from me, I wasn't about to give him that too. I went to a lot of AA meetings, attended grief counseling and support groups, and I leaned on my father greatly and let him guide me spiritually through a season spent wandering in the woods. More wandering seasons followed, with more grief to work through, more pain to confront, and more emotions to process; in sum total, more lost days than I could ever begin to count.

I relied on Mark Johnson to complete Jerry Corbin's house and I took on no new work, and when the Palm Springs job was finished I gave my business to Mark. My heart wasn't in it anymore, and I had no desire to go through the process of selling out, so I simply gave it away.

I never went back to the house in Newport, moving instead to the Edgewood Apartments. I literally left everything I owned in Kelli's house, and to this day I've never gone back to get any of it. I lived off my savings and did handyman work for Ahn Tran, the kindly old Vietnamese woman who'd managed the Edgewood from the time I first moved there all those years ago, and who was like a second mother to me. Nine months later Ahn passed away from a heart attack and I moved to a small apartment in the High Desert, far away from the coast. I was sick of all the goddamn death around me. I started writing and I learned to play the guitar, and I spent long afternoons walking the canyons and arroyos near my home, baking in the desert heat, contemplating this thing we call life. I kept a bottle of rye and the pistol Jerry gave me, always loaded with one in the chamber, prominently displayed on my mantle over a fireplace that was never used. Every day I'd come home from my long walks and look at that pistol and bottle of booze, and after some brief contemplation I'd say out loud, "not today". Sometimes I'd scream it so loud the neighbors could hear.

Winston Styles remained at my side through that long period of healing, and he made sure the liquor and the bullet never won. He buffered me from the relentless questions by detectives from so many jurisdictions I lost track. The Huntington Beach Police closed the case on Larry Peters, hanging his murder on Garrett. Fingerprints found at the scene, in addition to the witness who'd actually seen Garrett's truck, closed the case. The box Garrett left for me proved to be a crucial piece of evidence as well. Later, a search of the Twin Lakes Lodge turned up similar pieces of evidence relating to those other disappearances. Not all twenty, but a good number of them. Interestingly, there was also evidence found of victims who were not part of Kelli's investigation. It seemed Garrett liked to keep souvenirs of his crimes, and they proved to be the only physical link for investigators. In the end he was credited, if you will, with fifteen official murders. I guess you'd consider that a win.

Pete the Fisherman's murder didn't get much play. The lead detective handling Larry's case seemed to agree with me that Garrett was responsible, the old Cajun likely having witnessed Larry's murder or some part of it. But that was as far as it went, and the cops were disinclined to spend resources investigating the death of a man no one seemed to know or even care about. I was pretty disgusted, but I bore the detective no ill will over it. It was just one more shitty part of the whole sorry affair.

I see Tom Flynn from time to time, try and do my part to see that he's taken care of. There's really no one else to do it, outside of some distant relations who can't seem to be bothered with it. It's not too far of a drive to Grass Valley, a few hours if the traffic isn't bad, and occasionally I'll continue on to Lake Tahoe since I'm nearby, and I'll spend long days on the water contemplating the vastness of a world I'm slowly learning to rejoin. I'm not too concerned about Tom liking me anymore, because frankly, the Alzheimer's has gotten so bad he doesn't even know who I am. Each time I see him he acts pleasantly surprised, and once in a while it clicks in what's left of his memory that I'm that nice guy from San Francisco who brings him sweet things from Ghirardelli Square. Soon Tom will die, and even though I'm prepared for it, I dread the inevitability.

I found out a year ago that Kelli had named me the beneficiary of her life insurance policy. I was stunned by this. But to be honest, I have no desire to take the steps necessary to have her declared dead in absentia. With her father's condition eliminating him from the process, it leaves only me to see it through. I understand it's a sizable amount of money. I also understand you've got to wait seven years after the person has disappeared to file the paperwork. I've turned the whole thing over to Winston, the handling of Kelli's assets and such, and asked him to do what he thinks is right. Yeah, I trust him *that* much.

And why wouldn't I?

You see, we're partners now. It was Winston's idea, but it took some time to convince me. The bond we'd developed through the events of that horrible winter and the long aftermath ran deep, and once I'd made the decision to end my career as a homebuilder, the thought of becoming a private investigator intrigued me. When I finally made the decision I had three requests as a condition of joining with Winston. He agreed to all three.

One, we changed the name of the company from Apex Investigators to the Styles & Tanner Detective Agency. Remember, I have a thing about names.

Two, I opened a satellite office in the Bay Area. It was no good for me to stay in Southern California. Too many memories. Too many ghosts.

And three, I take on only missing person cases. It's become my obsession, my mission in life, if you will. It's the only thing I can do, channel my pain and loss into something that might help others.

Winston helped me get licensed, showed me the ropes, and nine months ago I made the move up here and hung my shingle. I've had some successes, along with too many failures, but the wins balance out the losses in a way that mere numbers cannot convey. I operate out of a little storefront office on the Embarcadero. I get inspiration from reading Dashiell Hammett. Sometimes I even wear a trench coat and a fedora. Yet despite the affectations, I'm all business, and when I take on a case I'm determined to bring closure to my client. Because in the end, that's all I ever wanted with Sam. But I never really got it. Sure, I found his killer, but the how and why eluded me. And now that Kelli has joined Sam, all that I'm left with is what I can make of this cruel and crazy world.

There's a cute woman who works the front desk of an insurance agency located in the same building as my office. I see her regularly at the little coffee joint down the street. I can tell she likes me, and at times I've felt a flutter in my heart at her flirtations. But it's too soon for that. Sadly, I feel too old and used up. Though I'm only forty-four, inside I feel ninety.

But sometimes a glimmer shines through, a vision of a different life, one free of pain and haunting memories, of feeling old before my time. I see myself as in a dream, that pretty insurance company lady by my side, love blossoming between us. And I see Kelli and Sam looking down at me from heaven, and they're smiling, for if there is anything I've learned from having two of the most beautifully perfect human beings in my life it's this: life is a gift and it's meant for the living, and we dishonor our dead by squandering that gift in favor of the destructiveness of our self-pity.

So I move through my days with Kelli and Sam in my heart, one foot in front of the other, making amends where amends are needed, and breathing in the gift with each new day. And in time I will heal, and in time I will move beyond the here and now, and all of my tomorrows will bloom beyond my wildest dreams. Because that's the only way for this story to end.

About the Author

John Turner lives in South Orange County, California. When he's not overseeing construction projects for a Los Angeles-based general contractor, he's banging away at his keyboard, trying to get the words right. *The Wicked Kind* is his first published novel.